Debrett's
Guide to Britain

Debrett's
Guide to Britain
Where to Go and What to See

Edited by Joanna Household

Webb & Bower
EXETER, ENGLAND

FRONTISPIECE: Race-goers at Epsom on Derby Day,
traditionally the first Wednesday in June.

First published in Great Britain 1983 by
Webb & Bower (Publishers) Limited
9 Colleton Crescent, Exeter, Devon EX2 4BY
in association with Debrett's Peerage Limited
73–77 Britannia Road, London SW6

Designed by Vic Giolitto

Picture Research by Anne-Marie Ehrlich

British Library Cataloguing in Publication Data
Debrett's guide to Britain.
  1. Upper classes—Great Britain
  2. Great Britain—Social life and customs—1945–
  I. Household, Joanna
  941.085′8′0880621   HT653.G7

  ISBN 0–906671–81–7

Typeset in Great Britain by Keyspools Ltd, Golborne, Lancs

Printed and bound in Italy by New Interlitho SpA

Contents

Introduction

For such a small country, Great Britain has an exceptionally rich and varied tradition of seasonal events and activities which are still almost as much a part of life as they were before the world wars irrevocably changed the old social order. There is still a calendar which strongly influences the leisure of those members of society with the time and usually, but not always, the money to continue in some degree the way of life of their fathers. To many the fact that people wear evening dress to the Glyndebourne opera season and still take precariously to the river in punts after the Oxford and Cambridge May balls is a sign that the true spirit of the nation is not dead, in spite of what might seem considerable evidence to the contrary.

What has undoubtedly changed, and few would argue that it is not for the

The Princess of Wales (then Lady Diana Spencer) on Ladies' Day at Ascot. Her distinctive style immediately set a fashion through all walks of life.

One of Christina Foyle's literary luncheons of 1955, given for Roger Bannister to launch his book *The Four-Minute Mile*. Miss Foyle is seated fourth from the right (wearing a hat) with Roger Bannister on her right.

better, is that the 'democratizing' process has reached almost everywhere, and such pleasures as an evening at Covent Garden or rubbing shoulders with the Royal Family at the Badminton Horse Trials are no longer exclusive to the rich or well-connected. It is now possible even to spend a weekend at one of the great country houses of England, if only as a paying guest, and it is certainly possible to attend most, if not all, the events traditionally the preserve of the privileged few.

It is unlikely that anyone will have the time or inclination to attend every event or occasion listed, but many people do regularly spend much of the year in this way, and with much enjoyment and satisfaction. To participate in some of the more demanding sports takes more than most of us are capable of, but anyone who wants to can watch a game of polo in Windsor Great Park without having the skill of the Prince of Wales, or watch the world's greatest tennis players on the Centre Court at Wimbledon without matching up to a Bjorn Borg. The traditional field sports, however, do offer an opportunity for the enthusiastic amateur to do more than just watch, and England, Scotland and Wales contain salmon rivers, grouse moors and hunting country to equal any in the world. With the right equipment, a few lessons and information about seasons and licenses, these former bastions of the landed gentry are now open to all.

Many of the events listed here will be familiar to most people, if only by repute, and there will be few who do not know that to row in the Henley Royal Regatta is the height of ambition for serious crews from all over the world, or that the Aldeburgh Music Festival commemorates the work of that great English composer, Benjamin Britten, but it is not perhaps so widely known that the ancient ceremony of Swan Upping traces its origins to the Plantagenet Kings of England or that Nottingham Goose Fair is so called from the centuries-old

The victorious Oxford team of 1911. In spite of a recent run of success, Oxford are still behind Cambridge in the number of times they have won. Only once, in 1877, has a draw been declared.

practice of selling geese at Michaelmas in preparation for the long winter months ahead.

Somewhere in this mixture, it is hoped, can be found that elusive and indefinable element which can be appreciated not only by those who trace their origins from Great Britain or who share the language and a common heritage, but by everyone who can appreciate a way of life unique to these islands.

January

Twickenham Rugby Football Internationals

On two Saturdays during the coldest months of the year, more than sixty thousand Rugby enthusiasts muffled up in sheepskins and their warmest clothes (ski clothes do not look amiss), and many carrying rugs for good measure, converge on Twickenham Ground, the home of Rugby Union Football. It is some twelve miles from London and each year is the venue of two of the ten International games fought between England, France, Scotland, Ireland and Wales. Each contestant hosts two matches during the season but England's Twickenham, as the oldest ground and the headquarters of the Rugby Football Union, has become known as the Mecca of this great amateur sport.

The ground occupies thirty-two and a half acres of former horticultural land known as 'Billy William's Cabbage Patch' after a great cricketer and keen but moderate Rugby player, W. Williams, at whose instigation the first portion of the ground was bought by the RFU in 1907. On 15 January, 1910 the first International—England v. Wales—was played there. It was a thrilling occasion as D. R. Gent, England's scrum-half recalled:

> In my case, the thrill largely lay in the fact that here was the new Home Ground of Rugby Football, that I had played on it for the the first time and that, wonder of wonders, we had beaten Wales for the first time since 1898.

The match was played to a capacity crowd of thirty thousand—more than half of them standing spectators. Today, with double the capacity for both categories, tickets for International matches are like gold dust. The majority go to England's four thousand Rugby Clubs and County Unions, Schools and Sports' Societies who apply each year by early October. However applications are always over-subscribed and each organization only receives a small proportion of its request.

Nevertheless, disregarding the inevitable ticket touts and less reputable agencies who supply tickets at highly inflated prices, there are ways for those, not even directly associated with the game, to get tickets. The Secretary of the RFU, Twickenham, TW2 7RQ will advise those who write at least five months ahead of a match and sometimes he keeps a few places up his sleeve for particularly deserving overseas visitors.

Some leading ticket agencies and industrial companies belong to Rugby Clubs or are debenture holders. As an outcome of the debenture scheme 'Package Tours' are run by several reputable agencies and prices vary for a seat in the South Stand, lunch in the new banqueting suite there and plenty of liquid refreshment at suitable intervals, or a luxury day out (run by Keith Prowse of 34 Store St, London WC1E 7BA). Participants meet at a private marquee adjoining the ground for a champagne reception at 11.30 am followed by a four-course lunch with wine and liqueurs and a talk by a leading Rugby personality. They are given

ENGLAND. Rugby.   SCOTLAND. Rugby.   IRELAND. Rugby.   WALES. Rugby.

FRANCE Rugby.   N. ZEALAND. Rugby.

S. AFRICA. Rugby.   IRELAND *VERSUS* WALES.   AUSTRALIA. Rugby.

ENGLAND. Association.   SCOTLAND. Association.   IRELAND. Association.   WALES. Association.

A page from the pre-war *Boy's Own Paper*, showing the International caps for Rugby Union and Association Football. The Irish side is still a united team from both the Republic of Ireland and Northern Ireland, and members can be picked for the team of 'British Lions' which challenges international sides at home and abroad.

a small bottle of brandy to take to their reserved seat in the West Stand. Afterwards, in the marquee there is soup, coffee and sandwiches and the bar is open for another two hours. A rating of the popularity of Twickenham Internationals is that these tours are fully booked three months before England play Wales, two months before they play Scotland and two or three weeks before a home match against Ireland.

Certainly the Welsh game is the most exuberant with thousands of ticketless Welshmen descending on London two days beforehand in the hope that somehow a ticket will materialize. But however beautifully their voices are raised in song the ticketless are unlikely to find a last-minute way into the ground. Weak spots have been detected and sealed up and rotating spikes installed on top of surrounding fences to foil gate-crashers.

The 1961 Home International game between England and France at
Twickenham, with the England Captain, R.E.G. Jeeps passing the
ball out from the scrum. France is the only country other than the
'home' teams (i.e., England, Scotland, Ireland and Wales) to play in
this championship.

For anyone who has a ticket and wants a day out without travel or car-parking
problems, luxury coaches are operated by an ex-England Captain, Jeff Butter-
field, from his Rugby Club in London's West End. He offers breakfast at his club,
coffee and drinks on board, refreshments in the North Car Park followed by
lunch with wine, coffee and 'heartwarmers' and, after the match, afternoon tea
with whisky.

But such cushioned comforts for seasoned 'Twickenhamists' are the exceptions. The majority come by train on the frequent service from Waterloo—a
twenty-minute journey followed by a twelve-minute walk to the ground, or bring
their cars, arriving soon after noon, in good time to find a parking space near the
ground for pre-match picnics. Car-parking space in the ground is reserved and
incredibly difficult to come by.

The car journey from London can take a good hour and a half but it is well
worth it because these picnics from well filled hampers stowed in car boots, often
with collapsible chairs and tables, are an integral part of the Twickenham
scene—even on improvised car parks such as in a local churchyard which seizes
the opportunity to swell church funds. Afterwards, a stroll in the West Concourse
is the best way to meet up with old friends.

Given a choice, the best seats are in the centre of the West and East stands, along the length of the pitch. But even high level ones at the ends of the stands are not to be despised for, the game apart, Twickenham is a party occasion—a day out for devotees of the sport, to meet old friends, one-time team mates and opponents; to relive great moments of games long past, like Prince Obolensky's classic pre-war tries and Andy Hancock's ninety-five yards dash to equalize for England in the last moments of the match against Scotland in 1965.

Unconventional attractions add to the party atmosphere, like the American drum majorettes who supplement the military band which plays for up to an hour before the game begins. So do impromptu incidents such as the streaker who, at half-time in an England–France match sprinted naked from the East to the West Stand where Princess Alexandra and her children were watching from the Royal Box. Propriety was delicately retrieved by a policeman who deployed his helmet for a discreet cover-up. Recently, such is the tolerance and good humour of the Twickenham crowd, a feminine counterpart, Erica Rowe, was not even arrested after her much-applauded topless dash across the pitch.

Hooliganism is virtually unknown. The police are hardly in evidence and the two or three hundred volunteer stewards are all ex-Rugby players. There is a long waiting list for these coveted positions. Anyone carrying cans or bottles is denied entrance but, in the seasonal weather, a flask of whisky or brandy secreted in a pocket or handbag can be a medical necessity. Public bars on the ground open at midday, close five minutes before kick-off and are no longer allowed to reopen.

The five-minute interval at half-time during the eighty-minute game hardly allows one to leave one's seat but it affords the chance to discuss the finer points of the game with friendly neighbours. For this friendliness, among a predominantly English crowd (only a comparatively small allocation of seats is allowed to supporters of visiting teams), is the very essence of this great amateur sport.

Recently, a tented village of hospitality marquees, out of sight of the pitch, has appeared. These are taken by companies who provide associates with lunch and a seat for the match. Also new are thirty-five hospitality boxes in the new South Stand for debenture holders. In each a dozen spectators can eat, drink and watch in uncharacteristic Rugby comfort.

The main difference between Twickenham and Internationals at Murrayfield in Edinburgh and Cardiff Arms Park in Wales is the car-parking arrangements. At Cardiff, the home of the Welsh National Game, there are none because the ground is only a short walk from the centre of the city. There are no bars in the ground and meals are eaten in local hotels and restaurants.

In Scotland, weather permitting, well-drained rugby pitches surrounding the ground provide unreserved space for fifteen thousand cars. However, the ground is only a twenty-minute walk from the city centre and there is plenty of public transport. No drink is allowed within the stadium. Tickets are very hard to come by but not as 'desperate' as at Cardiff where most are sold on a life debenture system. There the singing that echoes across the Welsh capital on match days is poor compensation for those who long to get inside the ground. However, an appeal to the Welsh Rugby Union Secretary at Cardiff Arms Park, Cardiff CR1 1JI, a few months before an International could work a miracle for overseas visitors, as indeed might one to his Scottish counterpart at Murrayfield, Edinburgh 12, before an International is played there.

February

Salmon Fishing

The renowned eighteenth-century writer and talker, Dr Johnson, is said to have dismissed all angling as 'a worm at one end of a stick and a fool at the other', though no such quotation is to be found in Boswell's volumes. Both salmon and trout may indeed be caught on a worm, in certain waters not illegally; but on the whole it is considered more sporting, as well as more effective either, in the case of salmon only, to 'spin', or else to cast for salmon or trout using for bait a hook cunningly garnished with bits of feather or hair so as hopefully to resemble a living insect, crustacean or even small fish, this approved method of course being known as fly-fishing.

The *modus operandi* has little in common with that of the 'coarse' fisherman who may be observed with his folding stool and large umbrella on river or canal bank, surrounded with tackle boxes and bait cans. In Britain none but salmon and trout are designated 'game' fish, all others being dubbed 'coarse'; and though certain coarse fish are not unpalatable it is customary for every one caught to be returned alive to its element, a procedure unlikely to appeal to the salmon man.

An important point for the prospective game fisherman to consider is that of all field sports fishing is the least sociable—a sport essentially for the benefit of the participant and not the spectator. Nobody who cannot bear being out of sight and sound of other people should take it up. If some game anglers do, on occasion, fish with a congenial companion similarly engaged, many—perhaps most—prefer complete solitude or only the company of a gillie (which may indeed be essential on some salmon rivers).

Both salmon and trout are fished for in unspoilt, unpolluted waters in surroundings often of considerable natural beauty; when sport is slow there will always be interesting beasts, birds or wild flowers to look at and enjoy; and outings in the course of which nothing may find its way into the creel—by no means uncommon—can never be regarded as entirely wasted. Expert and tyro alike learn something new every time they pull on waders.

Salmon have been captured in Britain by one means or another for centuries. Private salmon-net fisheries existed in mediaeval days, and until the river became too foul for them at about the period of Queen Victoria's accession they were to be found in the Thames. (Now that London's river is cleaner, efforts are being made to re-establish them.)

Salmon do their feeding in the sea and their breeding in fresh running water. Having spent two, three or even four years in their natal river the young fish don a silver coat and descend to sea in the spring of the year. They are then six or seven inches long and known as 'smolts'. Before changing colour to migrate, the juveniles, or 'parr', resemble young brown trout and feed similarly on little aquatic creatures. In the ocean, eating small fish, krill (shrimp-like crustacea) and other marine fauna, salmon grow very rapidly. A proportion may 'run up' the

Prince Charles salmon fishing on a favourite stretch of water where the River Dee in Grampian passes through the Balmoral estate.

river of their birth after spending one summer and winter at sea; such fish are called 'grilse' and offer fine sport. They may weigh anything from three or four to about ten pounds. Other salmon will spend two or three winters at sea before returning to perpetuate their species as fully adult fish.

Having spawned in November or December, after spending up to ten or even eleven months fasting in fresh water, the vast majority of the fish then die, or at least never return to their river. Many salmon recover condition to the extent of reassuming silver livery—the fish at spawning time become reddish or dull-coloured—and are all too often caught by rodsmen hoping for 'clean', fresh-run fish. These recently-spawned salmon are called 'kelts' and are never fit to eat; anglers return them to the water unharmed, though the inexperienced may find it difficult to distinguish a 'well-mended' kelt from a fresh-run fish.

'Salmon' as opposed to grilse will weigh anything from six to forty pounds, depending to a great extent on the river of their birth, though in Britain fish of the latter weight are very rare anywhere. On any water a thirty-pounder is a fine fish and many lifelong anglers have never killed one of twenty pounds. In plenty of rivers specimens of twelve pounds are better than average. The official rod-caught record for Britain is a salmon of sixty-four pounds, taken from the Scottish River Tay by a Miss Ballantine in 1922. She was fishing with a natural bait (a dace), from a boat manned by her father, a professional boatman. One of $69\frac{3}{4}$ pounds is said to have been caught in the Tweed by an early eighteenth-century Earl of Home, and very probably it was; but after so many decades the circumstantial evidence of its weight is not accepted as positive by the pundits keeping the record books.

Salmon—known to many Scots gillies simply as 'fish', no other piscine species being worthy of notice—have, unquestionably, an ambience of glamour. They are very large and shapely; they taste delicious on the table (especially when smoked) and salmon fly casting is apt to be regarded as the quintessence of the angler's art, though trout men would vigorously dispute this. What is quite certain is that as well as being, in general, considerably more expensive, salmon fishing is a more chancy business altogether. At the best of times the salmon enthusiast will land fewer fish than the trout angler and indeed may well catch none in a fortnight if conditions are unhelpful. The best salmon fishing must be arranged well in advance; thus there can be no certainty that enough rain will have fallen to swell the river and encourage fish to run. In any case salmon numbers fluctuate greatly from season to season.

Salmon are far less predictable than trout; even if they should be plentiful in river or loch it by no means follows that even a skilled man will catch any by legitimate means. All must depend on water temperature, colour and height: on how much or little rain has fallen. For adult salmon do not feed in fresh water. They seize lure or fly not because they are impelled to by hunger but because it seems to arouse their anger, their irritation or their curiosity. Alternatively it may be a reflex action touched off by vague memories of sea feeding or of early river life.

The tackle needed by the game fisherman who casts a fly, or spins, is much less extensive than the paraphernalia assembled by the coarse angler. It has to be; the seeker after salmon or trout doesn't sit or stand in one spot. Unless fishing from a boat he must be mobile.

The salmon rod, principal tool of the trade, may be constructed of the traditional 'split-cane', hollow glass fibre or —most modern—of carbon fibre. Fly rods vary in length from about ten feet to fourteen or even fifteen depending on the width and character of the river one fishes or intends to fish. Thirteen feet is a useful all-round length. Rods of eleven feet or more are made for double-handed casting: long rods impose an impossible leverage on the wrist if used single handed like a trout rod. Glass fibre rods, the least expensive, are perhaps the best for a beginner. Carbon rods are remarkably light, cast very well and cost much the same as a good cane rod, which is lovely to use but a good deal heavier. The advantages of the long rods used in Britain—Americans and Canadians prefer them single handed—are that they give the fisherman more control over his fly and enable him to cast considerable distances with less effort, besides making it easier to master and subdue a powerful and heavy fish.

Of almost equal importance is the tapered plastic fly line. Fly lines may be constructed either to float or sink, each employed according to river and circumstances. (The fisherman may want his fly to 'work' or 'swim' deep in the water in certain conditions and nearer to the surface in others.) To contain the fly line and its 'backing' a fly reel is a necessity. There are plenty in all price ranges to choose from. The salmon reel must have a drum wide enough to house line and plenty of 'backing', be absolutely reliable and of sturdy construction (one may drop the thing). Basically, it is just a winch; if economy must rule, start with the reel. Backing is thin but strong nylon or terylene line attached to the 'wrong' end of the fly line, which itself is only thirty to forty yards in length. A salmon may pull two hundred yards of backing from the reel—although this is not likely— so there should always be plenty in reserve. The 'leader' or 'cast' attached to the business end of the fly line is of nylon monofilament and nine to twelve feet long;

A nineteenth-century gillie gaffing a salmon.
This method of landing a fish is now frowned upon by many fishermen because
of the damage done by the long steel hook.

its breaking strain depending on size of fly and strength of current. (There is nothing 'sporting' about using too light a leader for any kind of angling 'to give the fish a chance'. What you will be giving it, probably, is a hook in its mouth to swim away with.)

Salmon flies, up to about forty years ago, were beautiful, elaborate creations made of snippets from the plumage of tropical and other birds to very precise patterns and with names such as 'Jock Scott', 'Thunder and Lightning' or 'Green Highlander'. No salmon fly, ancient or modern, actually resembles any insect, nor is it intended to; indeed these showy creations looked more like humming-birds. The many salmon caught on them would undoubtedly have condescended to seize with equal alacrity the much simpler flies, less exotic and beguiling to the eye, that are now in common use, take a quarter of the time to construct and cost a quarter of the money.

Once the salmon is hooked and 'played out' it must be safely landed. This may be accomplished by 'gaffing' it, by 'tailing', by 'beaching' or by means of a landing net (universal for trout). The gaff is a steel hook with a gape of about $2\frac{1}{2}$ inches, either telescopic or fixed to a long stick. When exhausted the fish is 'stroked' amidships with it and lifted from the water. Gaffs are bound to make deep punctures in the flesh; their use is generally forbidden late in the season when salmon are gravid and also early in the year when kelts may be about. Many salmon fishermen never use them. Tailing is accomplished by means of a kind of steel snare made for the purpose, or performed by hand. In either case the salmon is gripped by the 'wrist' in front of the tail fin and lifted clear of the water. To beach a salmon it must be run head first on to a gravelly or sandy margin or miniature bay if one should be handy. The fish, by flopping, unwittingly assists; the job is not difficult. If a landing net is used it must be a big one, which is probably awkward to carry. Salmon landed from boats are often secured thus.

The salmon man will, on many rivers, need chest-high waders; thigh waders are nearly always essential. He will also require a waterproof fishing jacket of top quality and a hat, plus fly boxes, scissors, a pocket knife, spare leaders (or nylon spools to make them from) and, if fishing without a gillie, a short, heavy instrument called a 'priest' for administering the last rites, i.e., to knock the salmon hard on the base of the skull in order to kill it cleanly. A gillie of course is a water keeper employed by estate or hotel, one of whose duties is to act as guide, assistant and general mentor to the rods who fish the beats he looks after. His company may be obligatory and in any case is very well worthwhile, for he is the fount of all wisdom. If your knots are unreliable, his are certain; if you don't know where the fish lie, he does; if you haven't the right fly, he has. A gillie should be tipped and would appreciate a nip of whisky.

Spinning for salmon is frequently resorted to early and late in the season when the water is cold and deep and salmon are hugging the bed; and at other times when the river is high and coloured. Some fishermen will never spin, others do little else; but most salmon fishermen employ fly or spinner (where spinning is permitted) according to conditions. A spinning rod is noticeably stiffer than a fly rod and much shorter, somewhere between seven and nine and a half feet long. Reels used for spinning differ from fly-fishing reels, and the line is of light nylon monofilament.

Spinning baits may be of metal, plastic or painted wood and are supposed to give the impression of a small fish—to the salmon, that is. Some of them, continuously or intermittently flashing in the water, are known as 'spoons'; others, called 'Devons', revolve more or less rapidly. Spinners are armed with double or treble hooks, perhaps with a pair of them. Artificial or preserved prawns and shrimps, or real live worms may also be permissible in certain conditions on certain waters.

Whilst fly fishing is always approved there are likely to be local restrictions on the use of spinning baits. Probably they will be permitted only on particular beats, or only when water levels reach a given height. All such provisos must be investigated and rigidly adhered to.

A stranger to fly casting for salmon or trout—or to spinning for that matter, though it is much easier to master—should have a good idea of what he is trying to accomplish before starting to fish his beat or he will be wasting time and money. Rather than relying on a friend's advice and instruction, or attempting to learn the art from books, the absolute beginner is strongly urged to attend a fishing course (which lasts only a few days) or else to take private lessons from any one of a number of fully qualified professional instructors who are also expert fishermen. This applies equally to the prospective trout angler. The advertisement pages of the monthly magazine *Trout and Salmon* is the place to look for them, and courses will also be detailed.

Tackle is provided, and it is best for the tyro to have the lessons before deciding exactly what to buy for himself. The whole salmon outfit, from rod to waders, will cost a great deal less money than a good shot-gun.

The finest water in England is the Wye (which in fact rises in Wales). The Hampshire Avon, lower Test, the Tamar (Cornwall) and the Eden and Coquet in the North are good too. In Wales, of many the Welsh Dee is perhaps best. But Scotland is the premier country for salmon, beyond argument. Tweed, Tay, Spey, Aberdeenshire Dee and Helmsdale—very prestigious—are all first class. Other good waters are Conon, Thurso, Deveron, Don, Oykel, Beauly and a dozen more according to personal preference or experience. But—and the 'but' is a big one—unless privately invited, able to pull strings or very lucky, the hopeful angler will find the most productive beats at peak season on rivers such as these very hard to come by in the absence of advance planning. There exist agents for good fisheries who should be contacted in case some beat has for one reason or another not been taken up (and also, of course, for booking ahead). A list of agents will be found in *Where to Fish*, of which more in a moment. Herbert Hatton and Bernard Thorpe of Hereford are two for the Wye. London Agents include Jackson-Stops and Staff, 14 Curzon Street; Knight, Frank and Rutley, 20 Hanover Square; Sporting Services International, 109 Jermyn Street. There are also a number in Scotland.

Hotel water exists on the Tay (much of the fishing in this huge river is from boats) and association water at Grantown-on-Spey whereon a visitor may try his hand.

Let not the salmon fishing sportsman unable to secure a first-class beat on one of the most famous rivers despair. There are the Border Esk and the Annan in the North; the Taw, Torridge and Exe in Devon (with some good hotel water); the Usk, Conwy, Dovey and Towey in Wales—the last three containing fine sea trout also; Brora, Findhorn, Garry, Ness, Nith, Orchy and a number of others north of the border. All or nearly all offer facilities for salmon fishing which may be of good quality if conditions are propitious.

It is important to bear in mind that while some rivers are best in late winter and spring, others will be at their prime during certain summer or autumn months: salmon have an awkward habit of running up different rivers at different periods of the season. An indispensable general guide to this and much else is the latest edition of *The Field* magazine's *Where to Fish*. Its 500-odd pages provide details of every sort of fishing on every British and Irish river, lake or loch—or lough—including stretches available to the visitor, hotel water, associations, costs and so on. *Salmon Fishing in Scotland*, the Haig guide, is another excellent book to study should that be the only country on which the fisherman's heart is set.

The Regional Water Authorities of England and Wales determine the local opening and closing dates for salmon and trout fishing on every river within their jurisdiction and also issue licences. The *statutory* open season for salmon is from 1 February to 31 October, but this means that salmon may be fished for between these dates only in default of other provision by the Water Authority; and there always is 'other provision'. In effect the different Authorities impose seasons of their own.

A River Authority licence must be taken out even by a riparian owner fishing his own river. But although such a licence is essential it gives the holder no right to cast on any water without permission from owner or tenant: for a game fishing poacher to claim that he has a rod licence is no excuse whatever. There are separate licences printed for every river or group of rivers; separate also for salmon, trout and coarse fish—that for salmon, not surprisingly, is easily the most expensive. Such licences are readily obtainable from fishing hotel, local tackle shop or perhaps post office.

In Scotland, at the time of writing, no licence is yet necessary. District Boards fix local open and close seasons and, as in England and Wales, they vary from river to river.

Crufts Dog Show

The greatest accolade for any show dog and its owner is to win the 'Best In Show' award at Crufts Dog Show when the endless days of grooming, waiting, smiling politely at the judges dim into obscurity. At last the most distinguished crown of all is held. The cameras click to capture the victory of the Champion of Champions.

There would be no Crufts in its present form without the Kennel Club, and to trace the history of Crufts Dog Show one must first look at the inception of the Kennel Club.

The Kennel Club was founded in 1873 by Mr Sewallis Evelyn Shirley and the first headquarters were at 2 Albert Mansions, Victoria Street, London. The first duty of the Kennel Club was to produce a *Stud Book* which contained the pedigrees of over four thousand dogs. It also contained a 'Code of Rules for the Guidance of Dog Shows and Field Trials'. In 1874 the membership was limited to

Judging one of the most popular breeds at Crufts Dog Show—the Old English sheepdogs. Each of these splendid specimens has already won at least one regional championship.

one hundred and the Committee consisted of only twelve. The first Trustees of the Kennel Club were appointed in 1877. The *Kennel Club Gazette* was founded in 1880 and in the same year a system of registration of dogs was devised.

In 1973 the Kennel Club celebrated its centenary year and since its foundation it has built up a reputation throughout the world for efficiency and the organization of everyone connected with dog breeding, dog shows, trials and indeed anything canine. Outside 1 Clarges Street, Piccadilly, London, the present headquarters of the Kennel Club, stands the most famous dog of all which is known as the Kennel Club Hound. The original was cast in 1925 from a sculpture by Captain Adrian Jones who used a hound from the Old Berkeley Pack for his model. The statue was presented to the Kennel Club in 1928, and he now proudly guards the main entrance.

The Committee structure of the Kennel Club has been revised many times during its long life but its aims remain the same. To quote from the Kennel Club Rules: 'The Kennel Club exists mainly for the purpose of promoting the improvement of Dogs, Dog Shows, Field Trials, Working Trials and Obedience Tests, and its objects include the classification of Breeds, the Registration of Pedigrees, Transfers etc., the Licensing of Shows, the framing and enforcing of Kennel Club Rules, the awarding of Challenge, Champion and other certificates, the Registration of Associations, Clubs and Societies, and the publication of an Annual Stud Book and a monthly Kennel Gazette.'

Every year over four thousand dog shows are held in Britain as well as about three hundred field and working trials. The Kennel Club is responsible for all of these and each one must comply with its Rules and Regulations.

There are some thirty or so Championship Shows including Crufts which allocate Challenge Certificates, these being the much sought-after 'green cards' which are issued by the Kennel Club. If any dog wins three Challenge Certificates under three different judges he becomes a Kennel Club Champion. The number of CCs (as they are commonly called) allocated to each breed varies considerably, depending on the size of the breed numerically and the number of registrations with the Kennel Club. The breed must also prove to be well represented at shows before it can qualify for the allocation of Kennel Club CCs. Crufts is the only British dog show which requires qualifications for entry.

In 1852 Charles Cruft was born. As a young man he started work for James Spratt selling dog cakes, much to the consternation of his father, a jeweller who had hoped that his son might follow in his footsteps.

It soon became apparent that Charles Cruft had quite a flair for organization, and in a selling capacity he visited many dog breeders and large estates. He even went abroad to visit kennels and in 1878 the French dog breeders invited him to organize and promote the canine section of the Paris Exhibition. The success of this venture led him to the management of the Allied Terrier Club Show in 1886 which was held at the Royal Aquarium, Westminster with an entry of over six hundred dogs.

Charles Cruft became General Manager of Spratts and stayed with them for thirty years; during this time he had an arrangement with his firm which allowed him to organize dog shows on his own account. In 1891 he held the first Crufts Dog Show at the Royal Agricultural Hall, Islington. In those days there were no quarantine restrictions and Mr Cruft encouraged many entrants from the

Winning any award at Crufts means hours of preparation and grooming, but
the achievement is worth every minute of unstinting labour and devotion on
the part of both owners and contestants.

Continent. Obviously this created a good deal of excitement in the dog world and
furthered Mr Cruft's reputation as a 'dog man' of some repute.

Charles Cruft died in 1938. His widow personally managed one more Crufts
Dog Show in 1939, but the work load was too much for her, and in 1942, in order
to always keep her husband's name as a prefix to this great show, she came to an
agreement with the Kennel Club that they would take over the future
organization. Six years later at Olympia the first Crufts was held under the
management of the Kennel Club. It was a huge and immediate success and has
indeed continued to be so ever since.

In 1964 Crufts attracted an entry of 16,022 from 8,277 dogs, with most of them
entered in more than one class. This posed a serious problem at Olympia
regarding space and a further problem for the judges who had to inspect each dog
thoroughly in the time allowed for each class and breed. It was decided by the
Kennel Club Committee that restrictions on entries must be enforced. Since then
more restrictions on qualification for Crufts have had to be brought in. In 1979
the show moved to Earls Court and the Crufts Committee stiffened their
qualifications even further. Only first-prize winners at Champion Shows during
the preceding year were eligible to compete, with special consideration being
given to Champions, CC winners and Reserve CC winners.

Something in the region of 55,000 people descend on Earls Court for Crufts
Dog Show every year, making it a somewhat stifling atmosphere for the exhibitor
who has to arrive with his dog by 11 am and is not allowed to remove his dog until
6 pm the same day, regardless of when and for how long he actually appears in the
Ring. There is little doubt that the Champion Shows held throughout the
summer, such as the East of England Show at Peterborough in July are much

more friendly and relaxed. Also being held in the open air the atmosphere (in more ways than one!) is less heavy and oppressive. The noise at Crufts can reach an intolerable level and I defy any exhibitor to leave at the end of the day without a splitting headache! Nevertheless there is something about Crufts that ranks it high among the great sporting events held in Britain.

It is a long, hard, tough journey to compete at Crufts. Having qualified, the dog is entered with others of its breed and sex and has to win the class. It then goes on to challenge the other winners of the classes in its breed before entering for Best in Sex. It must then compete against the Best Opposite Sex for Best of Breed. One breed judge makes all these decisions. Once declared Best of Breed the dog must then stand against others declared Best of Breed in its particular Group. There are six groups in this country for all shows including Crufts, Terrier, Working, Utility, Hound, Toy and Gundog. Each group is judged by a different judge. If the dog then wins its group he or she will stand with the other group winners to compete for the best exhibit in the Show under yet another judge. The six best dogs in the country line up for Best in Show at Crufts. One will win—and only one—until next year when they all try again.

Crufts Dog Show is held at Earls Court, London, over three days in the second week of February.

It is worth mentioning that apart from the main competition, there is also an Obedience Championship, Agility Competition and a Puppy Competition. In addition, there are over a hundred trade stands at Crufts, selling and displaying a very wide range of products and services for dog owners.

The Kennel Club issues an information leaflet which gives details of dates, times, prices of admission and how to reserve seats. Send a stamped, addressed envelope to the Secretary, The Kennel Club, 1 Clarges Street, London W1Y 8AB. Telephone bookings are not accepted. No dogs, other than exhibits, are admitted.

Foyles Literary Luncheons

Highlights of the London book scene for over half a century have been more than five hundred Literary Luncheons run by Christina Foyle, daughter of the co-founder of the world-famous bookshop in Charing Cross Road that bears her name. They have become something of a national institution.

It was in 1930 that nineteen-year-old Christina had the idea. During that great literary period authors including Rudyard Kipling, Arnold Bennett and Sir James Barrie used to call at the shop and chat with her father. She was fascinated to hear them talk and, one day, after lunching with her father and John Galsworthy, she suggested to her father that their customers might enjoy small literary luncheons. With his encouragement she organized the first one later that year at the now demolished Holborn Restaurant.

'I aimed very high,' she recalled. 'I wrote to the six best-known authors of the day—among them, Bernard Shaw and H. G. Wells. I thought they would all accept and I gave them each a date, beginning in October 1930. Bernard Shaw wrote back saying that if we wanted him to come we would have to hire the Albert Hall because otherwise we would never get all the people in! H. G. Wells replied that, from the letters he received from his readers he had no wish to meet any of them in the flesh!'

Eventually, both those gentlemen came and joined a list of speakers that reads like a roll-call of outstanding men and women and celebrities from all countries and all walks of life; from the Duke of Edinburgh to Paul Robeson, from Eleanor Roosevelt to Emperor Haile Selassie. Sir Gerald du Maurier was the Chairman who introduced the first ever speaker, Lord Darling the famous Lord Chief Justice on 21 October 1930. Ironically, among the guests at that first luncheon was Lord Alfred Douglas who appeared before Lord Darling several years before for his part in the Oscar Wilde case.

For the past thirty-five years the luncheons have been held at the Dorchester Hotel, Park Lane, every month except January and August. Between four and five hundred people paid £12 for a luncheon ticket in 1983 which originally cost less than twenty-five pence.

Invitations are sent to a list of applicants only two to four weeks before each lunch and anyone wishing to be included on this list should apply to the Luncheon Secretary, W. & G. Foyle Ltd, 119–125 Charing Cross Road, London WC2.

It is an occasion on which to be smartly dressed although it is no longer necessary or particularly usual for ladies to wear hats. By tradition the Chairman and the guests at the top table are friends or associates of the guest speaker or reflect his interests. For instance, when Gayelord Hauser spoke on the publication of his book *Look Younger, Live Longer* in June 1951 its message was reflected by a top table comprised of extremely elderly notables. Similarly, when Reginald Reynolds, author of a book on beards, spoke there was not a beardless man at his table.

The rest of the guests at this three-course luncheon sit at tables for ten or twelve. They are handed a guest list on arrival and many of them elect, in advance, the friends they would like to sit with.

Celebrities are chosen to speak around the time of the publication of their books and, for the sake of topicality, the programme is not arranged far in advance. There are, however, a few notable exceptions like the luncheon in honour of Noël Coward to mark the publication of his biography, *A Talent to Amuse* by Sheridan Morley. Held on 19 November 1970 it promised to be one of the great literary and theatrical gatherings of the year, until the previous evening when disaster threatened: Noël Coward collapsed at the opening of the Coward Bar at the Phoenix Theatre; Sheridan Morley could not attend because his father was taken ill and Dame Sybil Thorndike, a guest of honour, injured her leg at the last minute. The occasion looked like developing into something of an anti-climax. Then, as the guests arrived, among them was Charlie Chaplin who had previously made a half-hearted acceptance, depending on whether he happened to be in London at the time. There could not have been a more popular reserve speaker.

Nine years later the guest of honour, Earl Mountbatten of Burma, was killed a month before the luncheon to mark the publication of the book *Mountbatten— Eighty Years in Pictures*. That time it was decided there should be no reserve speaker. Instead the luncheon on 27 September was devoted to tributes and anecdotes by his great friends including Barbara Cartland and Lord Zuckerman.

Point-to-Point Steeplechases

Held between February and June, all point-to-point meetings are run under the sanction of the Jockey Club and under rules entitled 'Jockey Club Regulations for Point-to-Point Steeple Chases', published by the Stewards of the Jockey Club.

The meetings may be held by one hunt on one day annually or by two or more adjoining hunts, the Royal Navy, the Army, the Royal Air Force, the United Services, a naval or military formation or unit, or by a club or other society approved by the Stewards of the Jockey Club. The majority of point-to-points are run by a hunt, under the control of the Master of Hounds and a committee appointed by him.

The programme usually consists of five or six races in the following categories: Hunt Race (confined to the members, subscribers and farmers of the hunt organizing the meeting); Adjacent Hunts Race (confined to members, subscribers or farmers of the hunt, or hunts promoting the meeting and approximately ten or eleven adjoining or neighbouring hunts); Mens Open; Ladies Open; Maiden Race—Open or Adjacent—(confined to horses which have never won a National Hunt flat race, flat race, hurdle or steeplechase under the rules of any Turf Authority or a steeplechase at a point-to-point meeting).

To run in a Members' Race the horse must be owned by a member, subscriber or farmer of that hunt and have been regularly hunted with the hunt concerned. The Master's agreement is usually required. For all other races a horse must have a 'Hunter's Certificate' and its name must be registered with Weatherby's (the administrators of all racing for the Jockey Club). A Hunter's Certificate is issued

Coming towards the finish in a race at the South Shropshire Point-to-Point.

by the Master of Hounds of the hunt with which it has been regularly hunted and of which its owner is a member, subscriber or farmer. The certificate must be sent to the Racing Calendar Office where it will be lodged on payment of the registration fee (at present £10.35). No horse is eligible to run in a point-to-point if it is under five years old, or since the previous July, has won any race under the rules of racing other than a Hunters' Steeplechase. If a horse has run in a steeplechase or hurdle race in the current season, on or since 1 November, other than a Hunters' Steeplechase or a race confined to amateur riders run between 1 March and 30 June it will also be ineligible.

Riders must hold a Rider's Certificate issued by the hunt of which they are a member, subscriber or farmer. A person who has held a professional rider's licence from any recognized Turf Authority, or been paid for riding in a race, or who has worked in a licensed or permitted trainer's yard in the last twelve months is not allowed to ride. All riders must have reached their sixteenth birthday.

Originally a point-to-point steeplechase was a race run across country, from steeple to steeple, crossing natural obstacles along the route, which may have even included crossing a river. This progressed to having a racecourse, with natural obstacles such as banks, walls and hedges, while today the fences are a smaller edition of those found on a recognized National Hunt racecourse. Today the course is over farmland, which may be undulating and have a ploughed field. The distance of a race is not less than three miles, with eighteen fences. There are usually eight or nine individual brush fences, one of which is an open ditch. All the fences are standardized, and the whole course is inspected by the Area Course Inspector before the meeting takes place.

All owners choose their own colours for the jumper which the jockey will wear. These colours are included in the race card produced for the day's racing. The colours only have to be registered for horses running in a Hunter Chase at a National Hunt meeting and not for point-to-point racing.

All horses and jockeys must be declared to run at least three-quarters of an hour before the time fixed for their race. The jockey must weigh out, wearing his colours and carrying his dressed saddle at least fifteen minutes before his race. The weight to be carried will be in the specifications for each race, but a general guide is that eleven stone will be carried for a Ladies' Race and twelve stone seven pounds for all others. All five-year-old horses have a seven-pound allowance, and any horse carrying overweight will have the amount announced and put on the number board. After a race the first four jockeys have to weigh in and any objections must be lodged within the first five minutes after the race.

Anybody may attend a point-to-point meeting. There is a charge at the gate depending on the area in which the meeting is held (West Country meetings are usually cheapest). Some meetings have two charges, the highest price being charged for parking adjacent to the course where most of the proceedings can be viewed from the car. The charge is for the price of admission of the car, including all occupants, which can provide a very cheap day out for all the family. Having entered the course all the facilities are usually free and available to everybody. A few of the larger point-to-points still have an area, including one side of the paddock, with its own facilities, just for members and officials of the hunt promoting the meeting, owners, riders and sponsors. Long traffic queues may occur at some meetings and it is advisable to aim to arrive at the course about an

A point-to-point meeting at Melton Mowbray in 1939. This is the
home of the Duke of Rutland's Belvoir Hunt.

hour before the first race. In wet weather extra time should be allowed for getting
in and out of the course as the car parking area may become rather boggy.

A bar refreshment tent will be found on the course, although many people
choose to take their own picnic. As at a racecourse proper, there will be a whole
host of bookmakers in attendance. Odds are generally short and it is wise to find
out the in-form horses and riders.

The crowd at a point-to-point meeting will be largely made up of the local
farming community and hunting people, although the event always attracts many
townspeople.

Generally the horses will have been entered by their owners just for fun. Many
will be home-bred and owner-ridden, but often these horses will be a real family
affair with the horse being owned by one parent, led up in the paddock by another
and ridden by the owner's son or daughter. Point-to-point racing is very closely
allied to National Hunt racing and often provides a good early education for
horses going on to a career in steeplechasing. Many leading steeplechasers have
emerged from the ranks of point-to-pointers. Spartan Missile, second in the
Grand National in 1981 and The Dickler, a Cheltenham Gold Cup winner, are
two such horses. Many horses having finished their careers in National Hunt
racing will turn to point-to-pointing, the older, better jumpers often acting as
schoolmasters for inexperienced riders.

Many of our leading National Hunt jockeys have also started life riding in
point-to-points. As with horses, the experience gained in this form of racing
stands them in good stead. Many riders have said that it is far more difficult to
ride a winner at the local point-to-point than at a race meeting on a National
Hunt racecourse!

The local meetings will be well advertised in the area, with advertisements in
the local press and also pinned up in pubs and hotels. Point-to-point racing forms
a colourful and exciting part of British country life which should not be missed.

March

Trout Fishing

If salmon fishing tends to bring before the eye romantic pictures of stern Caledonian rivers and mighty fighting fish, trout waters encourage gentler images of buttercup-rich Wessex water-meadows in May, bubbling moorland brooks, Highland loch or lowland reservoir.

Two separate trout species are to be found in the British Isles, one native and the other an importation. The native is the brown trout—which in fact varies considerably in appearance and may, if migratory, be as silver-scaled as any salmon—and the introduced foreigner the rainbow, whose natural home is Western North America. This fish is thick, silvery, often green-backed and always decorated with a pink sash along the flanks. It boasts a speckled tail-fin, an uncommon feature in brown trout; and is, in short, unmistakable in the hand and usually so in the water.

Brown trout live in most of the clearer and less sluggish rivers of Britain and Ireland including all the salmon rivers and also in natural lakes having suitable spawning streams: like salmon, trout will only spawn in running water. But brown trout nurtured in hatcheries are released into reservoirs without any breeding stream and into many rivers, too, including some of the famous Hampshire chalkstreams—anywhere, indeed, where heavy fishing pressure would otherwise rapidly exterminate such indigenous trout as survive. It is unfortunately the case that most brown trout of more than a pound in weight caught on the rod in Britain have been artificially reared and then transferred to river and lake either as juveniles or as fish of already keepable size.

Brown trout on the River Test are now of greater average weight than when all the fish on it were truly wild and a two-pounder was considered a good one. Many fishermen find this sad; others, having seldom if ever caught wild-bred trout, enjoy capturing a big fish regardless of its ancestry. And after all the vast majority of pheasants shot have been hand-reared.

Wild browns, however, are still to be found, especially in Scottish lochs and in moorland districts where rivers are rain-fed rather than perennially issuing from deep natural wells like the favoured chalkstreams of Southern England and a small part of Yorkshire. Trout in most rain-fed waters are likely to be small, a half-pounder perhaps an event, but may be numerous still. There are several limestone rivers in Gloucestershire, Yorkshire and Derbyshire that possess chalkstream characteristics such as alkaline water, profuse weed growth and clarity, encouraging trout of better size.

There exists a natural race of brown trout of migrating habit called sea-trout; like salmon they feed in salt water and ascend rivers to spawn, but unlike salmon they may breed for several successive years. Sea-trout are magnificent sporting fish, occasionally running up to fifteen pounds but more commonly weighing between one and four. In appearance they resemble small salmon. Wales, Devon

Casting for trout on the River Itchen near Ovington in Hampshire. The Itchen flows through the ancient city of Winchester into Southampton Water and like its neighbour, the Test, is one of the great trout rivers of England.

and Cornwall, North-West England and much of Scotland are strongholds, a disadvantage for poor-sighted or less adventurous fly-fishermen being that in many of their haunts good catches can only be achieved during the hours of darkness.

The rainbow trout cannot reproduce and maintain itself in Great Britain in natural conditions (if one excepts a mere handful of rivers) and must therefore be artificially reared: ninety-nine of every hundred rainbow trout caught by the angler in still or moving British waters will have been placed there by human hands.

Rainbows attain a good size in the stew ponds much more speedily than browns and given favourable conditions will continue to grow fast when 'planted out'; they display considerably more dash and vigour when hooked than hatchery-bred browns; and, being greedy feeders, seem less cautious of the artificial fly.

Another sporting fish the trout angler may well come across in running water, especially chalkstreams and in northern England, is the grayling, a distant cousin of the trout. It lives in small shoals and is silver with a large and conspicuous dorsal fin. Rising eagerly to the fly, it is good to eat in late summer and autumn but early in the season may prove a nuisance. Grayling are not, strictly speaking, game fish.

Some knowledge of the trout's domestic larder is a necessity. Strictly predatory, both brown and rainbow trout eat the living prey species most readily available at any given time: trout are not inclined to waste their energy. Little fish (not excluding their own relatives), frogs and tadpoles, shrimps, water snails and a great variety of aquatic insects, together with terrestrial creatures finding their way into the water such as worms, slugs, beetles, crane-flies and perhaps even mice are all eaten: little that lives and is small enough to swallow comes amiss. Of these, aquatic insects form from the angler's viewpoint by far the most important items; they are, so to speak, the fly dresser's raw material.

For the river trout fisherman the water-bred mayfly and its smaller relations (spring olive, iron blue, 'pale wateries' of several species, medium and blue-winged olives) bulk large. The familiar mayfly itself appears in clouds towards the end of that month over favoured waters, providing days of feasting for chaffinch, swallow and trout and days of great excitement for the frenzied fly fisherman. All these 'duns' undergo a further metamorphosis unique to themselves—those successfully running the gauntlet and taking wing from the water surface, that is. They change into 'spinners', translucent and gauzy-winged, the females depositing eggs in or on the water and then, to the satisfaction of the trout, dying upon it.

Caddis grubs complete with their cases are devoured and so—enthusiastically—are the moth-like 'sedges' into which they change. On still waters the items already mentioned, or at least their near allies, are also taken, in addition to many species of aquatic 'midge' larvae and pupae, leeches, dragonfly nymphs, water boatmen, daphnia and so on. It is, however, aquatic insects in their various life stages that are most imitated as artificial fishing flies.

These come in infinite variety, from still-water lures resembling those used for salmon to the most minute and dainty creation made in as exact an imitation of some specific water-bred insect as ingenuity can devise. The salmon fly, so called only by courtesy, is fished 'wet', that is, under the surface at greater or lesser depth; but the trout fly may be either a wet or a 'dry' pattern, the dry sort being designed to float—which, anointed with water repellent, it really will if cast lightly. The wet fly is dressed with soft 'hackle' sloping towards the bend of the hook; the dry fly with stiff feather hackle standing at right angles to the hook's shaft, and a moderately practised eye is able to distinguish each at a glance. There is, too, a separate kind of wet fly known as a 'nymph', representing a water insect in its larval stage. It has a bunched thorax and little if any hackle. Largely for still-water use, the ambitious have also invented 'flies' in imitation of shrimps, snails and tadpoles—indeed, malicious rumour has it, even of the food pellets on which stocked trout are reared!

Traditionally the chalk and limestone streams are the bastions of the dry fly and—in more recent years—the nymph also, other wet flies often being prohibited. The many rain-fed rivers may be fished either dry or wet according to choice; seldom are there restrictions. In the north the wet fly, fished up or down stream, is preferred. On still waters, whether natural or man-made, whether situated in Cornwall or the Hebrides, the wet fly in its many guises is considered by most enthusiasts to be more successful than the dry. As always, of course, there will be exceptions to any such general statement. Sea-trout are usually caught on large wet flies embellished with gold or silver ribbing: these fish are not too particular at night.

If salmon patterns may be counted in dozens, trout flies—dry and wet, winged and hackled, very large and very tiny—are numbered in hundreds if not thousands. For the beginner this is confusing, but his choice must depend upon where he intends to fish; above all on whether he plumps for still or moving water. For still water perhaps two dozen patterns will be all he requires initially; for a river, a dozen should prove ample throughout the season even on the very best water. Professional instructors are well qualified to advise the aspirant and so are fellow fishermen haunting the same waters as himself.

The dry fly is pre-eminently the one to use when trout are perceived actually 'rising' to suck in floating insects. The fly is cast upstream, or up and across, ahead of the fish (which faces upstream), the angler hoping for a take as it floats past the trout's nose. The fisherman must then raise his casting arm to set the hook, or 'strike'. In clear rivers weighted nymphs are cast upstream to visible trout sometimes lying quite deep; good eyesight is needed to time the strike correctly, while in still waters the nymph may be fished speculatively. Conventional wet flies, popular for boat and bank fishing on loch and reservoir, are on the swifter rivers fished either upstream or 'across and down', again more often than not speculatively. Though three wet flies are frequently to be seen on leaders the dry fly is fished singly.

The tackle needed for trout fly fishing is similar to that for salmon though literally on a smaller scale; trout rods vary from six and a half feet to ten in length and are all used single-handed. The short rod is brought into play on narrow, bushy brooks; the nine and ten footers are employed for sea trout and also on still waters where long casting from the bank may be essential. The prospective trout fisher who buys a cane rod of more than eight and a half feet long is ill-advised. Its weight will tend to tire him; longer rods should be of glass fibre or carbon fibre construction. Every rod must be matched with a fly line of the correct weight (marked on the rod butt). The casual fisherman, content with just one for all purposes, could do worse than to select a rod—carbon or glass fibre—eight and a half to nine feet in length and designed to cast a weight six line.

Floating tapered fly lines are needed for dry fly and nymph fishing and both 'sinkers' and 'floaters' for the wet fly, 'fast sinkers' being employed by those reservoir anglers who delight in athletically casting a very long line and retrieving big lures in a series of line-stopping jerks, as though trying to spin with the wrong tools. What has been written of salmon fly reels applies to the trout reel also, but the river man needs little backing on it unless he is after reservoir or sea-trout.

Landing nets are essential and are legion in pattern, some being telescopic. Size should be suited to the size of trout anticipated, or approximately so; for the rest, carrying comfort and speed into action without the mesh becoming entangled are what matter most. Easily the best thing to carry dead trout in is the cheap bass or frail made of plaited (Chinese!) rush, obtainable from ships' chandlers and some mail order tackle firms, to which a strap should be attached. It is very light, keeps fish beautifully fresh and will last a season. Some prefer a handsome and expensive slung bag both for tackle and fish (presumably in separate compartments); other anglers carry their tackle in the pockets of fishing coat or waistcoat. Never put any kind of fish into plastic bags unless they are to go into the freezer immediately. Nothing deprives them of freshness more quickly.

Chest-high waders will seldom be needed, but thigh boots are necessary for wading and ordinary rubber knee-boots for fishing from a bank. The trout man will require the same sort of clothing and general odds and ends of tackle as the salmon fisherman, plus a pair of polarizing sunglasses for seeing into the water, not forgetting a priest of more modest weight; he will rarely be accompanied by a keeper and must get his knots right unaided.

Spinning for ordinary brown trout and rainbows is frowned on much more often than not. It is considered less sporting than fly-fishing as well as less satisfying; and treble hooks damage the mouths of young trout. For sea-trout however, it may well be allowable, particularly in Wales or Scotland. In high, coloured water the worm can be a deadly bait for these noble fish but while worming is permitted on some association waters the rule is by no means universal. In spite of the occasional advantages to be derived from spinning or the lowly worm, the majority of trout seekers never dream of wielding any weapon other than the fly rod.

Many consider the southern English chalkstreams the finest of all British rivers for trout, certainly for big trout and for fishermen preferring dry fly or nymph to wet, in spite of the heavy stocking deemed necessary in parts of some. The Test, Itchen and Kennet are premier names; there are too the Anton (a Test tributary), the Avon from Salisbury up, the Wylye and Nadder (both Avon tributaries) and the Dorset Frome. (There exists a small Dorset chalkstream with the enchanting name of Piddle.) Others less well-known may be found as good, any unpolluted chalk river is likely to prove more than satisfactory. There is a magic about its pellucid, leisurely flow, rich insect life, trailing skeins of bright green weed and boldly spotted trout that irresistibly appeals to many a trout angler. Until a few years ago it was hard, at short notice, to find fishing on chalk rivers, but day tickets for some stretches are now available as well as season 'rods'—often advertised in *Trout and Salmon* the winter before. Advertisements for ticket and season fishing must be closely scanned, or else the agents named in the salmon section consulted. Chalkstream fishing is never cheap.

Rain-fed rivers are altogether too numerous for all but a few to be named. In Scotland (without chalk rivers) the Deveron and in particular the Don contain very good brown trout: hotel water is easily obtainable. On the Border flows the Tweed and its many tributaries; there is the Eden in north-west England and in Yorkshire numerous rivers, some limestone. But in Derbyshire the limestone Dove, Isaak Walton's beloved river, is no longer what it was; though Derwent and its tributary the Wye are good, the latter is interesting as one of the few rivers in which rainbow trout breed naturally. In the West Country Exe, Taw and the Tamar tributaries provide good sport for small and lively trout, several very well-known fishing hotels having much water.

For the sea-trout hunter many Scottish rivers will provide sport, best known is the Aberdeenshire Ythan where there is good hotel fishing. Many if not most Welsh game rivers have good runs, sometimes of really heavy fish. In Devon the Taw, Torridge and Teign, and in Cornwall the Fowey, can be good.

Still water fisheries exist almost everywhere, a considerable number of reservoirs having been opened for (stocked) trout fishing within the past ten years. Famous are Blagdon and Chew in Somerset and the vast Rutland water in the Midlands, also the more recently opened Wimbleball on Exmoor, day ticket waters all. But there exist dozens more, great and small, on which day tickets are readily available without notice. A few 'artificial' waters, however, are open only to season ticket holders, the highly reputed Two Lakes fishery at Romsey by the Test being one.

Wild trout may be caught in Lake District waters and of course on dozens and dozens of Scottish lochs on the mainland and all the isles, not necessarily small ones, either.

The choice is bewildering; it is certain that better waters than some of those mentioned are waiting to be fished by the conscientious researcher. Once hooked by trout fishing, the victim is unlikely ever to free himself.

As for salmon the Regional Water Authorities of England and Wales determine the local opening and closing dates for trout fishing on every river within their jurisdiction. However, seasons and licences for trout fishing are a simpler business altogether. Unlike the unpredictable salmon, both species of trout are confined to fresh water throughout the year and must feed in it, the one exception being the migratory sea-trout. The choice of time—of exact 'season within season'—becomes a great deal less critical. While on every water some months may be better than others, at any period of the open season fish can be caught, weather allowing: and if, for example, he selects May or June the trout fisherman should scarcely fail anywhere unless after sea-trout, which may be more plentiful later in the summer. Some rain-fed rivers open in mid-March, but their inhabitants often remain in poor winter condition until April. Many chalkstreams do not open until 1 May. Still water dates more or less correspond to those of rivers. At the end of September, perhaps mid-October, river trout rods will be put away, but certain reservoirs stocked with 'put-and-take' rainbows remain open until the year's end.

Precise dates of seasons on different catchment areas may be discovered by consulting the pages of *Where to Fish*, plus details of rod licences—a rod licence for trout in England and Wales being as necessary as for salmon. If in pursuit of sea-trout the fisherman must expect to pay more for his licence than when brown or rainbow trout are his ambition: they are accounted fish more valuable.

Coursing: The Waterloo Cup

Coursing is the testing of the agility, strength and speed of two greyhounds in action against their natural quarry, the hare. There are two ways of coursing, walked up and driven. In driven coursing, a team of beaters is used to drive the hares slowly one by one into the running ground. The slipper or starter is hidden in a blind or hide and he watches the hare go by, having a good look at it to make sure it is fit and well and not in any way lame or damaged. Having given it some eighty yards start the two competing greyhounds are then slipped and the course is on. The greyhounds each wear a collar of a different colour, usually red or white, and the judge, who is mounted, carries two flags of the same colours so that he can signify the winner. The main object of the course being to test the dogs, and not to kill the hare, points are awarded for speed on the run up to the hare, for the first dog to do the turn, and also the angle of the turn. Points are not

The Waterloo Cup, from a painting by Richard Ansdell. Hare coursing is a very ancient sport, and the English greyhound is supreme in the field for its speed, agility and stamina.

usually awarded for the kill but if circumstances merit it, a maximum of one point can be awarded. The trip, i.e., an unsuccessful attempt to kill, is also awarded one point. In walked up coursing no beaters are used, but the competitors and spectators line out across the running grounds and with the slipper, the judge and the two dogs to be slipped in the centre of the line, walk slowly forward until a hare is put up, when, after the usual eighty-yard start the dogs are slipped and the course is on. The greyhounds compete on the knock-out system and the winner from each pair goes forward to meet another dog until by process of elimination the outright winner is found.

The normal number in a 'stake' is sixty-four dogs and if this number is run to a full and successful conclusion it is likely to take the best part of two days. Greyhounds hunt only by sight, and do not put their noses to the ground and search, so that there are no long hold-ups. Once the hare has gone through the hedge the hounds stop, and that is the end of that course. Every effort is made to allow the hare to get away, and to see that there is no suffering imposed. Around the edges of the running ground smeuses or small sleeves are built into the hedges which will let the hare escape and through which the greyhounds cannot follow. On some of the larger grounds, small underground cellars called sloughs are installed which provide a safe haven for the tired hare. At the average coursing meeting, something less than ten per cent of the hares get killed.

In Britain, there are several breeds of running dogs, or sight hounds which are used for coursing. The whippet, or mini greyhound, came into prominence early in this century as a rabbiting dog or food provider in the mining districts. There is now a thriving Whippet Coursing Club, which holds several good hare-coursing meetings every year. The saluki, or gazelle hound, also has a thriving coursing club, but in competition with greyhounds they come off second best, and although they appear to have a little more stamina than the English greyhound, they do not quite have the speed. The Scottish deerhound, a most delightful and romantic-looking animal, is also catered for in the coursing world. Last, but not least, comes the old favourite, the lurcher, the dog beloved not only by the gypsy fraternity, but also by the landed gentry. Lurchers hunt by scent as well as by sight and are supreme hare-killing machines, the ideal poachers' tool, but they do not do so well under strict competition rules. Coursing can vary a lot according to the breed being used, and also the type of land on which it is taking place. It is certainly one of the most exciting spectator sports available. The season runs from September to the end of March and as a lot of standing about is involved it is advisable to put on plenty of warm clothing and boots and to be prepared for a cold day. Don't forget to fill the hipflasks.

Meetings are held all over the country each year under the control of the National Coursing Club, 35 Grosvenor Gardens, London SW1, who will be glad to send details of any meetings. The most important meeting of the year is the Waterloo Cup which has now been held for nearly two hundred years on the marshes at Altcar between Liverpool and Southport. This is a stake for sixty-four dogs, the best in the land and is well worth a visit; all the best British dogs will be in action striving to win the Blue Riband of the coursing world. Coursing is one of the oldest, if not actually the oldest, dog sports known to man, having been handed down to us from as far back as the ancient Egyptians, and it is still thriving.

Hunting

The British have been hunting with hounds since mediaeval times. Today you can hunt deer, fox, hare and mink with hounds and there are some 346 packs of hounds. Some are hunted on foot but most from horses, in which case it is taken for granted that you need to be a competent horseman.

Some homework is needed before embarking on a hunting tour. It is important to contact the Masters or Secretaries of the packs with which you wish to hunt. Details of the various hunts can be found in *Baily's Hunting Directory*, published by J. A. Allen and Co Ltd, a book which is essential when planning a hunting tour. *Horse and Hound* and the *Shooting Times* are weekly magazines which can be found on most newsagents' shelves, and are full of information about hounds and hunting. The *Shooting Times* often includes a feature on sporting hotels and will always produce a back copy. If you don't have your own hunting clothes you can hire them from Moss Bros, of London. Take care to choose the correct kit; good quality and a good fit make for a more comfortable day's hunting, but don't expect the staff at Moss Bros to advise you.

The hiring of a horse is a problem with every pack, but the Hunt Secretary will be able to put you in touch with a good hireling yard, and they will usually also be able to give advice on good hotels in the area. It is from the Secretary or the Master that you must get permission to hunt. Useful information can also be obtained from the Master of Foxhounds Association whose Honorary Secretary is Mr A. H. B. Hart, Parsloes Cottage, Bagendon, Cirencester, Gloucestershire (028 583 470).

Spring staghunting begins in early March and goes on until the last day of April.

Three- and four-year-old stags are hunted as a culling exercise and this is a very popular form of hunting with both locals and visitors from foxhunting packs who will normally have finished their season.

In all deerhunting only the Joint-Masters and the hunt staff wear scarlet. Both men and women of the field wear ratcatcher dress. Men wear a tweed coat, boots and breeches, collar and tie and a bowler hat. Women wear a tweed coat, coloured tie, boots, breeches and bowler hat or a hunting cap.

Stags, horses and hounds are very fit after a long season so you will have to ride hard. Do not push your horse early in the day. A good tip is to try and stay on the hill top and to follow a local farmer. You may not see every move of hounds, but the chances are you will still have some horse-power left at the end when you will need it.

In the West of England where staghunting takes place it rains a good deal. Take a good waterproof with you or you can get very wet. Be sure to check with your hotel that they have drying facilities.

Hiring horses is always difficult, but bring your own only if it is exceptionally fit. There is no jumping, but much galloping up and down lots of hills and very steep they are. There is little chance of a clever horse 'jumping his way to the front'. When hiring a horse a personal recommendation is a great help. Nothing is more wasteful than paying good money for a bad horse. The Hunt Secretary will help if your hotel can't. Hounds meet at 11 o'clock and carry on until they catch their deer or until lack of daylight forces them to finish.

The stag is harboured before the meet and not until the harbourer has returned with news of where the stag is lying will the hounds move off. The tufters are some of the older, steady hounds and are taken to rouse the stag while the rest of the pack are kennelled. Only when the stag is running on its own and a line has been established are the tufters stopped and the pack called for. When it arrives the stag is given twenty minutes' law before the pack is laid on. Then the hunt proper begins. Hold on to your hat for you will be riding hard until the stag is taken. During the hunt the stag will often lie down and this may cause a short delay. Make good use of this by giving your horse a break. When, eventually, the stag has had enough it will stand at bay, almost always in water. Hounds will be whipped off and one of the local farmers who is carrying the gun that day will dispatch him at short range. The paunching is done by the huntsman and it is he who gives out the trophies. The head becomes the property of the Master who will give it to someone who has helped the hounds throughout the season. The slots (feet) are given away as are the liver, heart and kidneys. Should you be lucky remember that a financial thank-you to the huntsman is usual. The offal goes as a reward to the hounds and the carcass goes to the farmers in the parish where the stag was found since it is they who have been feeding him on their land all the year.

The Cheltenham National Hunt Festival

The Cheltenham Festival Meeting, held in mid-March every year, is arguably the most prestigious event of the winter racing calendar. Cheltenham produces the champions of the season, as the best steeplechasers and hurdlers from England and Ireland meet here. Although this meeting is regarded as the climax to the National Hunt Season, the 'Winter Game' season runs on into June, spanning some ten months and racing on forty-four different racecourses throughout the country.

Even the setting of the course, beneath the Cotswold Hills at the edge of this attractive spa town, makes the Cheltenham Festival meeting unique. There cannot be a more picturesque racecourse than this, or one on which so many great battles have been fought. Although racing takes place at Cheltenham all winter it is of the Festival Meeting that one thinks when Cheltenham is mentioned. It is held over three days in mid-March and often produces the most exciting finishes and unexpected results that one could imagine. The famous Cheltenham uphill finish, with the crowds surging either side of the rails, has stopped many fancied horses from winning races as their stamina was sapped by it.

In recent years many improvements have been made to both the course and its facilities. Cheltenham is a group one racecourse, meaning that it is one of those at the top of the grade. (Racecourses are graded according to their racetrack and amenities, from group one to group four.) New grandstands have been built and improvements made to the paddock and weighing-room areas. The course has changed over the years, but the present arrangement with two courses seems to work well. At one time runners in four-mile chases passed behind the grandstand and were therefore out of view of the public. A bronze statue of Arkle, Gold Cup victor in the 1960s, can be seen at the side of the parade ring.

The Prince of Wales and Queen Elizabeth the Queen Mother
watching a race at the Cheltenham National Hunt Festival.

The Cheltenham Gold Cup, run over $3\frac{1}{4}$ miles, is the race at which every owner
and trainer of a staying chaser sets his sights. First run in 1924, the race was
overshadowed in its early days by the Grand National, held two weeks later at
Liverpool (Aintree), but gradually it caught the imagination of the public and its
prestige was soon firmly established.

Many famous horses and jockeys have won the Gold Cup, including the great
Golden Miller who won it five times (1932–36), a feat not yet accomplished by
any other horse. Cottage Rake won the race three times (1948–50) and Arkle, one
of the most beloved steeplechasers, achieved victory in 1964–66. Of late the Irish
have had their fair share of Gold Cup successes, winning it six times in the 1970s.

Cheltenham's $3\frac{1}{4}$ miles is a gruelling test of a horse, especially as all Gold Cup
horses carry twelve stone and many a horse has been caught coming up the
Cheltenham Hill after the last fence. No horse has yet won both a Champion
Hurdle and a Gold Cup, but Night Nurse, a double Champion Hurdle winner in
the 1970s, nearly won in 1981 but was narrowly beaten by stable companion
Little Owl, ridden by his part-owner Jim Wilson. He was only the third amateur
rider to win a Gold Cup. Whatever the result at Cheltenham in the Gold Cup, one
can be certain that the winning horse is a good one, but oddly enough very few
favourites have ever won the race, other than the mighty trio of Golden Miller,
Cottage Rake and Arkle.

The 2 miles 200 yards Champion Hurdle is the Crown for hurdlers: the race,
first run in 1927, is that which every hurdler's owner and trainer wishes to win,
and is run on the Wednesday of the Festival Meeting. Several Champion Hurdle
winners have captured the imagination of the racing public. Hattons Grace,
victor in 1949, 1950 and 1951, Sir Ken from 1952 to 1954 and Persian War from

1968 to 1970 have each won the race three times, but of late it has been the battles between Monksfield, the Irish challenger, and Sea Pigeon which have produced some dramatic finishes. The jockey Tim Molony won the race four times from 1951 to 1954.

Other major races of the Festival Meeting include the Daily Express Triumph Hurdle which is the highest achievement for four-year-olds who would usually have had an introduction to racing as three-year-olds the previous autumn. This race often provides the top hurdlers of the future.

The National Hunt Two-Mile Champion Chase often produces interesting finishes and is the premier chase for two-mile chasers, while the Arkle Challenge Trophy and the Sun Alliance Chase provide championships for novice horses over two and three miles respectively. 'Novices' are horses that have not won a race before the beginning of the season. The 'novice' hurdlers are catered for by the Sun Alliance Novices Hurdle and the Waterford Crystal Supreme Champion Novices Hurdle, the former run over $2\frac{1}{2}$ miles and the latter over 2 miles.

Another aspect of the Cheltenham National Hunt Festival is the two Hunter Chases, the Foxhunters' Challenge Cup and the Cathcart Champion Chase. Hunter Chases are open to horses which have hunted with a recognized pack of foxhounds during the current season and are ridden by amateur jockeys. These horses are commonly home produced and are often owner ridden. Hunter chasers of this standard are usually very useful individuals and many such as Grittar, winner of the 1982 Grand National, and Spartan Missile, second in the Grand National the previous year, go on to greater achievements.

The Cheltenham National Hunt Festival Meeting is naturally the most popular meeting held at Cheltenham, so the racecourse is packed to capacity, especially on Gold Cup day. With this in mind it is often easier to go to the course by coach as long queues for car parking are the norm.

Under normal circumstances it is possible to obtain food and drink in the racecourse restaurants, but on Gold Cup days this could prove somewhat difficult. Accommodation in the Cheltenham area can also prove difficult to obtain as it is usually booked up months in advance. When seeking accommod-

Smartly dressed and aristocratic spectators
at the 1911 Cheltenham Gold Cup meeting.

ation it normally pays to read the classified advertisements in the sporting press.

Cheltenham provides a real showpiece for National Hunt Racing and despite the crush at the Festival Meeting it is well worth attending. Dress in the Paddock Area is smart, but elsewhere on the course anything goes!

For information about tickets apply to the Secretary of the racecourse.

The English Rowing Season and the University Boat Race

As with many other famous events in our sporting calendar, the English rowing season is a Victorian legacy, and unashamedly 'Oxbridge' based. This is fitting, for it was at Oxford and Cambridge that the foundations were laid of a supremacy in English rowing never seriously challenged until 1906, when a crew of Belgians carried off the Grand Challenge Cup at Henley Royal Regatta. To add to this catastrophe the Belgians, as was noted in near-outrage by one organ of the press, *rowed in purple sock-suspenders.*

Since that black day rowing in Britain has steadily recovered to a point when British crews, today recruited from a plethora of rowing clubs across the nation, regularly win medals at the Olympic Games and the great International Championships. But it is pleasant to reflect that this success has not been won at the expense of the original Victorian highlights of the English rowing season. Though of little relevance to the international rowing scene (Henley Royal Regatta excepted), they still provide the opportunity for convivial gatherings, to see and be seen—irrespective of any direct interest in events on the water.

Oxford oarsman in 1829.

The Oxford v. Cambridge University Boat Race—'*the* Boat Race', as it is invariably known—is more than a great national institution: it is a phenomenon. Perhaps the Oxford don Dacre Balsdon gave the best summing-up of the Boat Race in his book *Oxford Life*, when he wrote (more in sorrow than anger, one feels)

> Here are the two most famous Universities in the world, Oxford and Cambridge, and the world in general knows and is interested in one thing only about them—the fact that nine men from one and nine men from the other go to London some time round about Easter to see which nine can travel three and a half miles in a boat faster than the other. In this, however, the world is interested, and the newspapers are there to see that the world does not lose its interest.

Despite its international fame the Boat Race is basically a private challenge event; it cannot take place without last year's losing University Boat Club formally challenging the other. The first race was held in 1829, not on the London Tideway but at Henley-on-Thames; and to this day an 1829 gold sovereign is used when the two captains toss for stations before the race. The event was moved to Putney when it was agreed that only the London river offered proper scope for a really testing endurance race over three miles.

Cambridge oarsman in 1829.

Hammersmith Bridge on Boat Race Day in the 1860s, from a painting by Walter Greaves. The bridges over the Thames are still popular for viewing the race, although, needless to say, spectators are no longer allowed to perch on the suspension cables.

Only the iron hand of tradition could possibly keep crews racing, year in and year out, over a course which is so wickedly unfair. On the map the Boat Race course looks fair enough: an inverted 'U' shape, with the advantages and disadvantages of the two sides cancelled out. In practice, however, records show that the long inside bend of the Surrey (left hand) station has won more races than the Middlesex station, whose crew is favoured only briefly at the beginning and end of the race. The crews have only one advantage in common: the flood tide on which the race is always rowed, from Putney upstream to Mortlake. Even the tidal current can only be exploited to the full by one crew. It flows strongest in the deepest part of the river, an invisible, narrow track which meanders to and fro and can only be learned from hard experience in training. When the boats are racing neck and neck, each cox tries to push the other 'out of the tide' by edging across—gamesmanship pure and simple, calling for vigilance from the umpire heading the following armada of launches.

Given the worldwide interest and psychological build-up to the race, only the vilest of weather conditions normally justify postponement. The culprit is always the wind, which when blowing from certain directions can whip up standing waves to swamp the boat which tries to forge through. Here again it is up to the coxes to decide whether to risk 'staying in the tide' and shipping heavy, perhaps excessive amounts of water, or head out into calmer water and lose the push of the tide.

Though tradition is the essence of the Boat Race, there have been two notable innovations in recent years. The first, dating from 1966, has been a 'warm-up' race between the University second crews, 'Isis' for Oxford and 'Goldie' for Cambridge ('Isis' being the name of the Thames at Oxford and 'Goldie' that of a pillar of Cambridge rowing in Victorian times). The Isis–Goldie race has become a regular fixture on Boat Race Day, and is rowed an hour before the Boat Race itself. The second innovation came very recently, when the all-male restriction was lifted and ladies were allowed to compete, the first to win a Rowing Blue being the delectable Miss Sue Brown who was Oxford's cox in 1981 and 1982.

The Boat Race is the world's only rowing event in which bad weather can render the course unfit for play. It has been raced in blizzards, and in conditions so still and warm that crews have suffered from the heat. Keep a close eye on the pattern of the weather over the forty-eight hours before Boat Race day, and do not be misled by the weather conditions on Boat Race morning. In late March weather conditions are particularly susceptible to rapid change, so dress with particular care before setting out for the river. Above all choose comfortable boots or shoes which will stand up to slush, crowd trampling and cold. Wherever you are you will have a lot of standing about to do, and places to sit down are rare. Even if you or your driver are familiar with parking conditions in Putney, Barnes and Mortlake, the press of the crowds can make it all too easy for you to end up soaked by an untimely shower, far from the car or other shelter.

Unless your party is embarking to follow the race in a private launch, there are three main choices of viewpoint with shelter close at hand. These are the start at Putney (Surrey bank), the halfway point at Hammersmith Bridge (Middlesex bank) and the finish at Mortlake (Surrey bank again). There are public houses at all three where you can get a drink if you haven't brought a flask (particularly recommended if the weather is cold).

All the excitement and bustle of the pre-race 'warm-up' is to be found opposite the start at Putney. Here, with the boat-houses of the famous London Tideway rowing clubs conveniently to hand, good vantage-points may be found from which to watch the embarking crews, the start, and the first quarter-mile of the race; or to meet friends before taking a stroll along the towpath towards Hammersmith.

A pleasant alternative is an early snack lunch at the Doves (just upstream of Hammersmith Bridge on the Middlesex bank). From here you can watch the Isis–Goldie Race before strolling across Hammersmith Bridge and going down to the towpath; then, with the bridge at your back and the river on your right, walk on to pick your vantage-point above the long Corney Reach, by Duke's Meadows, in time for the main race.

The third choice is the finish at Mortlake, which may be reached from the Surrey side via Barnes or the Middlesex side via Chiswick Bridge. If you want to *see* the finish, get to the riverside at Mortlake in good time, before the Isis–Goldie Race starts; snacks and drinks may be had at the riverside hostelries close at hand.

Finally, a word on betting, always tempting with such a partisan event. No matter how well you think you know the form by studying the performances of each crew during training (there is no other clue), remember what an unusually open race this can be. Though there *is* nearly always a clear SP favourite, *do not lay any sizeable bets without covering yourself,* as with a bet on whether or not the result will be closer than three lengths (most unusual). One Boat Race forecast is nearly always safe: that the odds against a neck-and-neck finish will be the longest of all.

April

Lurchers

Some years ago, one was always being asked the question 'What is a lurcher?' but since the advent of the Lambourn Lurcher Show some fourteen years ago, the question does not pop up quite so often. A lurcher is a hybrid greyhound, not a mongrel or a haphazard crossbreed, but a greyhound crossed with another breed to improve its stamina, performance and intelligence.

The pure greyhound is the athlete of the dog world. It is an unbeatable machine for dog-racing or coursing, and, while all this is very good in its way, it will not fill the larder. Something more is needed. The greyhound hunts by sight and rarely uses its nose. It has terrific acceleration, but its brakes and steering would fail the MOT Test, and it soon burns up all its available energy. To combat these faults and improve the quality of the dog's work it is necessary to use an outcross to one of the working breeds which will provide the endurance, stamina and brains. This can be done by crossing with Border collies, deerhounds, salukis, or retrievers. The Scotch or Border collie, which can run thirty to forty miles a day without tiring, and at the end of the day's work can catch his own supper, sleep rough and still be ready for another day on the hill sheep gathering, is the favourite choice. With this cross one loses a little of the original speed, but this is made up by the increase in intelligence and endurance. The best results appear to be obtained by taking the progeny of the first mating and putting them back again to another greyhound, resulting in a dog that is three-quarter greyhound and one-quarter sheepdog.

A good well-bred lurcher is a very versatile dog and has many uses. They are the ideal poacher's dog, and as such the owners do not like to say anything about them unless they know the person they are talking to very well, so for many years and for obvious reasons, not much was known about lurchers except in certain sections of the community.

When the Lambourn Lurcher Show was first started, it was in a very small way

The lurcher, a carefully bred cross between a greyhound and one of a number of breeds known for intelligence and stamina, such as Border collies, deerhounds, salukis or retrievers.

and the success of that first show must have startled the organizers. It certainly brought lurcher owners into the limelight. Most lurchers at that time seem to have been owned either by a duke or a dustman, who all gathered together bound by their affection and admiration for the most versatile and hard working member of the canine world. The show grew from what was just about a Sunday afternoon tea party into, in a few short years, a major show. The most recent shows were attended by between 15,000 and 20,000 people with over 2000 lurchers. The number and standard of the entries were fantastic, with over one hundred and fifty in each class. The obstacle racing kept going all day, and at the end of the day, the lurcher racing held sway for several hours. Unfortunately, in the first year, as with all these good things, a doubtful element crept in and now the show has had to be abandoned. It just outgrew itself. If you can imagine large furniture vans arriving with twenty men and some forty dogs inside, large numbers of them camping for the full week, and then thousands of spectators turning out on the Sunday, it is clear that the countryside was just unable to absorb them all. The fighting and generally bad behaviour was more than a quiet little place like Lambourn could possibly survive, so regretfully, the committee had to cancel any further shows. This does not mean that there are no other lurcher shows. Most Hunts now have their own and there are many good shows taking place across the country every year between April and September.

It should be borne in mind that most if not all lurchermen are dealers by nature and cannot resist a deal, or a swop, so that most lurchers can be purchased, at a price, except for some of the very best which are priceless. The best lurcher shows are all advertised in the columns of the *Shooting Times*, which is published weekly.

Mink Hunting

This summer sport has taken over from otter-hunting following the decline of the otter population. The disappearance of the otter was not caused by hunting, but by pollution of rivers and the destruction of its quiet habitat by so-called aquatic sports. The wild mink, a descendant of those bred for their fur, has adapted well to life in modern rivers and is the major farming pest of today. They will kill almost anything that comes their way, from lambs downwards.

Mink hunting begins as early as Easter and goes on until October when the rivers become swollen. As a summer pastime this form of hunting has much to recommend it.

English rivers in the summer are as beautiful as any in the world and to walk in and alongside them with the cry of hounds to spur you on is a perfect way to spend an afternoon. The people you will meet are generally most amusing, if a little intense. Some packs of mink hounds are reluctant to publish their meets, so you should ask around the pubs and once the locals realize that you are keen to follow and support you will be made most welcome.

Mink hunting involves much 'water-work' and clambering over fences, so clothing should be light, tough and quick drying. Whatever you do don't wear 'wellies'. Shoes or plimsolls are much more suitable.

There are packs of mink hounds all over England and Wales, but not all are listed in *Baily's Hunting Directory*. Local enquiries will usually bring results.

The Grand National

The Grand National is regarded by many as the premier steeplechase of the National Hunt season in Britain and as the finest horse race in the world, but others consider the race to be far too stringent a test of a horse. Run in the first few days of April over a unique course at Aintree, a district six miles north of Liverpool, it is 4 miles 856 yards in length.

The origins of the race are quite fascinating. It was a Mr Lynn, landlord of the Waterloo Hotel in Liverpool who laid out the course at Aintree where the first Grand National was run. At this stage the race was called the Grand Liverpool and Captain Becher made a name for himself by falling into a brook, now called Becher's Brook and thought to be the most famous fence in the world. In 1843 the race became a handicap and continued to grow in prestige until the Second World War put a stop to racing.

After the war the National started to emerge in the way that one knows it today. When the weights are published in February, there is immediately a public upsurge of interest. In recent years there has been a shift of interest away from Aintree, but the course still provides a wonderful three-day meeting of chasing and hurdle racing, culminating in the Grand National on the Saturday, although this is now the only race meeting of the year staged at Liverpool.

The Grand National course at Aintree is only used for three races a year: two steeplechases and the National. The former two races are run two days before the National and only over one circuit of the course, instead of two as in the National. The course is designed to test the stamina of the most experienced horses and jockeys.

Every horse which goes round Aintree must be at the peak of its fitness, which will have taken months of preparation to achieve. In a race like the National with so many runners and, inevitably, many fallers it is by no means certain that horse and jockey will return unscathed, but all being well and with luck a good jumper and brave jockey will get round intact.

The famous fences of Aintree—the Chair, Valentines, Becher's Brook and others—create the spectacle that is Aintree. The horrific Canal Turn, with the horses jumping at a sharp angle, is equally fearsome.

In 1977 Charlotte Brew became the first lady to ride in a Grand National on Barony Fort, having qualified to enter the race by finishing fourth in the Foxhunters the previous year. She managed to get to the third last fence before her horse refused. In 1982 Geraldine Rees became the first woman to complete the course on Cheers.

There have been many thrills and spills around Aintree, not least in 1967 when almost the whole field was brought down in a massive pile-up. Foinavon, ridden by Johnny Buckingham, managed to avoid the grief and romped home at 100–1.

In recent years it is hunter chasers who have shown the way. In 1982 Dick Saunders became the oldest man to win the Grand National, at the age of forty-seven. An outstanding amateur rider, farmer and Master of Foxhounds, Dick chose this moment to 'hang up his boots'.

In 1981 a real fairytale ending was provided when Bob Champion and Aldaniti won from John Thorne on Spartan Missile. Bob Champion fought off cancer with the aim of winning and Aldaniti once broke down so badly that he was

Racehorses flying over Becher's Brook during the Grand
National. The Aintree Course is famous for its fences, such as
the Chair, Valentines and the fearsome Canal Turn.

nearly destroyed. If the stories behind the winning combination were not
sufficient it was John Thorne, amateur rider, grandfather, fifty-four years of age,
on his home-bred Spartan Missile who nearly stole the show.

Much has been said recently about the future of the National. The Jockey Club
have now pledged to raise £4,000,000 to buy the course so that this marvellous
spectacle will not be lost. Certainly an important part of the British heritage, it is
something one cannot afford to lose.

Generally speaking the amenities at Aintree are poor. The grandstands are old
and badly in need of renewing, which is part of the future plan. It is intended that
the oil paintings of famous National winners and memorabilia associated with
National heroes will always be on display in the new grandstand, as permanent
reminders of the race's glory. If one chooses to view the horses in the paddock
before the National the chances are that one will miss the race as it is impossible
to push one's way to the stands.

Endless queues for drinks and lavatories are to be expected. It could easily take
up to twenty minutes to obtain a cup of tea.

Dress is smart in the enclosure, but be prepared to be squashed and jostled.

Aintree is situated on the A59 road out of Liverpool where extremely long
traffic delays are to be expected.

Flat Racing

Throughout the flat racing season, which begins at Doncaster at the end of March or early April and continues until the first week of November when the final meeting is also held at Doncaster, more than five hundred race-meetings are held in England, Scotland and Wales under Jockey Club Rules. It is usual for each meeting to commence at 2.0 pm, with a minimum of six races which are run at thirty-minute intervals. In midsummer some evening meetings are held with the first race at 6.0 pm. The principal meetings are Newmarket, where there are two separate racecourses, Chester, York, Epsom, Ascot, Goodwood, Sandown, Newbury and Doncaster. The fixture list for the season is published in the late autumn of the previous year in the Racing Calendar and details appear in the national press.

On every racecourse the grandstand enclosures are divided into Members', Tattersalls and Silver Ring, with the Members' Enclosure being the most exclusive. The cost of annual membership, which on some courses requires being proposed and the payment of an entrance fee, brings considerable financial concessions over day-to-day admission charges. Vouchers are not required for day-to-day admission other than at Epsom on Derby Day and for the four-day Royal Ascot meeting in June. Restaurant and bar facilities are provided in every enclosure, on all racecourses, but nowadays it is becoming increasingly popular for racegoers to take their own picnic hampers from which they eat and drink in the car parks. These car parks are ample in area, but not necessarily free other than to annual members. Bookmakers willing to accept cash bets will be found in Tattersalls and the Silver Ring whilst the Tote also operates a cash and a credit service. Bookmakers who accept bets from clients with credit accounts will be found 'on the rails' which separate the Members' Enclosure from Tattersalls.

Commentaries are broadcast on every race at all racecourses so that spectators in each enclosure can be kept informed as to how the race is being run. This service is invaluable, for many English racecourses, unlike those in other parts of the world, have starts more than a mile from the grandstands. In addition to the broadcast commentaries, a photo-finish camera, race-timing apparatus, starting stalls and a public address system are provided by Racecourse Technical Services. Closed-circuit television is also provided on many racecourses for executives wish to do all in their power to make an afternoon's racing as enjoyable as possible from the viewpoint of the spectators, for whom no rules about dress are laid down except for the Members' Enclosure at Epsom on Derby Day and the Royal Enclosure at Royal Ascot where men must wear morning dress and top hats. It is accepted practice, however, that at the major meetings men wear suits and a hat, whilst the apparel for women is left to their taste and discretion. This discretion results in regular women racegoers dressing for stylish comfort without ostentation.

A Turf historian once commented: 'It would be as whimsical to imagine New York minus Wall Street, or Canterbury denuded of its cathedral, as to think of Newmarket without the Jockey Club.' His comment was justified for the Club, whose existence was first mentioned in print in 1752, gradually increased its benevolent despotism until its authority was so great that in 1842 Lord Abinger told a Court of Exchequer jury, 'neither you nor I are called upon to settle any controversy between members of the Jockey Club. They are gentlemen of high honour, and in consequence of the law not making any provision for the transactions in which they are engaged for their own amusement, have a law amongst themselves which they are competent, if they think fit, to decide upon ...' Until the middle of the nineteenth century Jockey Club members wore a uniform consisting of a cutaway brown coat with gilt buttons above doeskin breeches and boots when they raced at Newmarket.

Newmarket, twelve miles to the east of Cambridge, had become the headquarters of horse-racing in Britain more than a century before the establishment of the Jockey Club. King James I, who enjoyed hunting and hawking, discovered the sporting potential of the area which is so called because traders from the ancient village of Exning had founded a 'new market' soon after the plague of 1227. King Charles II, who loved Newmarket with even more passion than his grandfather, frequently took his Court and his courtiers to the town to avoid the dreary never-ending intrigue of politics in London, and rebuilt the palace which had fallen into disrepair during the Commonwealth. His patronage brought prestige to Newmarket and it was recorded in both 1671 and 1674 that he rode in races. Sir Robert Carr wrote in March 1674, 'Yesterday His Majesty rode himself three heats and a course, and won the Plate—all four were hard and neer-ridden* and I do assure you that the King won by good horsemanship.' One of his stallions was called Old Rowley which became his rider's nickname, and also the derivation of a part of the racecourse which is known as the 'Rowley Mile'. The Town Plate was founded by King Charles II in 1665 and is still run over a distance of four miles across the heath on the second Thursday in October.

The 'Rowley Mile' course is 1¼ miles straight, with races of longer distances starting beyond the Devil's Dyke and bearing right-handed into the straight. The straight is level until descending into 'The Dip' beside 'The Bushes' 2½ furlongs from the winning post.

From 1685 when the King died until the advent of the Jockey Club the reputation and renown of Newmarket declined. However, during the later decades of the eighteenth century the town regained its fashionable place, owing to the influence of such men as the Dukes of Queensberry, Grafton and Bedford, the Prince of Wales, and Sir Charles Bunbury who became acknowledged as the 'perpetual President' of the Jockey Club. At the beginning of the century horses were seldom raced until they were five-year-olds, but four-year-old racing began in the north of England in 1727. The first race for four-year-olds at Newmarket was contested in 1744 and twelve years later races for three-year-olds were held. The fundamental principle for these innovations was the effort by bloodstock breeders to improve the speed of racehorses by racing them over shorter distances, carrying lighter weights, at a younger age. The racing of three-year-olds grew in popularity particularly as a result of the success of the St Leger. Consequently in 1809 the Two Thousand Guineas was inaugurated at Newmarket, the distance of the race being one mile, and the winner Wizard owned by Mr Christopher Wilson who lived at Oxton Hall near Tadcaster and whose father was a Bishop. Wizard was a useful colt who started favourite for the Derby

* 'neer-ridden' (near-ridden) implies that the King neither gave nor expected any quarter.

five weeks later but was beaten by a neck by the Duke of Grafton's Pope. In 1814, inspired by the evident attraction of the Two Thousand Guineas, the One Thousand Guineas was instituted for three-year-old fillies, with Charlotte winning in the colours of Mr Christopher Wilson who thus completed the unique double of winning the inaugural running of both 'Guineas. The year before Charlotte's victory Smolensko became the first colt to win both the Two Thousand Guineas and The Derby. Another forty years were to elapse before West Australian was hailed as the first Triple Crown winner, having taken the Two Thousand Guineas, The Derby and the St Leger. By the time of West Australian's triumph the Two Thousand Guineas, the One Thousand Guineas, The Derby, The Oaks and the St Leger were accepted as the five Classics, with the prestige attached to victory being huge. Foreign bred and foreign owned colts and fillies attempted to win all of them, and the 1865 Triple Crown achievement of the French colt Gladiateur caused him to be named 'The Avenger of Waterloo', whilst Wall Street went hysterical when news was received that the American colt Iroquois had won the 1881 Derby.

During the past one hundred years there have been some immensely popular royal victories in the Two Thousand Guineas and the One Thousand Guineas. Minoru won the 1909 Two Thousand Guineas for King Edward VII and two

Trainers exercising strings of racehorses on the gallops at Newmarket, the headquarters of the Jockey Club and the National Stud.

An early eighteenth-century engraving by Pieter Tillermans of
'The Watering Place at Newmarket with a View of the
Course and the String of Horses belonging to His Grace the
Duke of Devonshire'. The popularity and prestige of this
Suffolk town was established by Charles II who was a keen
supporter of all the equestrian arts.

days later his filly Princesse de Galles finished second in the One Thousand
Guineas. In 1928 Scuttle won the One Thousand Guineas for King George V, and
Big Game and Sun Chariot achieved a notable success for King George VI by
taking both races in 1942. Hypericum won the 1946 One Thousand Guineas in
the royal colours and Pall Mall triumphed in the 1958 Two Thousand Guineas
for Her Majesty The Queen, who also won the 1974 One Thousand Guineas with
Highclere.

There are twelve meetings held annually at Newmarket, beginning with the
Craven meeting in April followed by the Two Thousand Guineas and One
Thousand Guineas meeting two weeks later. Throughout the summer major
races including the Cherry Hinton Stakes, the Bunbury Cup and the July Cup are
held on the July Course which has a straight mile, with races of longer distances
starting on the Cesarewitch course before turning into the straight. It was on the
July course, situated less than half-a-mile from the Rowley Mile, that the
substitute Derby and Oaks were run during the two World Wars. Several of the
meetings on the July course are held on Saturdays. In the autumn racing reverts to
the Rowley course where significant races held during October include the
Champion Stakes, now sponsored by the Ruling Family of Dubai, the Middle
Park Stakes and the Dewhurst Stakes which are considered two of the most
important two-year-old races of the season, and the Cambridgeshire and the

Cesarewitch, the two handicaps which have been the medium of some of the heaviest gambling in Turf history. The Cesarewitch acquired its name in honour of His Imperial Highness the Grand Duke Cesarewitch of Russia who generously gave three hundred sovereigns towards the prize money when the race was inaugurated in 1839. The Cambridgeshire was also run for the first time in 1839 and nine years later the Jockey Club passed a resolution that 'the winning owners of the Cesarewitch and Cambridgeshire Stakes shall each pay 30 sovs. to the Judge'. This unusual practice lasted until 1866 and may have been the reason for the Judge awarding a triple dead-heat in the 1857 Cesarewitch!

It has been claimed that Newmarket is the only place where a man can go racing. Elsewhere he merely goes to the races. Certainly the sight of hundreds of horses exercising on Newmarket Heath on a summer's morning is a spectacle of beauty, whilst the number of spring, summer and winter gallops gives thoroughbreds infinite variety. Historically Newmarket is steeped in Turf history, much of which is displayed in the National Horse-racing Museum which opened in the spring of 1983 and which relates the history of racing from earliest days to the present time. The Museum is housed in the Subscription Rooms in Newmarket High Street from where Harriet, Lady Ashburton once wrote to her brother: 'If I were to begin life again I would go to the Turf to get my friends. They seem to be the only people who hold together. I don't know why. It may be that each knows something that might hang the other, but the effect is delightful and most peculiar.'

The Badminton Horse Trials

The Badminton Horse Trials which take place in the middle of April are unique and could not be staged in any other country in the world. They were originally the brain-child of the 10th Duke of Beaufort who realized as he watched the British three-day event team's performance in the 1948 Olympic Games that unless something drastic was done quickly, then in the equine world of sport Great Britain should confine herself to show-jumping, polo and racing at which she still excelled.

So 1949 saw the birth of 'Badminton', and now more than a quarter of a million people flock each year to the Duke's park to enjoy a spectacle with an atmosphere all of its own. An equestrian version of the modern pentathlon, not only are the Trials a comprehensive test of all-round horsemanship, but over the three days in which it competes demands are made on a horse of every activity of which it is capable—dressage (a form of equine gymnastics), galloping and jumping across country against the clock, and finally show-jumping.

So popular have the Trials become with so many entries that now they extend over five days, and if you wish to savour them to the full it would be wise to book local accommodation or, better still, take your own caravan. Parking sites can be booked through the Horse Trials Office, Badminton, Avon (045 421 272). (This is the official address although the Duke himself maintains that he lives in Gloucestershire and still has Badminton, Glos.—like a superior brand of paint—engraved on his writing paper.)

The Wednesday of Badminton week is settling-in day for the competitors

ABOVE:
Princess Anne on Goodwill at the
Badminton Horse Trials. It was
there that she proved herself to be
one of the great names in 'eventing'
when she was chosen to be a
member of the 1976 British
Olympic team in Montreal. She had
already won the European Three-
Day Event Individual
Championship at Burghley in 1971,
and in the same year was voted
BBC Sportswoman of the Year.

RIGHT:
Queen Elizabeth the Queen Mother
watching the Badminton Horse
Trials with her hosts, the Duke and
Duchess of Beaufort. Members of
the Royal Family very often spend
the weekend of Badminton week
with them, and the Duke, Master of
the Queen's Horse until 1978, is an
old friend.

when, after receiving a full briefing, they inspect the course, taking in thoroughly what is expected of them and their mounts and planning the angle at which they will endeavour to take the fences. Out of the three cross-country courses they will have to cover, the first along roads and lanes, the second designed like a steeplechase, it is the third that draws the crowds where the fences are diabolically designed to terrify the riders when on their feet, but not to harm the horses providing they are of the right calibre—i.e., of Olympic standard.

That evening all the horses are given a strict veterinary examination which members of the public can attend on the north front of Badminton House, and on the Thursday the first stage of the competition begins, taking place in the vast arena surrounded by purpose-built stands which have mushroomed up a few days before, disappearing again just as quickly. This is the dressage, and no one will criticize you if you only give it your cursory attention, for you need to be an *aficionado* to appreciate its finer points. Instead, you can walk the cross-country course, examine the jumps closely and wonder at the temerity of the riders, before inspecting a huge complex of shops that lie outside the arena. Stocking every imaginable equine luxury and necessity, from the most expensive horseboxes complete with built-in caravan down to cheap rope halters and tail-bandages, there is an equally wide range of luxuries and everyday goods on sale—jewellery, clothes, pictures, books, antiques, porcelain, wood-burning stoves, food and wine and many others. The High Street banks are also there, providing havens where their customers can rest and refresh themselves.

If you join the British Horse Society (British Equestrian Centre, Stoneleigh, Kenilworth, Warwickshire—(telephone 0203 52241) early in the year, you will be able to make use of their catering premises which line the south end of the arena where you can not only watch what is happening but also eat, and introduce up to three friends as temporary members for a nominal sum. Members get early-booking facilities for the show-jumping on the Sunday, but you must act swiftly to make sure you get seats in the coveted West Stand—the 'right' place to be. You can also book seats through the Horse Trials Office and on the ground.

Dogs are permitted, but must be kept under strict control—the RSPCA runs a lost-dog stand. Leave them at home if you can, and the same goes for small children—though the Norland Nursery Nurses' Training College runs a crèche—and don't bring elderly grandparents, unless they are of the type peculiar to the British upper classes which never tire.

Saturday is the great day when you must start out early—enormous traffic jams build up very quickly at junctions 17 and 18 off the M4 Motorway. Wear comfortable water-tight footwear and clothing, for it will be a long and gruelling day. Picnics are almost an essential part of the general scene, usually taking place like Ascot in the car parks. Tables and chairs are out, though folding seats are permissible for those who cannot sustain the hard ground for long. Although there are catering tents, apart from that of the BHS, they are expensive, crowded and none too clean.

The car parks are ample (so much so that it can be difficult to find the car again at the end of the day) and invalids can apply to the Secretary for a place in a special car park which commands a view of several jumps. Car park tickets can be obtained at the gates.

Your own activity depends entirely on your stamina, but leap to the side of the course at the sound of a whistle, for it means a horse is coming. Drays, reminiscent of the tumbrils of the French Revolution, are parked here and there, providing excellent grandstands, but be prepared to vacate them quickly should a fleet of Range Rovers hove into view, bringing to the course most of the Royal Family who stay with the Duke and Duchess for the weekend to watch members of their family who often compete. If a solitary silver Range Rover, MFH 1, heads towards you, jump aside, for the Duke drives like he hunts: fast and straight.

Sunday starts with another veterinary examination of those horses remaining in the competition, followed at 11.30 am by a service in the Beaufort family chapel attached to the House which doubles as the parish church. To attend it, you will have to be really early, as the Royal Family are present and will walk back for luncheon through the garden.

That afternoon, suitably hatted, gloved and clad in smart tweeds, armed with field-glasses, take your seat in good time, for after a dressage display and some rousing military music played by the band of one of the smarter regiments, what by now has become a familiar flotilla of Range Rovers appears in the arena, setting down its passengers in front of the Royal Box in the centre of the West Stand. You can then indulge in a little celebrity spotting. The Duke of Beaufort is the tallest man, wearing a beige overcoat and bowler hat, while his cousin and heir, David Somerset, who will meet the party is also tall, dark and elegantly turned out, silk handkerchief flowing from his breast pocket. His wife, Lady Caroline—daughter of the Marquess of Bath—is equally tall and good-looking, and their three sons, Harry, Eddie and Johnson, top their father and have all inherited the family looks.

The show-jumping competition begins with a parade of not more than twenty survivors who enter the ring in reverse order, the ones with best marks coming last. Then follows an exciting display by horses you may be able to recognize from the previous days, when the outright winner eventually emerges. After the prizes have been presented, and there are many for it is a much-sponsored event, is the time when you can say thank you to the host, for the Duke of Beaufort's own hounds are paraded, and you can applaud him when he enters the ring to greet the pack—his pride and joy.

Other horse trials worth visiting during the year are the Windsor Horse Trials at the end of May, a three-day event, and the Stowell Park Horse Trials near Northleach in Gloucester, also in May. In September and October there are the Burghley Horse Trials and the Wylye International Three-Day Event. Wylye is where prospective Badminton eventers are tried out to see whether they are worth training and also where a lot of horse wheeler-dealing goes on—where rich fathers look for a suitable eventing horse for their daughters; and Burghley, very much part of the eventing scene, has the added bonus of being held in the grounds of a magnificent Elizabethan mansion, home of the Cecil family for many generations. It is important for visitors to Burghley to become a member of the Trials to enjoy the occasion to the full, and details can be obtained from The Burghley Horse Trials Office, Stamford, Lincolnshire (0780 52131). Ticket order forms are available from the same office from May onwards. For advance booking and membership details for Wylye write to The Horse Trials Office, Bathampton House, Wylye, Wiltshire (098 56 281).

The Harrogate Spring Flower Show

With the Lakeland Rose Show in July the Harrogate Spring Flower Show is a major social event for the northern counties of England. It is held in the centre of the Yorkshire spa town of Harrogate in a park called the Valley Gardens, towards the end of April, and for obvious reasons concentrates on displays of spring flowers. There are also marvellous exhibits of flower arrangements, alpines, landscaped gardens and a plant market organized by the leading nurserymen of the county. As at the other major horticultural and flower shows there is a formal reception attended by the Mayor and other VIPs by invitation.

Stratford-upon-Avon

Stratford-upon-Avon is an essential stopping-off place for the visitor to England because it may well be considered the cradle of our dramatic heritage.

Although Shakespeare's strange life is mostly a mystery, his beginning and his end are well recorded here. Holy Trinity Church contains the font where he was baptized, his grave and monument with parish registers that show his birth and burial entries. The house where he was born in 1564 has been restored and contains documents and relics. New Place, where he died, is now a museum surrounded with a fine formal garden. Within the old Guildhall building is the Grammar School where Shakespeare sat as a boy, and in the nearby village of Shottery one can explore the old thatched cottage where his wife, Ann Hathaway, lived. The sixteenth-century timbered house, Hall's Croft is worth seeing, and is now cared for by the Shakespeare Trust, while Mason Croft has connections with Marie Corelli.

The theatre which stages Shakespeare's plays is the second one on the present site. The first Victorian Gothic edifice was built in 1879 but burnt down in 1926. The present theatre (known irreverently as 'the Jam Factory') is of red brick and has a somewhat stern outline, though this is softened in a general view by the River Avon that flows beside it among grass lawns and fields. There is altogether a sense of peace and contentment here amid an otherwise busy town.

Sir Barry Jackson of the Birmingham Repertory Theatre took over the directorship of Stratford after the last war until the end of the 1948 season. From 1949 Anthony Quayle assumed sole control and encouraged the assistance of John Gielgud and Tyrone Guthrie as directors of plays. In 1952 Glen Byam Shaw joined Anthony Quayle as co-director. When Quayle resigned at the end of 1956, Shaw became sole director for three years. Every well-known actor and actress has played Stratford and when Peter Hall succeeded Glen Byam Shaw he had a going concern. Through his efforts the company not only gained the title of 'Royal' but established a London base at the Aldwych Theatre in 1960, so expanding their operations and fame.

Now the London end of the Stratford organization is established principally in the Barbican, with The Pit as an experimental theatre; while there is a similar stage called The Other Place (TOP) in Stratford. Trevor Nunn and Terry Hands are joint artistic directors now, whose responsibilities overlap across these four venues.

LEFT:
Donald Sinden as King Lear.

BELOW:
Sarah Siddons as Catherine
of Aragon in the trial scene
from *Henry VIII*.

'David Garrick's Jubilee in Honour of Shakespeare, 1769. The Scene at the High Cross, Stratford-upon-Avon.' David Garrick was one of the great eighteenth-century Shakespearian actors whose name is still as well known today as it was in his own time.

Both the town of Stratford and the theatre have a long experience of catering for visitors. There are first-rate hotels, including the only Hilton in Britain outside London and Gatwick; theatre meals have the advantage of a marvellous view over the river. The actors' 'pub' just across the road from the stage door which says 'Black Swan' on one side of its sign-board and 'Dirty Duck' on the other, is always known by the latter title, and is almost part of the theatre itself. There are innumerable photographs of artists, past and present, on its walls, and theatre talk goes on throughout licensing hours.

It is advisable for the visitor who wants to go to the theatre to become a member (or associate member) of the Royal Shakespeare Theatre Mailing List, which gives priority for booking tickets. There is also a joint membership that covers both Stratford and London and information may be had from The Mailing List Organizer, The Royal Shakespeare Theatre, Stratford-upon-Avon, Warwickshire.

But even if the casual visitor to Stratford fails to equip himself with this necessary passport to the heavily booked theatre season which starts at the end of March each year, there is a great deal to enjoy elsewhere. The surrounding countryside is full of beauty spots; Henley-in-Arden, where once there was a forest, still has the best ice cream in Britain; and there is always punting on the River Avon.

The County Championship

The first-class cricket season traditionally opens at Oxford or Cambridge Universities, towards the end of April. Both universities play two or three matches against county sides before the County Championship begins about ten days later. It is worth mentioning that admission is free for the Oxford and Cambridge matches, unlike those at all the county grounds.

Championship games are played over three days. John Player League games are one-day games, played on Sundays, usually between the county teams who are at the same time half-way through a championship game. The other one-day competitions are the Benson and Hedges Cup and the Natwest Bank Trophy—both knock-out cups.

The County Championship is a league competition played between seventeen counties. There is no system of relegation, just a division between first-class and 'minor' counties. Since 1921 no minor county has been invited to join the championship. There can be little doubt that this system—or lack of one—has contributed to the falling gates at championship matches.

The Benson and Hedges and Natwest competitions do, however, enable 'minor' counties, and indeed Scotland and Ireland, to play in matches against the first-class counties. The appeal of these games, therefore, for the spectators is something similar to the early rounds of the FA Cup.

'Cricket of late years is become exceedingly fashionable, being much countenanced by the nobility and gentlemen of fortune, who frequently join in the diversion.' So wrote Joseph Strutt in *Sports and Pastimes of the People of England*, published in 1801, but it was not until the 1870s that the County Championship was started on a formal basis, though County Teams had been playing for over a hundred years.

During the eighteenth century cricket was frowned on by the establishment as a fairly disreputable game. The following account of a match between Kent and Surrey in 1762 gives a reasonably clear picture of what could happen.

'One of the players being catched out, when Surrey was 50 a-head the first innings; from words they came to blows, which occasioned several broken heads, as likewise a challenge between two persons of distinction: the confusion was so great, that the betts were all withdrawn.'

Teams at this time, though they called themselves County teams, were not generally representative of the best players in the county; rather they were privately sponsored sides, under the patronage of some wealthy enthusiast.

Kent v. England on 18 June 1744 is the first match for which the score is known today; it is also the date of the earliest known written rules of the game.

Right up to about the middle of the nineteenth century cricket matches were played for money, and the stakes were frequently high. It seems that spectators, too, could wager all manner of bets during the course of a match.

In the early days cricket was played with a sort of hockey stick, which evolved gradually into the present blade-shaped bat during the eighteenth century: probably because the curved 'bat' was only suited to hitting balls bowled along the ground but quite useless once bowlers started to flight the ball. The bowler was bowling underarm and at a two-stump wicket.

The County Ground at Chesterfield in Derbyshire. County cricket is often played in very picturesque settings, and the traditional scene of an immaculate pitch surrounded by trees, with the church in the background, captures the essence of this most English of sports.

It was not until the opening of the railways that teams could travel long distances. This, together with the Factory Act of 1850—making Saturday a half-day, and making it possible for the average man to watch a match—caused cricket to become the major spectator sport of the time.

In 1872 twenty-five inter-county matches were recorded, and in 1873 championship tables were published for the first time. Only nine counties were involved: Derbyshire, Gloucestershire, Kent, Lancashire, Middlesex, Nottinghamshire, Surrey, Sussex and Yorkshire. For many years before there had been an unofficial champion county—decided on a challenge basis—but no detailed figures were reported.

The number of matches increased each year until by 1892 seventy-two championship games were played: each of the nine teams playing all the others twice.

Derbyshire dropped out of the championship for a while, being replaced by Somerset. Essex, Hampshire, Leicestershire and Warwickshire were admitted to the championship in 1895, when a total of 131 matches were played during the season. (Worcestershire joined in 1899, Northants in 1905; and finally Glamorgan in 1921—the last county to be admitted.)

At the start of the championship (1873), Gloucestershire were a formidable side containing the three Graces, with W.G. captain and the best batsman in the world. They became champions for the first time in 1874.

Before the turn of the century, Nottinghamshire, Lancashire, Surrey and Yorkshire were the most successful sides.

In the fifteen seasons prior to 1914 Yorkshire won the championship six times, Kent four, Middlesex, Lancashire, Nottinghamshire and Warwickshire once each. (Warwickshire were the first county outside the original nine counties to win the championship)

The First World War ended what might be called 'the golden age of cricket'. *Wisden* (the annually published cricketer's bible) records in 1916 and 1917 the deaths of some three thousand cricketers. Up to the beginning of the First World War the public schools had produced a seemingly endless stream of first-class players but after the war amateur players began to find it more difficult to devote their time to the game, and an increasing number of professional players began to make their mark.

From the 1920s to the early 1960s the County Championship (then played over five days) was at the height of its popularity, but by the 1970s county cricket as a whole was in desperate financial straits and without the sponsorship of Schweppes, it is doubtful if the Championship in its traditional form would still exist. The one-day competitions attract the crowds, but it is the Championship that is the training ground for Test cricketers, and to win it is the highest ambition of all county cricketers.

A list of fixtures and venues, including the championship games, cup matches, university games and Test matches, can be obtained from the Test and County Cricket Board, Lord's Cricket Ground, St John's Wood, London NW8 (01 289 1615).

May

Oxford May Morning

Oxford May Morning has nothing to do with the sport of rowing, but it is certainly a popular social occasion involving boating, and deserves a word or two here.

The actual proceedings are simple. Every May Morning, in the pre-dawn grey, the choir assembles at the top of Magdalen College tower. With the first rays of the sun (or at the official moment of sunrise if the sky is overcast) the choir sings an ancient Latin hymn in invocation of summer, 'Te Deum Patrem Colimus'. As their hymn ends, the bells of Oxford join in a glorious peal to salute the coming of summer.

The event is made by the crowded merrymakers who have kept vigil through the night, in boats and punts on the River Cherwell below Magdalen Bridge. This is a splendid way to end a party held the night before, but if it is to be enjoyed to the full it is wise to make appropriate preparations.

First, even if it is a fine night *it will be cold*, all the more so because of the chill rising from the water. A warm cloak or top-coat is therefore essential if you want to stay the course in reasonable comfort, together with gloves, warm headgear or scarf. Nothing dispels the party feeling quicker than freezing by inches, unable to escape because of the press of boats.

The vigil is traditionally a champagne occasion, but unless you are in an unusually opulent and well-stocked party the champagne tends to run out all too quickly. It is a prerogative of the truly wise to take a flask of what Winston Churchill once called 'other appropriate medical comforts'. The party's provisions should also include a flask of hot coffee to keep the pre-dawn chill at bay.

Boats and punts are hired from St Clement's above Magdalen Bridge, and it is wise to book early to make sure of obtaining a craft which can hold the entire party in comfort. Make sure that the person in charge of your boat really knows what he's doing; you may be sure that at least one boatload will capsize during the vigil, and it is bound to be a long cold walk to warmth and shelter for those who end up in the water. Keep an eye out for particularly uproarious parties and try to stay clear; it is a time for horse-play, which upsets even more boats than sober ineptitude.

It is bound to be cold; it may even rain; but there is an inimitable gaiety about the May Morning vigil that the above precautions will enhance even further.

'Why do they do it?' asked Soviet premier Nikita Kruschev during his visit in 1955. 'Because,' the President of Magdalen gently replied, 'they have done so for the past five hundred years.'

The choir on top of Magdalen College tower on May Morning in Oxford, a
ritual which is thought to date from the reign of Henry VII.

Magdalen Tower and May Morning by Harry Paintin, from the *Oxfordshire
Chronicle*, May 1909

Respecting the origin of singing on the tower on May morning, many and
conflicting theories have been advanced, some have maintained that the
custom originated in a charge made on the Rectory of Slymbridge by Henry VII
in order to provide a requiem for his obit on every first of May. It is true that
Henry VII permitted the transfer of the advowsons of Slymbridge and Furdon
to the college, and the latter undertook to observe an obit for him every year, as
it was customary to do for other benefactors of the college, but there is no
authentic evidence to connect this observance with the May morning
ceremony, and the £10 annually derived by the college from the Rectory of
Slymbridge was granted in 1501 by the Bishop of Worcester to augment the
general fund of the college, not to provide for the singing on the tower on May
morning. The statement submitted by Mr Wilson in his comprehensive and
informative contribution on Magdalen to the series on *College Histories* seems
the most probable account of the origin of the custom. He suggests that in the
first instance the observance was merely an inauguration ceremony associated
with the completion of the tower. Originally the singing not only took place an
hour earlier than at present, but the character of the proceedings was entirely
different from that which it contains at present.

In the succeeding century a contemporary writer alludes to the ceremony as
a 'merry concert both of vocal and instrumental music, ... lasting about two
hours.'

The change in hour and character was made, it is believed, in the closing
years of the eighteenth century, when according to Dr Bloxham adverse
climatic conditions on a particular occasion rendered it impossible for the
ceremony to be carried out in its ancient form.

The Middlesex Sevens

'The best day out in Rugby Football' is how the memorable scrum-half R. E. G. (Dickie) Jeeps, England captain and British Lion,* who was capped twenty-four times, describes the last fixture of the season at Twickenham, held usually on the first Saturday in May. From soon after midday sixteen teams from the three hundred who made the qualifying rounds compete in this seven-a-side competition, playing seven minutes each way, so by the end of the final match, some six hours later, spectators have watched fifteen hard-fought games by men at the very peak of their fitness and speed.

Seven-a-side rugby is a particularly strenuous form of the game, and requires a high degree of stamina, fitness and above all determination.

Moreover, this is a family day, starting from the car parks where cars converge soon after 10 am on a first-come-best-placed basis for, on this one important day, there is no booking space on the Twickenham car parks. Sometimes a family car-load boasts only two tickets but, no matter; in the (with luck) spring-like weather, this is a day for strolling about in informal seasonal clothing, meeting friends, drinking and eating. According to F. Boyden OBE, Chairman and Honorary Secretary of the occasion, 'this is the biggest picnic party of the year'. Applications for tickets may be made to him at 1 Liphook Crescent, Forest Hill, London SE23 3BN, to a leading ticket agency or, in desperation, to the Secretary of the RFU at Twickenham.

Seven-a-side rugby, one of the most strenuous games on record, was invented by the little Rugby Football Club of Melrose on the Scottish border in 1882. In a desperate attempt to get themselves out of financial difficulties they staged an

* A member of the touring side from the four home countries of Great Britain.

inter-club tournament in which teams of seven played a modified version of the game. Soon English and Welsh clubs were taking part in annual tournaments organized by other Border clubs as well as Melrose.

In 1926 the game was exported to Middlesex by a Scotsman, Dr Jimmy Russell-Cargill, a member of the Middlesex Committee who is commemorated by the name of the trophy presented to the winners of the Middlesex Sevens. Fifty clubs entered for that first tournament which, for the first four years, was won by the Harlequins. Proceeds from the event go to Middlesex and are donated to charity and deserving Rugby causes.

Another unusual feature of this end-of-season fixture is that true enthusiasts take their picnics into the ground so that they need not miss a moment of the exciting and exhausting games. The players are so exhausted that there is a twenty-five minute interval between the semi-final and the final. Then, to entertain the spectators and also keep them from straying on to the pitch, the organizers arrange displays by the Combined Services or massed bands, helicopters or the Police and, on occasions, Gaelic football, rugby-netball or lacrosse matches. It is usually 9 pm before the last players and spectators leave Twickenham Rugby Football ground to recuperate for another season.

The Royal Academy of Arts Summer Exhibition

The start of the London Summer Season was, until recently, marked by the opening day of the Summer Exhibition at the Royal Academy, Burlington House, Piccadilly, on the Saturday preceding the first Monday in May. However, over the past four or five years, due to the increased number of exhibitions held there, the date of this most important event in the British art world is no longer inflexibly fixed. This great show of some fifteen hundred works by living artists of any nationality lasts for a minimum of twelve weeks but may open anything up to a month later than the beginning of May.

Nevertheless, invitations to see and be seen at its opening are in such demand that there are now three successive private view days each attended by between four and five thousand guests. The first day's invitations go to the fifty Royal Academicians and thirty Associates, each of whom is entitled to show six works. This exclusive society consists of painters, engravers, sculptors and architects resident in the United Kingdom whose guests are also invited to the first opening day. So too are exhibitors of the other eleven to twelve hundred works hung and their guests, anyone who bought an exhibit from the previous Summer Exhibition, members of the Academy's ex-officio list of important officials in the art world and a number of fortunate members of the association of thirty thousand Friends of the Royal Academy with a guest, chosen by ballot, and any Friend who particularly wants to buy a picture.

Tickets for the other two 'Opening Days' are divided between the remaining Friends, alphabetically, according to their surnames, with the A–Ls alternating with the M–Zs in successive years. Afterwards, for three months, the Exhibition is open daily from 10 am to 6.0 pm for members of the public who buy tickets at

The Royal Academy Summer Exhibition of 1787. By 1868 the number of pictures exhibited had outgrown the available space and the Royal Academy moved its schools and galleries to Burlington House.

the door. But anyone wanting to be at one of the three open days should apply to join the Society of Friends through the Secretary of the Royal Academy of Arts, Burlington House, Piccadilly, London W1.

The Summer Exhibition has been held annually, without a break, for more than two hundred years since King George III declared himself the patron, protector and supporter of the Royal Academy. The first Summer Show was held in 1769 under the Presidency of Sir Joshua Reynolds and contained 136 works. During the following years a rapidly growing number of pictures was crowded from floor to ceiling and almost touching each other, initially in hired rooms in Pall Mall, then in Somerset House and then, with the National Gallery, in a building in Trafalgar Square. In 1868 the Royal Academy moved to its permanent home in Burlington House which it enlarged to accommodate schools and galleries. At times, two thousand works have been seen in the galleries during the summer by up to four hundred thousand people.

Artists of any nationality, professional or amateur, may submit up to three works for consideration by the Selection and Hanging Committees who choose those ultimately displayed through a rather involved process. Prices range from £5 to £50,000 and in 1982 four-fifths of the pictures were sold of which more than half of the total exhibits bore the coveted red dots after the first open day.

There is no age limit: the nineteenth-century English painter Sir John Millais exhibited at the age of fifteen, a record which was broken ten years ago when much interest centred around an abstract 'thumb painting' called *Monkey in a*

Tree by a four-year-old. Exhibitors also derive a certain satisfaction from having their work hung 'on the line'—at eye-level—but this is not so relevant now that there is ample room to display works to their full advantage.

However, in terms of human spectacle the opening of the Summer Exhibition is no longer the colourful occasion it was: summer dresses and lounge suits with a sprinkling of visitors in jeans are a poor consolation for the days when men wore tail-coats. Then, personalities such as the beautiful Lillie Langtry, the flamboyant Oscar Wilde, the Glenny twins in identical quaint outfits, or the rose-grower Harry Wheatcroft sporting one of his largest exhibits in his buttonhole, meant that the visitors were just as interesting as the works of art on show. One talking point persists: the public still take intense interest in assessing 'the picture of the year'. Each summer one wonders if any will achieve the universal approval of Annigoni's portrait of Queen Elizabeth II, about a quarter of a century ago, or John Merton's triple study of the beautiful Countess of Dalkeith of about the same period.

The Chelsea Flower Show

The first Great Spring Show at Chelsea took place in May 1913 in the grounds of the Royal Hospital on the Thames Embankment in London. The marvellous buildings of the Hospital, most of which were designed in the seventeenth century by Sir Christopher Wren on the site of the famous pleasure gardens of Ranelagh House, are themselves worth a visit, but during the third week of May, the centre of all attention is the vast marquee, covering three and a half acres, which dominates the twenty-three acres of the Show.

A group of Chelsea Pensioners at the Royal Hospital, since 1913 the site of the Chelsea Flower Show. The Hospital was founded in the reign of Charles II as a refuge for soldiers wounded in the service of their country.

Many of the exhibits at the Show are out-of-season varieties grown specially for the event, which takes place in late spring before many of the most spectacular blooms are normally seen.

The Chelsea Flower Show, as it is universally known, is the most famous in the world. Visitors come from many countries, and some of the exhibits are sponsored by foreign governments, notably Belgium, Holland, Colombia, Brazil, China and South Africa. The show has always been a Mecca for gardeners, and the social attractions have always taken second place; people go to the Show primarily to see the exhibits and meet fellow-gardeners, but it is still an important occasion in the social calendar.

The Royal Hospital was founded in 1683 during the reign of Charles II as a refuge for wounded soldiers who were receiving a pension from the Government in recognition of their services to the realm, and Wren's stately edifices are a fitting and dignified setting for the scarlet-coated 'Chelsea Pensioners'. The surrounding gardens developed over the years, notably with the building of the Chelsea Embankment in 1874, and by the time the Royal Horticultural Society, in the years just before the Great War, were looking for a new site for their Spring Show, the Hospital grounds provided the ideal answer.

The Horticultural Society (the appellation 'Royal' was added in 1861) was established in 1804 at a meeting in Hatchards' Piccadilly bookshop, as a 'Society for the Improvement of Horticulture'. There were seven founder members, who included the botanist Sir Joseph Banks and John Wedgwood, the son of Josiah of the great pottery family, who became the first president.

From its inception the Society encouraged research, experimentation and the growth of horticultural knowledge. (The Society's present garden at Wisley in Surrey which was established in 1903 is a remarkable testimonial to generations of dedicated botanists and horticulturalists.) By the 1880s competitions had become so popular that the first shows were held in a marquee at Chiswick, and in 1888 the RHS moved its by now well-established and extremely popular Show to the grounds of the Inner Temple off Fleet Street where it remained yearly until 1911. By then there were so many exhibits, and the popularity of the Show had grown to such an extent with non-exhibiting visitors, that the Benchers of the Inner Temple had become thoroughly fed up with the yearly devastation inflicted on their sacred confines and over the previous few years they had imposed stricter regulations which eventually led to the Society's search for an alternative location.

An important figure in this relocation was Harry J. Veitch (later Sir Harry), whose grandfather John Veitch had established the famous family nursery business at Killerton near Exeter. They followed the great tradition of travelling botanical explorers, and the Veitch Memorial Medal is one of the principal honours awarded by the Society.

In 1912, the year before the first 'proper' Chelsea flower show, a great exhibition was held in the grounds of the Royal Hospital—the Royal International Horticultural Exhibition. This turned out to be enormously successful, and involved commercial nurserymen, landscape gardeners, vegetable growers, Societies and individual competitors, and displays from home and abroad.

Socially, too, the Exhibition was a complete success. It was opened by King George V, patronized by foreign and British royalty and nobility, and gave an excuse for endless parties, banquets, picnics and general enjoyment. Ladies found the occasion, if not always the weather, perfect for showing off their prettiest clothes and making almost as much of a colourful display as the flowers. Coming at the height of the London Season, the Show was as essential a part of the daytime social scene as Henley and Royal Ascot.

But even at the height of the heyday of the London Season, the Chelsea Flower Shows remained first and foremost horticultural occasions of great importance for growers: the culmination of the year's hard work, its fruition in the form of awards, and a chance to meet fellow professionals or enthusiasts, to exchange ideas and catch up on recent gardening trends, discoveries or failures.

The energy and tireless, dedicated, sheer physical work that go into making the Chelsea Flower Show are often unappreciated by the visitor, but when it is remembered that all the exhibits and displays are only there for about a week in the year something of the scale of the enterprise becomes apparent. Everything, from a fully grown tree to the smallest miniature rock plant, is brought in containers to the site for the occasion. The trees and such water plants as Gunnera, etc., are lifted and crated sometimes months in advance, and grown on in the 'packed up' state so that when they are finally moved to Chelsea—often in full-sized pantechnicons—they are quite undisturbed and in perfect condition. That might be enough in itself, but some displays, the Royal Parks for example, include spectacular landscaping involving lakes with bridges and water gardens. It is the inspired grouping of plants in a naturalistic way that is the special artistic skill of British gardeners and designers, which has led to the *jardin anglais* being renowned for its charm of nature at its simple best, as opposed to the formality of the 'parterre' and 'carpet' planning of other European countries.

Other exhibits are of necessity concentrated in the open ground around the marquee, but even inside the vast tent it is difficult to remember that every single flower, shrub and tree has been transported here sometimes from another continent. There is a quite astonishing impression of permanency which is, as it should be, submerged in the breathtaking sight (and scent) of masses upon masses of immaculate, perfect and totally blemish-free flowers.

There are, of course, more than flowers. Vegetables are an important part of the Show, as are fruits, exotic plants, herbs, shrubs, rock-garden plants and succulents. The latest equipment, tools, garden furniture and gardening books are on display, and there are educational and scientific stands which preserve the link with the early pioneering botanists of the eighteenth and nineteenth centuries.

The Show usually opens on a Tuesday in the third week in May, but to the exhibitors the most important day is the day before—the day of the Royal Visit and the day of Judging. The Royal Family arrives at the Embankment entrance at intervals of a few minutes ending with the most senior member at 5.30 pm (usually The Queen or the Queen Mother). After their reception by members of the Council of the RHS, the Royal Family separate and tour the marquee so that each exhibit receives a visit. It is a great honour to be on the stand for the Royal Visit, and only one representative per exhibit is allowed. Members of the public cannot be present on this day.

Judging takes place before the Royal Visit, and the RHS Gold Medal in any category is the most sought-after award for any gardener, nurseryman or horticulturalist. There are various other medals and awards depending on the type of exhibit, but the Gold Medal represents the height of achievement in a very highly competitive field.

The Show officially opens the next day, Members' Day. This is the day to be seen at and to see, and although entry is restricted to Members of the RHS, anyone can obtain a ticket by joining the Society on payment of the subscription, which is done in advance by post from The Secretary, The Royal Horticultural Society, Vincent Square, Westminster, London SW1, or even on the spot from the Society's kiosks at the entrances to the showground. It is, however, a great advantage to be an exhibitor, or attached to an exhibit, because apart from any other benefits the exhibitors' refreshment marquee is much less crowded, particularly during lunch when the pressure in the public marquees can be considerable even in dry weather. This has led to the fact that the really dedicated gardeners tend to go to the Show early in the morning or late in the afternoon to get a better opportunity of viewing their particular interests. For the very privileged, tea is by invitation only with the President of the RHS, but failing this many people bring a picnic hamper full of early summer delicacies.

Visitors on Members' Day, as well as socialites, consist mainly of gardeners, both amateur and professional, from owners and head gardeners of great estates to council-house dwellers whose gardens are the envy of all. Dress nowadays ranges from classic 'tidy' country clothes to the latest extravagances of fashion, but it is no longer quite the setting for high elegance that it was in the past. It is, for example, no longer *de rigueur* to wear a hat, although on Members' Day, a sense of occasion still prevails which is reflected in the dress of visitors and exhibitors. Visitors usually arrive by taxi, as there is no Underground station in the immediate vicinity. The nearest is Sloane Square (Circle or District line), or there are buses to Chelsea Bridge Road. Entrances to the showground are on the Embankment and Royal Hospital Road.

Wednesday, Thursday and Friday are open to the public, and the crowds can

The Queen is a regular visitor to the Chelsea Flower Show, and tours the exhibits the evening before the Show opens to the public.

be considerable. The Chelsea Flower Show holds its appeal from year to year, in fair weather and foul, and attracts visitors from all walks of life. On the Friday at closing time, many exhibited plants are offered for sale and there is a frenzy of buying: gardeners can be certain of getting good specimens of every type of plant for the year ahead. After all, the Chelsea Flower Show is the most famous horticultural show in the world and the quality and variety of the plants and exhibits are unsurpassed. This is also true of the planning and staging of the whole exhibition. Infinite care is taken after the Show closes each evening in the gentle spraying of flowers and plants so that they are free of the film of dust raised by the tramping of thousands of feet milling round the exhibits during the day. Every sign of wilting is removed and the flower or leaf or whole plant is replaced. This attention to detail results in the Show's appearance of perfection as much to the last visitor as it did to those who attended the preview.

The Chester and York Race-meetings

Chester is one of the most historic racecourses in Britain, and when a meeting was held on Shrove Tuesday 1540 the Mayor presented a silver bell to the winning owner. Nearly three hundred years were to elapse before the Chester Cup was instituted—a handicap of such prestige that one Victorian journalist wrote, 'I should be inclined to place the race as the third most attractive of the year, the Derby and St Leger claiming first and second place.' In the nineteenth century the 1st Duke of Westminster patronized Chester races, entertaining on a vast scale at his home, Eaton Hall, which was only a few miles from the course. Curiously no horse which carried his colours ever won the Chester Cup for which the prizes included Cheshire cheeses for the owners of the first, second and third. One year an owner from Liverpool whose fancied horse failed to be placed, ruefully remarked: 'Those blooming cheeses! Why, if I kept one for a year it would cost far less and run a damn sight faster than my horse by next Cup day.'

Another highlight of the May meeting is the Chester Vase which has frequently proved a pointer to The Derby. In the 1930s both Hyperion and Windsor Lad achieved victory in the race before winning at Epsom, whilst in 1980 Henbit was successful before his Derby triumph. However, the left-handed flat circular race-track, on ground known as the Roodee, is so sharp that many long-striding horses are 'all at sea' on the twisting bends of its 1 mile 64 yards circumference, and fail to produce their best form. Nevertheless from the point of view of the spectators the smallness of the race-track enables them to watch every moment of each race with the naked eye. On Chester Cup Day thousands of these spectators sit on the high stone walls on the west side of the city adjoining the course, gaining a grandstand view free! The Dee Stakes, the Ormonde Stakes and the Cheshire Oaks are also contested at the May meeting.

The week after Chester heralds the equally popular meeting on the Knavesmire, half a mile to the south of the city of York. The word 'Knavesmire' is derived from the Anglo-Saxon 'knave', denoting a poor householder, and 'mire', alluding to the watery situation of the fields. Sylvanus, a nineteenth-century sporting author, wrote, 'There is no town in England more thoroughly imbued with the genuine spirit of Racing than the grand old city of York, and in none have there been greater exertions or more princely liberality displayed of late years for the encouragement of the noble pastime by all ranks, shades, sects and sexes than in venerable Ebor.' When the first race-meeting was held in 1731 the most distinguished county families patronized the occasion by entering their horses for the contests, donating prizes and attending with their magnificently liveried servants and outriders, in carriages and coaches which lined both sides of the course. In 1754 a red-brick grandstand was built by subscription for the race-meetings, and gave opportunities for the gentry and their guests to enjoy assemblies, balls and card parties. Royalty have always given their patronage to York races and on 19 August 1952 Her Majesty The Queen had her first winner after succeeding to the throne when her colt Aureole won the Acomb Stakes. The race-track, acknowledged as one of the best in the country, is a flat left-handed course, horseshoe shaped, of two miles, with two bends and a straight run-in of five furlongs. The five-furlong and six-furlong courses are straight, and the recently constructed seven-furlong course has one slight bend.

York Races are administered by a Committee whose members are drawn from Yorkshire families of influence and affluence. Highlight of the May meeting is the Mecca–Dante Stakes which is acknowledged as one of the final Derby trials and which was won in 1978 by Shirley Heights before he attained immortality at Epsom. Two other highlights are the Yorkshire Cup and the Great Voltigeur Stakes named after the famous colt, Voltigeur, who was Yorkshire bred and owned and won the 1850 Derby.

Many racegoers consider the 'Ebor' meeting in August to be one of the most enjoyable meetings of the Racing Season. The Benson and Hedges Gold Cup, the Sprint Championship and the Ebor Handicap, always a heavy betting race, are contested but historically and traditionally the most significant race is the Gimcrack Stakes which carries the honour of allowing the winning owner to make the principal speech at the dinner given by the Gimcrack Club every December. The Club has neither rules, meetings nor functions other than to act as hosts at the annual dinner, but it has been remarked: 'What the Gimcrack Club thinks today, the Jockey Club will think tomorrow.' Many wise, profound and entertaining comments have been made by winning owners, with Sir Abe Bailey smilingly suggesting in his 1937 speech, 'I do not say that all those who go racing are rogues and vagabonds, but I do say that all rogues and vagabonds go racing!' When Mr Paul Mellon, owner of winning colt Mill Reef, spoke to the Club in December 1970 he told his audience, who included the Prince of Wales, 'The sincere, the heartwarming and the so-human interest of the Royal Family over the centuries, culminating in the enthusiastic and knowledgeable and successful participation of Her Majesty The Queen, and the Queen Mother, in racing, chasing and breeding is another factor which has invested the sport with an aura of dignity and decorum coupled with restrained pomp and pageantry.'

No visitor to York, where six meetings a year are held, in May, June, July, August, September and October, should fail to visit the Racing Museum in the grandstand, for the exhibits form 'an inseparable link with the champion horses and famous men whose deeds have enriched racing and are part of our heritage'.

The Royal Windsor Horse Show

The Royal Windsor Horse Show could certainly be regarded as the showpiece of all British Horse Shows. Held every May at Home Park, off the Dorchester road in the shadow of Windsor Castle, and with the River Thames on the other side, its setting is exceptionally picturesque. Over five days the public are treated to high-class show classes, show-jumping, driving and main ring attractions.

The highspot of the Royal Windsor Show is the Musical Drive of the King's Troop, Royal Horse Artillery. When performed during the evening performances of Friday and Saturday night, by floodlight, it is a most moving sight.

A very wide social spectrum of people attend the show, in some cases to be seen as much as to see. In relation to other shows membership is expensive, but certainly worthwhile. The Member's Enclosure, situated at the ringside, provides excellent viewing of the main ring activities whilst drinking champagne and eating smoked salmon sandwiches. The Member's Grandstand becomes some-

Windsor Great Park provides a magnificent setting for the Royal Windsor Horse Show, which attracts some of the greatest international names in show-jumping and every form of equestrianism.

what crowded, particularly at the two evening performances on the Friday and Saturday nights so it is advisable to book seats in advance. Dogs are not allowed on the showground. The restaurant facilities are excellent. There is a certain charm in dining in a striped marquee, bedecked with flowers, and viewing the public figures, actors and socialites who are fellow-diners.

Although the main ring programme is very full it is certainly worthwhile to visit the outside rings where all aspects of the equestrian scene can be viewed. A showing class unique to Windsor is that for polo ponies, particularly appropriate in view of the town's long association with polo. Dressage is another event worth watching in these pleasant surroundings as it is not always possible for the public to see highly schooled horses performing what must considered the equine equivalent to ballet.

As Great Britain is acknowledged as a major producer of quality horses one of the finest sights of the show is the hunter competitions. On a fine spring day there is nothing more pleasant than to bask in the sun watching these beautiful horses. Show classes are also held for hacks, ponies, and other horses of various breeds.

Members of the Royal Family will be much in evidence at the Royal Windsor Show where it is not uncommon to see Princess Anne and Captain Mark Phillips competing. The Queen and her house party arrive for the evening performances, which with the floodlit castle above and the electric atmosphere of the crowds around the arena are a very exciting spectacle.

The driving events are yet another popular aspect of the show. In recent years the International Driving Grand Prix has created much interest, especially as the Duke of Edinburgh is a regular competitor. This kind of competitive driving is a

ABOVE:
Prince Philip is an enthusiastic participant in the driving competitions and has
achieved considerable distinction in this arduous sport.
BELOW:
A contender in the hack class is carefully looked over by judges wearing the
traditional habit for sidesaddle riding.

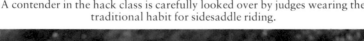

fairly new sport and is run along similar lines to a three-day event as it encompasses dressage, marathon and obstacle driving. The marathon course is around Windsor Great Park and provides quite a spectacle for those prepared to leave the showground to watch this. This Grand Prix tests the all-round ability of both drivers and horses as all three sections of the competition require a high degree of skill and precision. The dressage is held on the Friday—the presentation also being judged—the marathon on Saturday and on Sunday the obstacle driving is held in the main ring.

Other forms of driving can be found at Royal Windsor, namely the coaching marathon, turnout classes, pairs driving and often a meet of the British Driving Society. Over recent years, there has been an upsurge of interest in driving in Britain.

Many other events can be seen at the Royal Windsor Show. A meet of hounds during the Saturday evening performance, under floodlights, seems to be enjoyed by all and the inter-services show-jumping competitions are a real needle match between the teams. This event usually takes place on the Saturday afternoon.

Unlike most other shows the stabling is not on the showground but at Ascot Racecourse and other venues in the area, so a traffic jam in the mornings and evenings is commonplace and time should be allowed for this. The show opens daily at 9 am and it is advisable to arrive as early as possible to avoid the queues. As Home Park is only a short walk from Windsor town centre and the two railway stations it is worth considering using the train to avoid delays. After the evening performances of Friday and Saturday night British Rail usually operate special late trains. By road the M4 is nearby, and the exits are no. 6 (through Eton) or no. 5 (through Datchet).

At the Royal Windsor Horse Show the trade stands play a part in adding colour to the scene. They seem to increase in number and variety every year and it is well worth visiting them as many bargains are there for the picking. Saddlers selling items for horse and rider are in the majority, but it is also possible to purchase such unlikely items as an oriental carpet or a piece of jewellery.

The Royal Windsor Horse Show comes at the beginning of the British outdoor show season, which is one of the reasons for its popularity. Certainly it provides one of the first indications of the form of horses and it is interesting to follow the winners of classes here right through to the Horse of the Year Show in October.

Some international show-jumpers visit the Royal Windsor Show each year, which helps to give a more cosmopolitan atmosphere to the show. The show-jumping classes are of the highest standard in the main ring, but it is also interesting to watch competitions for novice horses in the other rings as some of these will go on to be the stars of tomorrow. In the main ring both the ladies' and gentlemen's show-jumping competitions are hotly contested. The ladies' championship usually takes place on the Friday afternoon and the gentlemen's on the Friday evening.

In all the Royal Windsor Horse Show and all it encompasses is a most enjoyable and well run show. Crowds are heaviest on Saturday and Sunday, owing to its close proximity to London. It is certainly one of the main events of the social calendar.

To become a member, the best way of enjoying the Show, write to The Secretary, Mews, Windsor Castle, Berkshire (075 35 60633).

The Rose Ball and the Caledonian Ball

Charity balls are an essential part of the London Season and two of the most enjoyable are the Rose Ball, in aid of Alexandra Rose Day, and the Caledonian Ball which, as its name implies, is very Scottish indeed and is held in aid of Scottish charities.

The Rose Ball has been held since before the First World War when its patron was Queen Alexandra, wife of Edward VII. Until 1976 the main ball in the social calendar was Queen Charlotte's, held in aid of the fashionable maternity hospital of the same name. Originally this ball was held exclusively for debutantes presented to the monarch, but now that presentations at Court no longer take place there is nothing to stop anyone buying a ticket, although they are much in demand and not at all cheap.

Both the Rose Ball and the Caledonian Ball are held in May at the Grosvenor House Hotel in London's Park Lane. There is a very elegant and extremely large ballroom, with a gallery running above the main room with extra seating. For the Rose Ball it is normal to make up parties of any number and to book one of the

Princess Margaret dancing a reel at the Caledonian Ball. Everyone entitled to wear the tartan does so, and the occasion has a uniquely Scottish flavour rarely found in the heart of London's West End.

tables round the dance floor or on the gallery. (It is as well to try and book early enough to avoid a table too near the band.) Music is always provided by one of the top dance bands of the day, or for anyone wanting some variety there is also a discotheque upstairs behind the gallery. Dinner, which is included in the price of the tickets, is served at the tables, and men wear dinner jackets or white tie. (As with all such 'smart' occasions, the dress expected will be specified on the ticket.) Ladies wear their most dazzling evening dresses and jewellery and this glittering event has now taken the place of Queen Charlotte's Ball in becoming the most important date in the debutante's season. Very often the deb's parents will make up a party for their daughter and their friends, so there is a wide age range attending.

The Caledonian Ball is also held at the Grosvenor House Hotel in May and is undoubtedly the next most important social event after the Rose Ball. Again, parties are organized in advance but this time it is essential that the numbers are in multiples of eight because most of the dancing consists of Scottish reels, which are usually danced in sets of eight or sixteen. Tables are labelled with the name of the host or person organizing the party and this time people arrive after dinner (the opening set does not start until after 10.00 pm). The ticket includes a bottle of whisky for each table of eight people and unlimited soft drinks—especially welcome as the physical exertion involved in dancing reels is considerable.

Dress is strictly formal with white tie for men and long ball gowns for women, with Highland Dress for everyone entitled to wear the tartan (this entails kilts for men and tartan sashes, which are usually worn over the left shoulder and fastened with a brooch, for women). Debutantes will usually wear their traditional long white evening dresses. Tiaras are not usually worn, but even so the ball does present without doubt the most glittering and eye-catching spectacle. It is a favourite occasion for members of the Royal Family, particularly Princess Margaret who is usually one of the opening set with representatives of the Scottish regiments.

With the tickets everyone is issued with a dance card listing the reels (which are interspersed with other dances such as waltzes and foxtrots—perhaps to give the dancers a breather) which is filled in with the names of partners. It is essential to know the steps of the main Scottish dances, and information can be obtained in advance from the organizers of practice sessions for anyone who is a bit rusty.

At some point in the evening a tombola is held in aid of the charities benefiting, with prizes donated by companies and individuals.

After the last reel everyone joins up in lines across the ballroom linking their arms and swinging round like the spokes of a wheel. The breakfast of bacon and eggs or kedgeree which, as at all similar balls, is served in the small hours is most welcome, and guests leave the ball probably much fitter than when they came in.

Other balls worth going to are the Highland Ball held at Claridge's and the St Andrew's Ball at the Grosvenor House (held on 30 November, St Andrew's Day). Or, for a really Scottish flavour, the Skye Balls and the Oban Ball in August are not to be missed.

Details of all the charity balls can be obtained from society magazines such as the *Tatler* and *Harpers and Queen*, the Court and Social pages of *The Times* and the *Daily Telegraph*, or by contacting the Chairman of the Ball Committee of the Charity concerned.

Eights Week and the Cambridge Mays

Eights Week at Oxford in the last week of May, followed by the Cambridge May Races, or 'Mays', at the beginning of June, are the great summer tournaments of Oxford and Cambridge College rowing, and notable highlights of the English rowing season. Each takes up four days of racing (perversely known as 'nights'), from the Wednesday to the Saturday. Even if it rains the Eights and the Mays are made gorgeous by the peacock costumes of the rowing men and their escorts.

The River Cam by St John's College, Cambridge.
Punting is a traditional pastime still popular with both
undergraduates and visitors. Manoeuvring the boats requires a certain skill,
and is much more difficult than it looks.

Eights Week at Oxford in the 1820s. Because the Isis is too narrow for side-by-side racing the winner is the boat which succeeds in 'bumping' its opponent, which then starts the next race in a lower position. The overall winner is known as 'Head of the River'.

Because neither the Isis nor the Cam is wide enough to permit side-by-side racing, the Eights and the Mays are 'bumping' races, with all boats following the same track. Races are rowed by 'divisions' of about ten boats each, crewed by different Colleges. When the starting-gun fires the line of boats, spaced out along the bank at 1½-length intervals, sets off hell-for-leather, intent on making physical contact with 'the boat, its oars or any member of the crew' immediately ahead: 'making a bump'. The bump is acknowledged by the defeated cox throwing up his arm; it has become common for the cox of a hopelessly outmatched crew to acknowledge without actual contact having been made, in order to save the boat from a costly collision. As it is virtually impossible for the pursuing cox to judge the decreasing distance from his quarry directly ahead, relays of dedicated supporters keep pace on the bank, emitting patterns of whistle-blasts or (more excitingly) blank revolver shots to let their crew know how fast it is gaining.

When a bump is made the two crews involved drop out, getting out of the way to let the rest of the division sweep by; and the next night they change places, yesterday's victor starting one place higher. The boat at the top of the First Division is the 'Head of the River' boat, and the Headship of the River is the ultimate prize—though it may take a College boat club many years to achieve.

Unlike the Cam, the Isis is wide enough to permit spectator craft from which the racing may be viewed. Boats and punts may be hired from St Clement's on the Cherwell or Folly Bridge on the Isis—but *only* with a really competent boatman in charge, able to make way quickly for the racing crews. Carelessly handled spectator craft can ruin the racing by getting in the way, and even cause thousands of pounds' worth of damage to a new racing shell. Given competent boat handling and fine weather, however, and a well-chosen and secure mooring safely off the course, there is nothing more pleasant than to watch Eights week as a member of a boating picnic party.

Allow plenty of time for parking (Oxford has a restricted 'disc zone') and the walk to the river. The best plan at Oxford is to walk down through Christ Church Meadows and try for a vantage-point on one of the College boat-houses or barges. Tea may be had at nearly all of them, though naturally preference is given to members of the Colleges and their guests. If you decide to watch from the towpath, either at Oxford or Cambridge, watch out for the surge of spectators keeping pace with each race. Remember, too, that recent rain will mean sludge on the towpath and muddy splashes on your costume; appropriate footwear should be chosen.

The bottom divisions start racing around noon, but unless you have a specific interest in one of the lower crews it is normally sufficient to arrive at the riverside in time for the Third Division (about 4.30 pm). The divisions race at 45-minute intervals and it is rare for the First Division to start before 5.30 pm.

On the Cherwell, from *Chamber's Journal*, 1876
Many a summer visitor to Oxford has pleasant memories of the little stream winding with its many branches amid Magdalen Walks, and then to Christ Church Meadow and so to the Isis. On sunny afternoons, especially during the time the Eights are practising for the world renowned boat-race, you may see boatload after boatload of fair visitors, decked in all the colours of the rainbow, pulled by no less bright-hued collegians, proceeding up the Cherwell to Magdalen, there to hear the afternoon service chanted by the famous choir, and then returning in the cool evening in time to see the second and higher division of the Eights.

Oxford weather, even in the summer term, is fickle, and this summer was more than usually cold; so it was quite late in the term that I conceived the idea of passing the afternoon in my favourite manner, by taking a punt, and proceeding at my leisure up the Cherwell until I found a shady spot where I could moor my roomy craft and doze away the sultry hours with a book. This is my favourite way of spending a hot afternoon at Oxford and on such days every nook of the Cherwell has its occupants, who stare lazily at the passing boats. Now everyone knows, I presume, that a punt is a flat-bottomed boat of heavy structure, propelled, even when the performer is skilful, slowly, by means of a long pole. A long pole I say advisedly, for narrow as is the Cherwell, its depth in some parts is considerably over twelve feet. These punts, common enough on every ornamental water, and used for fishing, are at Oxford provided with sundry large and small cushions, the former of which are termed beds and are exceedingly comfortable.

June

The Fourth of June Celebrations at Eton

Although known as the Fourth of June, the festivities celebrating the birth of that most maligned of kings, George III are held on the nearest Saturday to that date, and because Eton College is, after all, a school the occasion is as much as anything a parents' open day where the boys' work, craft activities and hobbies are put on display.

One of the boats in the river procession in the Fourth of June
Celebrations at Eton. When the crews stand up to salute the spectators
on the bank they are in some danger of toppling over as the boats are
extremely precarious unless one is firmly seated.

The centre of the event is the river, and Agar's Plough which is known to the world as the *real* scene of the victory of Waterloo—the playing fields of Eton. Throughout the day on this hallowed ground a cricket match is played between the College XI and the Eton Ramblers, and parents, friends and relations of the boys sit about on the grass eating delicious lunches of lobster and strawberries and cream from hampers. There is a festive feel in the air; girlfriends, mothers and sisters wear pretty summer dresses with hats, and the boys wear carnations in their buttonholes.

During the afternoon there is a marvellous procession of boats down the River Thames—Eton boats have stirring names such as *St George*, *Defiance*, *Britannia*, *Victory* and *Dreadnought*. The last boat to go past is the ten-oared *Monarch*, probably the only one of its kind in the world. The oarsmen (or 'oars') wear nineteenth-century sailors' dress with straw boaters bedecked with flowers and foliage. As the boats drift along the river past the spectators the crews put their oars up into a vertical position and pull themselves upright hand-over-hand on the oars. When they are standing up, rather precariously as the boats are extremely liable to topple over, they take off their boaters and wave them energetically at the onlookers, so that the flowers fall off and drift away on the current.

To get there by road take the Eton exit off the M4, or go by train from Waterloo to Windsor and Eton Riverside Station which is within walking distance of the College.

Lord's Test Match

The headquarters of cricket, Lord's, in St John's Wood, London, is a magnificent setting for any cricket match. It is the county ground for Middlesex and the home of one of the oldest cricket clubs in the world, the Marylebone Cricket Club, which is historically the most prestigious. As with many traditional British sports, there is one place and one occasion each year that matters more to the sportsman and spectators than any other; the Lord's Test is undoubtedly one of these occasions.

The match takes place in early June, beginning on a Thursday and ending on a Tuesday, or Monday if there has been play on the Sunday. A 'Test' Match is an international match, played over a series of three or five games (the other Test match grounds being The Oval, also in London, Trent Bridge in Nottingham, Old Trafford in Manchester, Edgbaston in Birmingham, and Headingley in Leeds).

Lord's is so steeped in cricketing lore and legend that it is difficult to summarize what is so special about the place. Perhaps the actor Boris Karloff summed it up when he was taken onto the players' balcony by Jim Laker: 'This is just like dying and going to Heaven', he said.

The first three days of the Lord's Test are the most crowded; for some reason that is difficult to understand, it is nearly always easiest to get a seat when the match is at its most interesting stage, over the final two days. Perhaps this has something to do with it being easier to take time off from work at the end of the week.

The atmosphere depends very much on who the tourists are (Australia, the

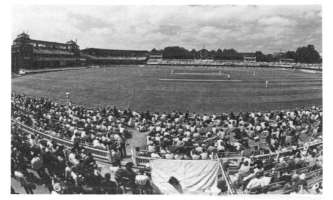

The Test Match at Lord's against Australia in 1981. To keep the turf in perfect condition occupies at least six groundsmen, but the result is one of the best surfaces for the game in the world. The first ever Test Match took place in 1884.

West Indies, Pakistan, India and New Zealand are the Test Countries) and from where you watch the game. The high-spirited West Indians, for example, turn large parts of the ground into a noisy carnival, and their banter and wit must now rival the famous Hill at Sydney. Many people bring a picnic hamper with them, or there are a number of bars around the ground serving food and drink.

A Test series against Australia (for the 'Ashes') always has a special significance, and even more so a Lord's Test during an Ashes series, recalling a mock 'obituary' of English cricket. In 1882 *The Sporting Times*, following England's defeat by Australia at The Oval, published an 'obituary' for English cricket: 'The body will be cremated and the Ashes taken to Australia.'

The next English team to tour Australia was popularly described as going to recover the Ashes. After the team had won two of the three-match series, two ladies presented the English captain with the ashes of a ball inside a pottery urn. This urn remains at Lord's to this day, and never returns to Australia whatever the result of a Test series.

Tickets are obtainable from the Secretary, MCC, Lord's Cricket Ground, London NW8 (01 289 1615). The most expensive seats are under cover in the grandstand. Members and their guests have their own stand.

Cricket has been played at Lord's, the headquarters of the oldest and most prestigious club of all, the Marylebone Cricket Club, since 1814, and in 1822, the date of this picture, the game was well established in England, with rules very much as they are today.

Epsom

The Derby, first contested in 1780, is the most famous horse-race in the world, and has become a part of Britain's tradition. In the nineteenth century Parliament adjourned so that Members, Ministers and ex-Ministers could drive to Epsom Downs and 'in their white hats with blue veils discuss the prospects of their favourites' while in the midst of the Crimean War the result of The Derby was recorded in general orders. Benjamin Disraeli coined the expression: 'It is the Blue Riband of the Turf,' and during the past two hundred years the history of the race has been packed with drama, for favourites have been nobbled, fortunes squandered, winners disqualified, and a suffragette killed after bringing down the King's horse. As Lord Rosebery wrote in 1901, 'In the last quarter of the eighteenth century a roistering party at a neighbouring country house founded two races in two successive years, one for three-year-old colts and fillies, and the other for three-year-old fillies, and named them gratefully after their host and his home. Seldom has a carouse had a more permanent effect. Up to that time Epsom enjoyed little more than the ordinary races of a market town ... now horses earn immortality by winning on Epsom Downs before hundreds of thousands of spectators.' Certainly on Derby Day all roads lead to Epsom, with the Downs, open and free to all, a kaleidoscope of colour as brightly painted charabancs and open double-decker buses hired for the day by clubs and companies, mingle with the striped awnings of the fun-fair sideshows and the gypsy caravans. In the grandstands sartorial elegance is less noticeable than in pre-Second World War years, but if elegance has declined and bears no comparison to that of Royal Ascot, the value of the Derby winner has soared to astronomic heights, with the hero of the hour being valued at millions of pounds and cheered to the echo by his supporters. Small wonder, therefore, that an American visitor once remarked: 'The roar of a great crowd is a wonderful noise, it seems to have as many distinct sounds in it as Niagara. If you can hear the sound of the sea in it, you can also hear the Carillon of Bruges, and the hooting of steamships on the Banks. But I believe that no crowd, not even a New York baseball crowd at a great baseball match, roars so long or so loud as the Derby Day thousands roar.'

Two men were responsible for establishing The Derby—General John Burgoyne, a swashbuckling gambler, soldier, playwright and wit, and his nephew by marriage, Edward Smith Stanley who became the 12th Earl of Derby in 1776. Burgoyne owned The Oaks, a large rambling house which he had created from an old inn near Epsom. Returning discredited from the New World after his ignominious surrender at Saratoga he spent more and more time at The Oaks where night-long reckless gambling parties were held. Sir Charles Bunbury, Charles James Fox, Richard Brinsley Sheridan and the youthful Lord Derby were frequent guests. Burgoyne, who knew Anthony St Leger, advised Lord Derby on his bloodstock interests, and the lackadaisical peer, who lived for the day and cared nothing for the past or the future, was content to be guided by him. In 1779 Burgoyne and Lord Derby, inspired by news of the St Leger at Doncaster, organized a contest for three-year-old fillies and gave the race the title 'The Oaks'. Much to the delight of Lord Derby his filly Bridget defeated her eleven rivals. Elated by this success he gave a riotous celebration dinner at The Oaks where before midnight it had been agreed to stage a similar race for colts and

Derby Day in 1928. From its inception in 1790 to the present time this race, named after the 12th Earl of Derby, has generated enormous excitement.

fillies the subsequent summer, with entries having to be made during 1779 when the nominated horses were two-year-olds. May 4, 1780 was the memorable day upon which Sir Charles Bunbury's Diomed won the first Derby. The race was, in reality, only a minor part of the afternoon's sport which included bear-baiting, tugs-of-war, cock fighting and wrestling matches. Many of the 'curled and scented bucks, with their cambrics and quizzing glasses and sparkling rings' who attended The Derby had been dancing at a ball the previous night. They arrived in their cabriolet and carriages and were a source of amazement and amusement to the locals who were unaccustomed to such luxury. Eight years later the Prince of Wales, wearing a green jacket, white hat and tight-fitting nankeen pantaloons, gave The Derby Royal Patronage when he watched his colt, Sir Thomas, win the race from a small wooden grandstand in company with the Dukes of Bedford and Dorset, Lord Jersey and Beau Brummell.

The Derby began to increase in popularity soon after the end of the Napoleonic Wars, due to the establishing of the Two Thousand Guineas and the One Thousand Guineas which made up the five Classic races of which The Derby was the most significant, and to the founding of the sporting newspaper *Bell's Life* which intimated that the Press were becoming interested in horse-racing. In consequence the coverage given to racing increased, and the middle and lower classes, many of whom had a passion for gambling, were brought into daily contact with the 'Sport of Kings'. In 1840 the young Queen Victoria paid her only visit to The Derby. No reigning monarch had previously watched the race, and the executive created a new paddock for saddling the horses so that the Queen could use the existing paddock as a promenade. Twenty-three years later her son, the Prince of Wales, visited Epsom on Derby Day. The weather was appalling and Charles Dickens commented, 'last year it was iced champagne, claret cup and silk overcoats. Now it ought to be hot brandy and water, foot baths and flannels.' Persimmon won The Derby for the Prince of Wales in 1896 and a telegram was received from the Queen who was at Balmoral. Her son replied, 'The scene after The Derby was a most remarkable and gratifying sight.' In the evening the Prince

The 1981 Derby winner
Shergar, ridden by Walter
Swinburne. In 1983
Shergar was kidnapped
while at stud in Ireland.
His value was estimated
at 20 million pounds.

entertained the Jockey Club to dinner at Marlborough House at which the wines drunk included Château Margaux 1875 and fifty-year-old Royal Tawny port.

Four years later Diamond Jubilee gave the Prince his second Derby victory and as he proudly led his hero into the Winners' Enclosure the huge crowd on the Downs showed their patriotic fervour by singing 'God Save The Queen'. An even greater triumph came in 1909 when Minoru won by a short head, and as the King went on to the course to greet his Derby winner the roar of the crowd was tumultuous. However, the King, ever mindful of his colt's safety, sensibly remarked, 'Please do not touch him or he will kick.'

Prime ministers, in addition to royalty, have patronized The Derby. The Duke of Grafton, a great-grandson of King Charles II, became Prime Minister at the age of thirty-one, and won The Derby three times. Lord Palmerston also loved his racing, and once was so carried away at having been successful in a Parliamentary debate that he exclaimed, 'I have won my Derby.' The 14th Earl of Derby, twice Prime Minister, won the 1851 Oaks and his colt Toxophilite finished second in the 1858 Derby. In 1857 he wrote a letter to the Stewards of the Jockey Club. 'My Lords ... it has become a subject of general observation and regret that the number of men of station and fortune who support the Turf is gradually diminishing and that an increasing proportion of horses in training is in the hands of persons in an inferior position, who keep them, not for the purpose of sport, but as mere instruments of gambling ...' When Lord Rosebery won the 1894 Derby with Ladas he had been Prime Minister for nine weeks and a friend sent him a telegram: 'Only heaven now left.' Two years later in a Gimcrack speech he admitted, 'I won The Derby, and what was the result? I, at that time, held high office under the Crown. I was immediately attacked for owning racehorses at all ... although without guilt of offence I might run second or third, or even last, it became a matter of torture to many consciences if I won The Derby ...' Winston Churchill also found pleasure on the Turf and was robbed of possible Derby victory in 1960 when his much fancied Vienna was withdrawn at the eleventh hour.

No one denies that The Derby and The Oaks, which is run over an identical distance, are unique, for they test the endurance of a three-year-old to the limit. The course is left-handed and 1½ miles in extent. It rises 150 feet in the first four furlongs and falls in varying gradients a hundred feet to Tattenham Corner with a considerable rise to the winning post. It is customary for The Derby to be run on the first Wednesday in June and The Oaks three days later.

A Derby winner must overcome the undulating twists and turns of the Epsom track, which is situated a mile to the east of the town, without becoming unbalanced and also be able to cope with the hubbub and excitement of the occasion. He must have stamina and speed, and be prepared to gallop at top speed for twelve furlongs uphill and downhill without interrupting the flow of his natural action. He must not change his legs as he descends to Tattenham Corner for if he does so he will lose ground—and probably the race. Finally he must have the courage and ability to 'pull out a little extra'. That 'little extra' has enabled such twentieth-century champions as Hyperion, Bahram, Sir Ivor, Nijinsky, Mill Reef and Roberto to be hailed as Derby winners before embarking upon a stud career which has enabled each of them to influence bloodstock breeding throughout the world and endorse the description of The Derby as 'the event which is the touchstone of equine greatness'.

Oxford and Cambridge Balls

The Cambridge May Balls, in spite of their name, are held in about the second week in June over the period of the May Races on the Cam, the Oxford Commemorative Balls ('Commem') fall at the end of the month.

In June 1861 in *The Leisure Hour* magazine, the following article about the Oxford Commemoration appeared:

The question is often asked by non-academic readers, 'what is the Commemoration at Oxford to which *The Times* devotes a long and interesting column every summer?' It is an annual festival held in the [Sheldonian] Theatre (never used for theatrical purposes) at the close of the summer term in honour of the founders and benefactors of the university; and it corresponds in some measure with the 'Commemoration' held in the senate house at Cambridge, which however is not made so much of.

As the time approaches, Oxford completely alters its appearance, and, as it were, bursts into flower. Caps and gowns are altogether outnumbered by 'lionesses' in summer attire, and the classic High Street shakes off for the nonce, its sombre and meditative aspect. Dear old Alma Mater is holiday-making, and she does not do it by halves. The few days preceeding the Commemoration are one continued round of promenades, concerts, balls, flower-shows, archery meetings, boat races, processions, elegant breakfasts, tasteful luncheons, dinners, suppers, picnics and all manner of entertainments.

Both in Oxford and Cambridge the annual revelries are very lively affairs and the college balls present scenes of unrivalled merry-making. Black tie is very much worn, with long evening dresses for ladies, and people usually make up parties who assemble beforehand for dinner, although there is always plenty to eat at the

RIGHT:
The Trinity College Ball at Cambridge during the May Week Celebrations, which in spite of their name take place during June.

BELOW:
After the ball is over, and perhaps after a spell on the river in the small hours, a delightful way to finish is with breakfast in the open air at Grantchester, a village two miles upstream from Cambridge immortalized by Rupert Brooke in his poem *The Old Vicarage, Grantchester*.

ball. It is best not to arrive too early—these balls tend to start later than most and to go on for longer into the not so small hours of the morning. Included in the price of the ticket (which is obtained from the lodge of the college holding the ball or from the Chairman of the Ball Committee) is breakfast and sometimes even the cost of a punt after breakfast. There is also the customary firework display at dawn. It is traditional to go on the river after breakfast, and nearly traditional to fall in. One Cambridge college recently offered breakfast in Paris for an extra £50, but more usually bacon and eggs are demolished in large quantities in the marquees. Some wine is generally also included in the ticket and there are several bars around the dance-floors. There will always be more than one dance band or orchestra playing different kinds of music, usually including a well-known group, and often entertainments similar to night-club cabaret acts as well in the college hall and specially decorated marquees.

Not every college holds a ball every year; some only occur every other year or once every three years, and the balls held at the larger colleges are correspondingly more lavish and more crowded, but not necessarily more enjoyable. Most people of course go to a college with which they have some connection or acquaintance, but tickets are by no means restricted, and colleges are always happy to include visitors from outside the academic world.

Trooping the Colour

In the Middle Ages a battle between soldiers either dressed alike and unrecognizable in suits of armour, or in a motley collection of any clothing they could lay their hands on, could be lost simply because the troops had no idea where, or who, their leader was, so identification symbols had to be established. These took various forms: a commander would devise some insignia depicting a particular event or object peculiar to himself or to his house which was then embroidered on to his surcoat and the coverings of his horse or he would use a password or battle-cry known only to his followers, and above all he would have his 'colour', or standard, held high, close to his person as a rallying point for his troops. As time went by his identification insignia became his family coat-of-arms and his battle-cry might become his motto, subject to the ancient and complicated laws of heraldry. With the organization of the British Army, however, notably under Cromwell in the seventeenth century, the colour became a symbol of a fighting unit and over the years a ceremony grew up round this essential piece of equipment. It was above all important that each soldier was thoroughly familiar with his colour and to this end the standard would be carried along the ranks every day. There was still the further function performed by the colour of providing a rallying point both in action and to identify the regiment's headquarters.

For these reasons the colours of a unit became objects of emotion, to be protected at any cost of life or limb, and today, when the hand-embroidered silk colours are 'laid up' after about twelve to fifteen years' use, they are never thrown away but preserved with great honour.

The ceremonious trooping of the colour to mark the reigning monarch's official birthday began in 1755 under George II and has continued ever since, though not necessarily on the sovereign's actual birthday. Since the days of Edward VII the ceremony has always been held in the summer when there is at least a chance of reasonable weather. Under Queen Elizabeth II it is held on the second Saturday in June.

Since the eighteenth century the regiments of Foot Guards of which the Sovereign is Colonel-in-Chief have formed the nucleus of the ceremony, but during the reign of George VI the Household Cavalry began to play a greater part. Today, their mounted band is one of the most popular attractions for onlookers, and their spectacular uniform of highly polished cuirass, high riding boots over white buckskin breeches and plumed helmets make them one of London's most photographed sights. (It is interesting to note the various differences in the uniform of the Cavalry regiments, such as the red tunics and white plumes of the Life Guards and the blue tunics and red plumes of the Blues and Royals. The Life Guards wear their brass helmet chains under the lower lip and the Blues and Royals under the chin.)

Before the day itself there are two full dress rehearsals, which are very necessary considering the complicated and very precise drill formations involved. At the first rehearsal the salute is taken by the Major-General commanding the Household Division, and at the second by the Colonel of the Regiment of the Colour. (The Prince of Wales is Colonel of the Welsh Guards, Prince Philip of the Grenadier Guards and the Duke of Kent of the Scots Guards.) The Guards

Her Majesty The Queen taking the salute, as Colonel-in-Chief of the Guards regiment whose colours are to be trooped.

regiments take it in turns to troop their colours each year, and it is a great honour to be the young officer chosen to carry the colour. It is no easy task to hold the heavy standard in the same position for what must seem like eternity, and it requires serious exercise of the muscles of the right arm for weeks beforehand.

The ceremony takes place on Horse Guards Parade in Whitehall, the headquarters of the Household Division, with William Kent's beautifully proportioned building on the edge of St James's Park in the background.

The Queen, riding sidesaddle and wearing the uniform of Colonel-in-Chief of the regiment whose colour is to be trooped, leaves Buckingham Palace with precisely enough time to spare so that she ends the mile-long ride to Horse Guards Parade on the stroke of eleven. The Mall is lined with guardsmen in bearskins and scarlet tunics spaced exactly six paces apart. The Queen is preceded by members of the Royal Family in carriages, and the spectacular mounted band of the Household Cavalry, who make their way past the Victoria Memorial and down the Mall to turn into the Parade.

Trooping the Colour on Horse Guards Parade.
The Guards regiments are famous the world over for their formation marching.

Before the Queen takes the salute of the guards on parade and the colour has been trooped, the massed bands perform a marching display in slow and quick time. While the colour is being trooped they also execute their famous spin wheel.

The best place to see this is from the specially erected grandstand which is open to ticket holders only. Tickets for the rehearsal and for the ceremony itself can be obtained from The Brigade Major, HQ Household Brigade, Horse Guards, London SW1. Applications should be made in writing between January and the end of February and should state whether tickets are required for the rehearsal or for the ceremony itself. A good view of the procession can be had from the Victoria Memorial or along the Mall.

The Bath Festival

The Georgian city of Bath is one of the most elegant and interesting places in Britain, with a history going back to the days of the Roman occupation when as *Aquae Sulis* (The Waters of the Iron-age Celtic goddess Sulis) it was a popular place for leisured Romans seeking the benefits of the natural hot springs. The lead-lined Roman baths with their elaborate under-floor heating system are well worth seeing, and the first-century Great Bath is still used for special occasions today. In the eighteenth century Beau Nash, a dandy with immense social influence, was responsible for the city's new status as a fashionable resort and centre of culture, and with the architect Ralph Allen he made it a showpiece of crescents, terraces and squares, much of which remains today in this saucer-shaped city. The elegant Assembly Rooms were burnt out in the blitz of 1942 but have since been completely restored, and with the Guildhall, Bath Abbey and the ancient pump room they now provide one of the more attractive venues for the Festival's concerts and lectures.

The Festival of music and the arts was launched in April 1948 as the 'Bath Assembly', under the direction of Ian Hunter, who had succeeded Rudolf Bing at Glyndebourne, but it ran into difficulties and was suspended in 1956. In 1959 the new management of the Bath Festival Society revitalized the event by appointing Yehudi Menuhin as artistic director. Since then it has flourished with Sir Michael Tippett in charge between 1969 and 1974 and, under the present artistic director Sir William Glock, the Festival has become established as one of the most important cultural events in the country. Much enjoyed by visitors today is the programme put on by the festival Fringe who organize walks, lectures, and tours of local places of interest. The Fringe, which is run by a sub-committee of the Festival Society, also arranges the spectacular opening procession and candlelit singing on the first day of the Festival. In the early evening a sort of carnival procession winds about the city and ends outside the Abbey. At dusk, the Royal Crescent, the Circus and Brock Street are closed to traffic, the street lights are switched off and the residents all put lighted candles in their windows. As it gets dark the flickering lights give a magical quality to the graceful buildings, and make a perfect setting for the choir singing madrigals under the trees of the Circus and the Royal Crescent.

The other main event organized by the Fringe is the open-air picnic held on the last Saturday of the Festival. This spectacular occasion is based on a different period theme each year, and everyone attending wears appropriate costume. The venue of the picnic varies from year to year, but always somewhere particularly attractive is chosen, such as a nearby stately home (one year, when the theme was the Elizabethan age, it was held at Longleat House) or even the Bishop's Palace at Wells. There are usually sideshows, music and entertainments appropriate to the chosen period, with strolling players and dancing till the small hours. Champagne is on sale or people bring their own—each year the picnic hampers brought seem to get more and more lavish, sometimes set out on tables covered in white damask sparkling with crystal and silver.

Tickets for the picnic, all the Festival events and a complete programme can be obtained from the Festival Office, 1 Pierrepont Place, Bath (0225 62231).

The Garter Day Ceremony at Windsor

Garter Day at Windsor usually takes place annually on the Monday before the Royal Ascot Race Meeting in June and provides a fine example of British tradition and ceremony.

The Most Noble Order of the Garter is the highest order of English Knighthood, and the oldest order of chivalry in Britain. The Order was founded by Edward III in about 1348, and honours twenty-four knights who have given service to their country. (There are also a few 'extra' knights.) Called the 'Order of the Garter' or 'The Blue Garter', there is a later tradition that it derived its name from an incident in the fourteenth century in Calais when a lady, possibly the Countess of Salisbury, lost a garter while dancing. This garter was retrieved by King Edward who proceeded to tie it around his leg, much to the amusement of the courtiers. The Sovereign rebuked them by saying 'Honi soit qui mal y pense'—evil be to him who evil thinks—which was to become the motto of the order. Most modern historians do not accept this tradition as fact, mainly because the military garter of the times bears little resemblance to a lady's garter. The Order was formed as a military organization to reclaim the throne of France for Edward III who had styled himself 'King' of France.

This oldest and most sought-after honour took Saint George as its patron, its Chapel being St George's Chapel, Windsor. For many years the Order was awarded for political reasons by the Prime Minister, but after the Second World War George VI took it back to his own personal choice, and one of his first investitures was of Princess Elizabeth and Prince Philip soon after their marriage.

The investiture of any new Knights is carried out in a private ceremony, in the Throne Room of Windsor Castle during the morning of Garter Day. Following the traditional format this ceremony is attended by the Knights and Officers of the Order. The Sovereign places the Garter on the left leg of the Knight or Lady, the Blue Riband over the left shoulder, the Star of the Order on the left breast, the Mantle on the shoulder and the Collar over this. At the end of the ceremony the Registrar, always the Dean of Windsor, presents each new Knight with a Bible and administers the oath in which the Knight swears to obey the statutes of the Order and the laws of the Realm.

After lunching in the Waterloo Room at the Castle the procession moves off to the Garter Service in St George's Chapel. The Service takes place every year whether or not there has been an investiture.

At the entrance to St George's Hall the procession is met by the Constable and Governor of the Castle and the Military Knights of Windsor, who are not Knights of the Garter, but retired senior officers living in lodgings within the Castle. They were originally known as 'Poor Knights' and their function was to pray in the Chapel for Knights of the Garter who were away on military campaigns. For Garter Day the Military Knights wear scarlet uniforms.

In the procession are the Knights and Ladies with the Heralds in their richly embroidered tabards and the Officers of the Order in their traditional robes. The Knights and Ladies of the Garter precede The Queen as Sovereign of the Order who is always accompanied by other members of the Royal Family. The Prince of Wales, the Duke of Edinburgh and the Queen Mother are the only members of the Royal Family who are Knights or Ladies of the Garter. Other distinguished

The procession leaving the Chapel of St George in Windsor Castle
after the Garter Ceremony. The route to the Chapel is lined with
footguards and troopers of the Household Cavalry.

Ladies of the Garter are Princess Juliana of the Netherlands and Queen
Margrethe of Denmark. At the rear of the procession will be a detachment of the
Queen's Bodyguard, the Yeoman of the Guard.

Crowds will have been lining the route in the Castle precincts to St George's
Chapel since early morning. The procession passes between lines of footguards
and dismounted troopers of the Household Cavalry, through Engine Court,
under Norman Gate and down the hill through the Middle and Lower Wards of
the Castle, under the arch into Horseshoe Cloister and up the steps to the West
Door of St George's Chapel.

At the West Door the procession will be met by an ecclesiastical procession
made up of Sacristans, Cross Bearer, Choristers, Lay Clerks, organist, minor
Canons, verger and the Canons of Windsor. When the procession passes under
the screen trumpets sound to show that the Queen has entered the Chapel.

The Knights take up their places in the Choir and the Queen, facing the High
Altar, will say, 'it is our pleasure that the Knight Companion newly invested be
installed.' The Chancellor calls the new Knight's name and Garter King of Arms
then conducts him to his stall.

Each Knight has his own stall in the Choir above which hangs a banner bearing
his coat of arms, which will hang in St George's Chapel during his lifetime.

After the Service the spectators will get another chance to see the Royal Family
as they return to the Castle in carriages and the Knights who return to the Castle
in cars.

This ceremony, one of the oldest traditions of Britain, provides a marvellous
spectacle, and it is advisable to secure a place early to view the procession as a

The Princess of Wales on the steps of St George's Chapel after the Garter Ceremony.

large crowd always gathers. In the event of rain the procession may be cancelled and vehicles will be used to transport participants in the Garter Service to St George's Chapel. Tickets of admission to the Castle and to the Chapel are issued by ballot by organizations such as The Society of the Friends of St George's and Descendants of the Knights of the Garter, and membership is open to anyone paying a small subscription. Write to the Honorary Secretary, The Curfew Tower, Windsor Castle, Berkshire.

Royal Ascot

Royal Ascot, which invariably takes place in mid-June a fortnight after The Derby, has always held a unique position in the world of racing for Classic winners, champion stayers and sprinters, and overseas challengers contest some of the season's most important races throughout the four-day meeting which is also incomparable for its pageantry and elegance of fashion. Few would deny that it is the highlight of the summer season, both as a sporting occasion and as the event where the glamour provided by an abundance of beautifully dressed women, particularly on Ladies' Day, reaches its zenith. The contrast of their dresses and hats (which are obligatory for ladies in the Royal Enclosure) with the sombre greys and blacks of their escorts' top hats and morning dress has been immortalized in the film *My Fair Lady* and brings to Royal Ascot the atmosphere of a garden party where sleek magnificent thoroughbreds steal the limelight. Champagne, lobsters and strawberries are proffered in vast quantities in the Club tents and the private boxes in the grandstands; a military band entertains those who wish their feet to be set tapping; and above all else the pomp and splendour of Royal Patronage dominates the Meeting.

Every afternoon the procession of five open landaus drives up the course, arriving at the Royal Enclosure half-an-hour before the first race. Only if torrential rain has soaked the course so that the carriage wheels sink into the softened turf is the procession cancelled. Outriders in scarlet coats and gold-laced

The Ascot Scene from the film version of Lerner and Loewe's musical *My Fair Lady*.

top hats precede the first carriage in which are the Sovereign and the Master of the Horse. In the following landaus are members of the Royal Family and guests who have been invited to Windsor Castle for race week. Each landau is drawn by four horses with postilions wearing buckskin breeches, top boots, a wig and velvet cap, and a scarlet, purple and gold jacket. For some years it has been customary to have four grey horses drawing the first carriage, preceded by two outriders also on grey horses, and four bay horses to each of the other carriages. The horses, Cleveland and Oldenburg mares and geldings, used in the Royal Procession are the responsibility of the Crown Equerry, the first of whom was appointed in 1854 with the additional tasks of being Secretary to the Master of the Horse and Superintendent of the Royal Mews. Every morning during Royal Ascot the horses are harnessed up with the historic harness which bears the Windsor ornamentation, and at noon are inspected by the Crown Equerry.

Although racing was interrupted by an interval of an hour between the first and second race until the early 1930s, and in the days of King Edward VII his chef, Gabriel Tschume, took to the Royal Box elaborate luncheons sometimes stretching to a dozen courses, in modern times it is usual for The Queen, the Royal Family, and her guests to lunch at Windsor Castle, three miles from Ascot, before the start of the Royal Procession which was initiated by King George IV. Previously King George III had ridden up and down the Ascot course in front of the grandstand with his family—the Queen and the Princesses being in a sociable—but this was a parade as opposed to a procession. In 1825 King George IV drove down the course in a carriage, with the Duke of Wellington on his right and his Lords-in-Waiting opposite him. The carriage was preceded by Lord Maryborough, Master of the Buckhounds, and a large number of outriders. King William IV continued the Royal Patronage and in 1831 Charles Greville commented, 'The King and the royal family came to the course on the first day with a great cortège, eight coaches, two phaetons, pony sociables and led horses. The Duke of Richmond was in the King's calèche . . .'

Four years later the King took Princess Victoria with him. Many years later she wrote to the Prince of Wales, 'Dear Bertie—now that the Ascot races are approaching I wish to repeat earnestly and seriously . . . as my uncle William IV and Aunt, and we ourselves did, confine your visits to the races to the two days, Tuesday and Thursday—and do not go on Wednesday and Friday to which William IV never went, nor did we . . .' The Prince replied, 'I fear, dearest Mama, that no year goes round without your giving me a jobation on the subject of Racing. The Tuesday and Thursday at Ascot have always been looked upon as the great days, as there is the procession in your carriages up the course which pleases the public and is looked upon by them as a kind of annual pageant.'

Today Her Majesty The Queen is greeted by her Ascot Representative when she arrives at the Grandstand. Until the death of Queen Victoria Ascot was under the control of the Master of the Buckhounds, irrespective of his interest in racing. King Edward VII abolished the Royal Buckhounds, and since then the Sovereign has appointed a Representative to administer the racecourse and its environment. In 1913 the Ascot Authority Act was passed from which the Ascot Authority— the three Trustees appointed by the Sovereign—derive their powers to manage and superintend any lands in their hands as if they were absolute owners. The Act also gives powers to maintain, improve, add to and alter any of the enclosures,

One of the sights of Ladies' Day at Ascot— the milliner David Shilling escorting his mother who appears each year in ever more exotic outfits.

approaches, conveniences, fences, gates, or other property for the time being vested in them, or to provide or erect new buildings, stands, offices, rooms, enclosures, gates, fences or other things deemed necessary for use in connection with Ascot races. The control exercised by the Sovereign is the right to appoint by deed the Ascot Authority Trustees. Since 1952 The Queen's Representatives have been Bernard, 16th Duke of Norfolk (1952–72); John, 5th Marquess of Abergavenny (1972–82) and Colonel Piers Bengough (1982–   ).

The first race-meeting at Ascot took place on 11 August, 1711 when Queen Anne drove from Windsor Castle with her courtiers and her maids-of-honour to attend a day's sport which had been organized at her command. Despite such Royal Patronage racing at Ascot did not flourish until William Augustus, Duke of Cumberland, was appointed Ranger of Windsor Great Park in 1745. The first member of the Royal Family to be elected to the Jockey Club, he revived interest in the sport, arranged for those who wished to run their horses for the King's Guineas at Ascot races to apply to the liveried huntsmen for tickets proving that they had qualified for entry by being present at the kill, and introduced his great-nephew, George, Prince of Wales, to the pleasures of racing. In 1791 the Prince saw his horse Baronet win the valuable Oatlands Stakes at Ascot. Even the King was pleased by this success and remarked to his son, 'Your Baronets are more productive than mine. I made fourteen last week, but I get nothing by them. Your single Baronet is worth all mine put together.' Within two years of this victory the Prince had lost all interest in racing, with the result that he did not patronize the Turf until his interest was rekindled in the 1820s. In 1829 he watched the Gold Cup from a pavilion built to the design of Nash in 1822. The Cup runners included two Derby winners, a St Leger winner, an Oaks heroine and the winner of the 1828 Cup. Understandably a contemporary wrote, 'Thursday was considered by all as the grandest day ever seen at Ascot, both as to numbers of people, elegance of dress, and rank in life . . .'

In the early 1830s the Ascot racecourse again seemed to be losing popular appeal. Consequently when William IV gave his annual dinner to members of the Jockey Club, at which five Dukes and eight Earls were present, he suggested that the future of Ascot should be discussed. The discussions were fruitful and in January 1839 the foundations were laid for a new grandstand which had a handsome balcony supported by Corinthian pillars, accommodation for almost one thousand spectators on the roof and refreshment rooms, retiring rooms and a basement where betting transactions were carried out.

The year before the building of the new grandstand was commenced Queen Victoria, attired in pink silk and lace and wearing a white bonnet trimmed with pink ribbons and roses, drove up the course in the Royal Procession. She was accompanied by Lord Melbourne who agreed with her at dinner on their return to Windsor Castle that it was not desirable to bet, for betting spoiled the grandeur of the occasion. After the death of the Prince Consort the Queen never went racing, but her son relished Ascot and pointed out to her that attending Ascot enabled the general public to see members of the Royal Family. He added, 'and after all Racing with all its faults still remains, I may say, a National Institution of the Country.'

When Queen Victoria died the 1901 Royal Ascot meeting was a sombre affair with the race programme encircled in black, the lawn below the King's Stand railed off and no admission allowed to it, and racegoers informed that they should wear black. Similar mourning was observed in 1910 when the Royal meeting was held only weeks after the death of King Edward VII. During the First World War there was no racing at Ascot which was used as a military depot, with the Silver Ring Grandstand being used as a hospital. Within a year of the conclusion of the Second World War King George VI approved plans for the reconstruction of the course and in addition proposed that there should be three extra Ascot Heath meetings later in the year. During the past three decades other major improvements have been made, with the most significant being the rebuilding of the grandstands. The Queen Elizabeth II Grandstand, 560 feet long and 74 feet high, contains 280 boxes each with its private luncheon room and was completed in 1961. The new Royal Enclosure grandstand followed four years later, and necessitated the rebuilding of the Royal Box. In the old Royal Box the staircase contained a newel post into the top of which a wooden star was inlaid. It was rumoured that The Queen often touched this star for luck. When the new box was completed the builders arranged for a similar star to be included on the staircase to continue the good luck.

It is not possible for Ascot visitors to see this star or any part of the inside of the Royal Box which contains a large viewing area, retiring rooms, and a high ceilinged tea-room on the walls of which are oil paintings by Henry Chalon of racehorses owned by King George IV. However, they are able to inspect the magnificent pair of wrought-iron gates erected behind the Royal Stand to commemorate The Queen's Accession. The design for these gates, which are used by the Royal Family when they arrive by car, was made by an Oxfordshire

The Black Ascot of 1910,
the year of the death of Edward VII. Mourning had also
been worn in 1901 after the death of Queen Victoria.

craftsman, and was based upon similar gates at Arundel Castle, home of the Duke of Norfolk who generously presented to Ascot a pair of stone lions which can be seen outside the Weighing Room.

The Ascot round course is a right-handed, triangular circuit of 1 mile 6 furlongs 34 yards with a run-in of three furlongs. There is a straight mile course, and the Old Mile course which joins the round course at Swinley Bottom. All races shorter than one mile are contested on the straight course. A galloping track, the turns are easy and there are no minor surface undulations to throw a long-striding horse off balance. All races are very much against the collar over the final half-mile. The major races run at the Royal meeting are: the St James's Palace Stakes, the Prince of Wales Stakes, the Coventry Stakes, the Queen Anne Stakes, the Ribblesdale Stakes, the Coronation Stakes, the Gold Cup, the Hardwicke Stakes, the King's Stand Stakes, the King Edward VII Stakes and the Queen Mary Stakes.

Throughout the past 270 years Royal Ascot has retained a splendour and a tradition which entitles it to a high position in the heritage of Britain. In addition it must not be overlooked that the June meeting is supported by the running of the King George VI and the Queen Elizabeth Diamond Stakes in July which is one of Europe's three most prestigious races, a Charity meeting in September and steeplechasing during the winter months.

Applications for admission to the Royal Enclosure, as announced in December in the Court and Social Page of *The Times*, must be made personally in writing to Her Majesty's Representative, Ascot Office, St James's Palace, London SW1, by March and require the signature of a sponsor, who is already on Her Majesty's list. Information and tickets to all other stands can be obtained from: The Secretary, Grand Stand, Ascot, Berkshire.

The Aldeburgh Festival

The Aldeburgh Festival was instituted in 1948 round the personality, the taste and the music of one man: Benjamin Britten. Together with his lifelong friend, the tenor Peter Pears, and Eric Crozier, writer and producer, he had already established the English Opera Group in 1947. Now, a year later, they launched their first festival so successfully that with their keen sense of musical style combined with the originality and quality of performance, they ensured that Aldeburgh would almost certainly outlive them all.

Britten was born at Lowestoft in 1913 and the East Anglian coast was part of his nature. He died at Aldeburgh, as Lord Britten, in 1976. After the success of his 'Variations on a Theme of Frank Bridge' in 1937, he bought a converted windmill overlooking the Aldeburgh estuary and Snape Maltings. There he composed much of his large output of instrumental and vocal music, none of which is more evocative of this landscape than the opera *Peter Grimes* based on a story by George Crabbe (born in Aldeburgh in 1754). This corner of Suffolk gave Britten his inspiration with its windswept skies and the empty salted river marshlands which echo to the cry of the curlew. And when there is a storm, it is a particularly fearsome one when the sea lashes the shore and threatens to eat away the coast even faster than it has been doing for as long as anybody can remember.

The first festival made use of Aldeburgh's Jubilee Hall and local parish churches for performances, but as the attraction of the Festival in this quaint little market town increased, a firm decision was made to buy the disused maltings at Snape, whose Victorian buildings were converted and the malt-kiln itself was turned into a concert hall. All this took nearly seven years.

The composer Benjamin Britten (right) with his great friend the tenor Peter Pears in 1943. From a painting by Kenneth Green.

The Queen opened the new hall in 1967, but only two years later, after the opening concert of the 1969 season, the hall was burnt to the ground. The degree of sorrow and sympathy which came to Aldeburgh may be judged by the fact that £20,000 was raised within two months of the disaster; then good will, hard work and perseverance created a new hall on the ashes of the old one in time for the opening concert of the 1970 Festival. Again The Queen performed the initial ceremony.

The wooden construction of the new Maltings and the clarity of sound inside it reflect certain aspects of the country outside it where wide open beaches and marshlands, clean, clear air and the feeling of a boundless sky and sea create a unique atmosphere.

The duration of the Festival is changeable. Since 1972 it has been curtailed from its former two weeks in mid-June to spread events elsewhere over a longer period. Public demand for tickets always exceeds the supply for this miniature festival excels in the presentation of intimate works by the great masters, by Britten himself—but not predominantly—and by young British composers, some of whom are protégés of the Snape Chamber Music Festival in October.

The whole atmosphere is relaxed and informal: a basis of friendship persists not only between the directors and other musicians who wait to be invited, but also among visitors and 'locals' at Aldeburgh. Accommodation is limited, and getting there is best done by road, although there is a (rather slow) train service as far as Saxmundham seven miles away, thereafter by a connecting bus.

Programmes become available in early March from The Festival Office, High Street, Aldeburgh, Suffolk, where they also take advance bookings.

The Royal Highland Show

Situated at Ingliston on the outskirts of Edinburgh, the Royal Highland is undoubtedly the premier show in Scotland. Although the show is very much on the national show circuit few invaders from south of the border can be found there. The competition in all classes is very intense as the ambition of every patriotic Scotsman is to carry off a prize at this show.

Unlike many shows in England and Wales the Highland is still very much an agricultural show. The main emphasis in the show ring is on cattle, and there are plenty of stands exhibiting farm machinery and items of special interest to farmers in the showground.

As one would expect, Scottish breeds are much in evidence. The lovely Highland cattle, with their long horns and shaggy coats, are a sight all too rarely seen these days. The large, stocky Highland pony is also much to be seen, and especially popular are the immensely powerful Clydesdale horses.

At this show, other than the usual events, special attractions in the main ring are not often as spectacular as those to be found south of the border. Most of the competitors in the show-jumping classes are Scottish, although a few of the big names make the long haul up to Edinburgh.

The trade stands are always of a high quality and although it takes a considerable time to inspect all the exhibits there are some most interesting ones amongst them. The Rare Breeds Survival Trust always has a large exhibit where endangered species of farm animals may be viewed.

Judging ponies at the Royal Highland Show at Ingliston, just outside Edinburgh.

Although the Royal Highland Show is small in comparison to English agricultural shows it is a unique occasion which certainly merits a visit. It has a strong Scottish flavour and you will certainly hear the music of the bagpipes and see plenty of tartan worn.

For details of membership apply to the Secretary, Royal Highland Show, Ingliston, Midlothian, Scotland. As at other similar shows a catalogue is a must to ensure that all events of interest at the show are seen. The showground is situated eight miles west of Edinburgh just north of the A8 towards Glasgow.

Polo

Of all games played in Britain, polo is the one which to the detached observer conjures up most strongly a vision of the upper classes at play, the British Empire and, above all, exclusivity. This is largely because it is so expensive to join in unless you happen to be a member of the Pony Club, a Guards Officer or educated at Millfield. In spite of its image, however, anyone can go and watch a polo match and feel most welcome. Polo is an exciting game to watch even if one doesn't understand the intricacies of the rules. It is at least obvious that the teams are trying to get the ball into each other's goal by using long-handled mallets.

There are four riders in each team, and substitutes can only be brought on in cases of injury. Polo ponies are not a particular breed of pony but a type bred specially from a thoroughbred stallion and a polo pony mare, usually Argentinian. Most of this country's top polo ponies have been imported from the Argentine. The game can be very hard on the horses, and collisions at high speed are commonly seen. Because of this a player will usually have more than one mount at the ready during a game so that he can change one whenever necessary.

During the height of the Raj in India under Queen
Victoria polo was firmly established as a popular
sport with British officers, seen here playing against
the Nawab of Baltistan in North Kashmir.

The game, which is made up of eight periods (called chukkers) of $7\frac{1}{2}$ minutes each, is thought to have originated in Persia or the Far East, but all that is certain is that it was played in the nineteenth century in the India of the Raj by officers in the British Army. It is now a popular game in both North and South America as well as in Britain and the Argentinian teams in particular reach very high standards.

In England the game is organized by clubs, notably the Cirencester Park Polo Club at Cirencester Park, Gloucestershire (0285 3225), the Cowdray Park Polo Club at Cowdray Park, Midhurst, Sussex (073 081 3257), the Guards' Polo Club who play on Smith's Lawn at Windsor Great Park, Englefield Green, Egham, Surrey (0784 34212), the Ham Polo Club, Richmond Park, Surrey (01 948 3627) and Orchard Portman at Taunton, where Millfield School play. The Hurlingham Polo Association, Pephurst Farm, Lexwood, Billingshurst, Sussex (0403 752738) will also provide information. The polo team at Millfield School in Somerset is very active but it is exclusive to members of the school.

The best way to go is in a car which can be parked on the sidelines of the polo ground, and this facility is not usually restricted to members only. Although all the clubs have separate areas for members and the public, there is not as much difference as at many other sporting occasions, and it is probably not necessary to become a member in order to enjoy an occasional polo match.

Matches at the weekend usually begin in the afternoon and most people bring a hamper of varying degrees of extravagance for a picnic before the start, although refreshments are also available in the Club Pavilions. Pimms and champagne are the most popular drinks. Dress is reasonably informal, but it is important to wear comfortable shoes, particularly if taking part in the odd custom at half-time and between games of 'stamping in the divots' when everyone flocks on to the ground

Prince Philip playing polo at Cowdray Park in Sussex.
The game has strong royal connections,
and Prince Charles is as keen a player as his father.

and stamps about, in theory to keep the ground in good condition especially where it has been heavily cut-up by the ponies in front of the goal posts. During the matches a commentary is broadcast on loudspeakers and complicated rules or moves are usually explained, and an effort is certainly made by the clubs to keep their visitors interested and fully informed.

The best matches to go to are the Warwickshire Cup tournament at Cirencester Park towards the end of June and the Cowdray Park Gold Cup in July. It is also worth visiting International Polo Day, which is held at the end of July on Smith's Lawn in Windsor Great Park, and is an occasion where the Prince of Wales has sometimes been seen as a member of the second English team.

Polo matches are enjoyable occasions with a light-hearted and informal atmosphere, and they can be almost as entertaining for the spectators as for the players. It is also, however, a game of skill and one which requires courage and a high degree of skill and fitness, and there can be moments of considerable drama. It is certainly never boring.

Wimbledon

The first lawn tennis championship of the All England Croquet and Lawn Tennis Club (later this became the All England Lawn Tennis and Croquet Club as tennis overtook the gentler game of croquet) took place at Worple Road in Wimbledon in July 1877, and since then it has never lost its place as the pinnacle of achievement in the highly competitive world of international tennis. It is still the highest ambition of players (since 1968 the Championship has been open to professionals as well as amateurs) and, in spite of periodic mutterings about inadequate prizes, out-of-date facilities or inaccurate line calls, players today will, on the whole, agree with Rod Laver's words as he took the trophy for the Men's Singles Championship at the first Open Wimbledon: 'What is there left to prove?'

The game of lawn tennis in the early years of the tournament had many obvious similarities to its ancestor real tennis, much played by the Tudors, ('real' means 'royal' and has nothing to do with the game's authenticity or otherwise), such as the snow-shoe shaped rackets and the fact that the net, which was five feet high at each end, dipped to three feet three inches in the middle. This of course made the tactics very different from today's, as did the underarm serving. Perhaps it was more courtly (the ground on which the game is played is still called a 'court' from its regal origins). Wimbledon's sporting connections started with croquet, a game which in the nineteenth century was almost as much favoured as the other upper-class games of the time, which of course included cricket, although even in

Major Wingfield's hourglass shaped sphairistike court in the 1870s, the forerunner of the modern rectangular court.

those heady days of gentlemanly sporting endeavour cricket had achieved a place apart—the first Championship had built into its programme a two-day break so that spectators could watch the Eton v. Harrow match at Lord's. Originally, indeed, in 1875, the Marylebone Cricket Club (as semi-official upholders of the sporting code of the British Empire) had set up a Tennis and Rackets Sub-committee to regularize the rules of lawn tennis but a couple of years later the All England Club took the control firmly into their own hands, and it is on their rules that today's game is based.

Lawn tennis developed on the solid Victorian suburban lawns, where the leisured classes acted out the social play with croquet and outdoor rackets. It presented an ideal opportunity for decorous flirtation in an acceptable setting.

The rules of lawn tennis in these early days remain much the same today, with the singular scoring system (based on the game's mediaeval French origins) leading to a set of six or more games. The rules were also influenced by that remarkable figure in the history of lawn tennis, Major Walter Clopton Wingfield, who styled himself the inventor of the modern game. His unique version was based on an hour-glass shaped court with the net at the 'waist', and was given curiously the Greek-sounding name of 'sphairistike'.

In 1880 the service 'let' was introduced and players were not allowed to play the ball before it had crossed the net; and in 1882 the height of the net posts at each end was set at a standard three feet six inches, with three feet at the centre, where it remains to this day throughout the world. In 1887 the most radical change came to the game with the first over-arm service (it also brought about the first known case of tennis elbow).

In 1884 the first ladies' singles championship was held, and was won by Miss Maud Watson, who beat her sister Lilian in the final. Thirteen ladies entered the championship. But it was the legendary Lottie Dod who established ladies' tennis, and, if not on a par with such stars of the men's game as the Renshaw brothers, Willie and Ernest, who were among the earliest of the truly dedicated and superbly inspired players, she did at least bring to women recognition as sportswomen in their own right, and prepared the way for such astonishing achievements in the next century as Billie-Jean King's (née Moffat) twenty Championship victories. (In December 1982 another milestone in women's tennis was passed when Virginia Wade, who won the Ladies' Singles title in The Queen's Silver Jubilee year of 1977, became the first lady player to become a committee member of the All England Club.)

There were several early pairs of brothers or sisters who are remembered with the great names of tennis, among them Wilfred and Herbert Baddeley and the Doherty brothers ('Big Do' and 'Little Do'), who for several years over the turn of the century were the leading lights of the tournament.

In 1888, after various internal wranglings in the All England Club, a new independent governing body was founded, and the British Lawn Tennis Association was inaugurated with Willie Renshaw as its first president. In practice, this was an excellent move, for it meant that the onerous tasks of organization were passed to the LTA while the All England Club retained its exclusivity as a private club, so achieving the most desirable effect of pleasing everybody.

The Lawn Tennis Association published its first book of rules in 1889, and

The legendary French tennis star of the 1920s, Suzanne Lenglen. She was a spectacularly athletic and graceful player.

with minor changes it remains standard throughout the world to this day.

In the years leading up to the First World War the popularity of the Singles Championships at Wimbledon, and indeed international contests such as the Davis Cup (donated by the great American player Dwight Davis in 1900), established the game as an important part of the sporting season, and by the 1920s when the Championships moved to its present site in Church Road, the scene was set for such charismatic stars of the courts as Suzanne Lenglen and W. T. Tilden, and also saw the rise of other glamorous players from abroad who made Wimbledon truly international. In 1934 The Lawn Tennis Association signed an agreement which gave them joint ownership of Wimbledon with the All England Club, and they also handed over the administration of the rules of the game to the International Lawn Tennis Federation on the understanding that the rules should always be published in the English language. The popularity of the tournament was such that in 1925 it was found necessary to introduce the Qualifying Competition which is today, for the players, almost the most agonizing part of the whole Championships. (Out of several hundred would-be players nowadays, there are only places for sixteen men and eight women for the singles titles. The rest of the places are taken by players whose record in other tournaments justifies their automatic inclusion.)

Royal interest in Wimbledon really started with King George V and Queen Mary. The King had first visited the tournament as Prince of Wales in 1907 and became President of the Club, an office he retained until 1909, and in 1926 he saw his second son, the Duke of York (later King George VI) play left-handed in the Men's Doubles with Wing-Commander Louis Greig. Although his son never achieved the coveted men's singles title, King George donated the silver cup that is now triumphantly flourished before the packed crowds of the Centre Court, and the press and television of the world, at the end of the match—a trophy that has been won by such superb players as Fred Perry, Lew Hoad, Rod Laver, Jimmy Connors, Bjorn Borg and John McEnroe. In more recent years royal patronage has been led by the Dukes of Kent and their families, who have followed the tournament avidly since before the Second World War, particularly Princess Marina who is remembered by players and officials with much affection.

Such is the popularity and prestige today that the demand for Centre Court tickets far outstrips supply, and apart from the lucky (and rich) owners of debenture seats and members of the All England Club and LTA Council Members who have their own enclosure, the best way for the public to get in is to be invited to join the select parties in the private marquees (mostly owned by companies), or to take part in the annual ballot for seats. Applications for this have to be sent to The Chief Executive of the All England Club by 31 January each year on the official form which is obtained from the same address on receipt of a stamped addressed envelope at the end of the year. A number of daily Centre and No 1 Court tickets are available at the ground. There is also the chance that you might get a seat for a short time if you go in person: if a ticket holder leaves the court before the end of play the ticket is put into a special box and then resold at very cheap rates to anyone waiting at the time.

Apart from the main tournament matches some excellent tennis can be seen in the Gentlemen's 35 and Over Singles and Doubles events, and Juniors' and Ladies' Plate Championships which are played during the second week.

The organization of the tournament is a marvellous mixture of tradition and efficiency. On court nearly everything is in the green and purple colours of the All England Club from the uniform of the ball boys and girls (all specially trained and chosen from local schools) to the umpire's chair. Even the famous ivy-coloured walls of the main building continue the colour scheme. The All England Club provides a completely sheltered and self-contained environment for the players with fully equipped dressing-rooms, trained physiotherapists, a private restaurant and even a Post Office with the Club's own special postmark.

Out of the eighteen grass courts, by far the most popular, obviously, is the Centre Court with No 1 Court coming a close second. The Centre Court provides a grass surface which is 'the fastest, hardest and truest in the world' and to achieve this takes a great deal of work throughout the year. After the close of each tournament the court is reseeded, and on the Saturday before the first game of the Championships a doubles game made up of four lady members of the exclusive All England Club 'play the grass in'. The match also provides a rehearsal for the ball boys and the scoreboard team. (The Court is officially closed by a game played by the Chairman's four.)

To protect the court from the ever-present threat of rain, there is a tarpaulin weighing over four tons which can be pulled over at a moment's notice. It is, unfortunately, often brought into use.

Outside the courts much work goes into making the occasion enjoyable for the spectators. Refreshments of various sorts are on sale, including the famous strawberries and cream. Many people bring a picnic and eat it on the delightful lawns, drinking Pimms or champagne, although the private marquees usually lay on sumptuous spreads for the more privileged. Every day the grounds are tidied up and all litter cleared so that when the gates open at noon each day everything is immaculate again. Highlights of the occasion (after the tennis!) are the Garden Party before the tournament starts, and the Wimbledon Ball and the Champions' Dinner at the end. This is for players and invited guests and VIPs, and is very difficult to get into.

To get to Wimbledon either drive, although parking can be a problem, or go by train from Waterloo or Blackfriars stations, or by Underground District Line to Southfields or Wimbledon.

July

Deer Stalking

Stalking the red deer in the Scottish Highlands in the autumn is one of the most exhilarating of sports but one which demands considerable stamina and patience. It is also one which can be extremely expensive for anyone lacking a useful acquaintance who happens to own a forest. (Deer stalking terrain is called a forest although it is not covered in trees. Most of the land is more likely to be open hillside with not a tree in sight, and stalking is much more enjoyable on the mountainsides than in woodland, in which the deer can be difficult to find, and are more likely to see you before you see them, and which can be awkward to get through. The term 'forest' is used because Scottish deer, like the red deer of England and the Continent, were originally forest animals, but they have adapted to the bare Highland expanses and are more often seen in the open on the heather and bracken-covered slopes.)

It is possible (at great expense) to rent a forest for the season and there are estate agents in centres such as Inverness in the main stalking areas of the Highlands which specialize in arranging lettings. Magazines like *Country Life*, *The Field* and *Shooting Times* sometimes carry advertisements for whole forests

Spying out the deer on Ben More in Sutherland.

or for the individual gun and there are also certain inns and hotels offering stalking as part of their amenities which can be found through the Scottish Tourist Board.

Not a great deal of equipment is necessary but an obvious and important requirement is a good high velocity sporting rifle usually of .270 calibre, 030–06 or .318, bought or hired from a reputable gunsmith known for his knowledge of rifles who will also put the novice in touch with a rifle club through which he can obtain a firearms certificate and where he can practise target shooting at leisure. It is essential that the stalker is familiar with his rifle. Opinions vary on the desirability of telescopic sights, which can be misused to take excessively long shots but are properly used only to make certain that the aim will ensure a killing shot. They do, however, have the advantage over the traditional open sights of considerably improved accuracy of aim and this of course reduces the risk of wounding deer. Nowadays very few modern stalkers shoot over open sights. Normally the heart or neck shot is taken as there is a better chance of instant and humane death by a bullet in these areas. Soft-nosed bullets that expand on impact are used as when well placed they are more instantly fatal. If a deer is wounded it is essential that it is followed and killed, not left to die a lingering death or live on in a maimed condition in the wild.

Anyone stalking deer should wear clothes as inconspicuous as possible which blend with the surrounding country; normally people wear breeches in a not too lightweight tweed with strong nailed or studded boots with good ankle support. Some sort of tweed hat should also be worn; even the famed deerstalker is commonly worn as it is ideal camouflage. There is a sort of competition of camouflage between the deer and the stalker, with the deer having the advantage of several thousand years. As a result they can be extremely difficult to spot except on open ground. It is essential to avoid clothing which rustles or crackles, and this is an important consideration when choosing waterproof jackets, coats or over-trousers. It is also essential to take binoculars or a telescope in a case which is worn on a strap over the shoulder, and which is used for spying the deer. Although the stalker, who fulfils the same function as a gillie in relation to a fisherman, will spy out the deer, the rifle will be anxious to take an active part with his own telescope. Many people take a good strong stick with them, and this can be used in helping to hold the telescope steady as it can be difficult when lying down in the bracken to get one's balance right. (Of course anyone who is foolish enough to stand up to take a look is more than likely to be spotted by the deer.) The only other equipment needed is a packet of cartridges, a bag (usually a green canvas haversack) containing sandwiches for lunch, suitable liquid refreshment, often carried in a hip flask, and spare clothing. A compass can be useful and many people also take a basic first-aid kit.

Before setting off in the morning with the stalker, often in a Land Rover, it is very desirable to check the sighting of the rifle by shooting at a stationary target from 100–150 yards, particularly if the rifle has not been used for a few days. It is as well also to have a good breakfast; it can seem a long time until dinner.

Normally each rifle is accompanied by a stalker, and if there are two rifles they take it in turns to shoot. Sometimes a pony man also goes out who will help to bring the deer down from the hill and will carry the carcass home on the pony at the end of the day. The stalker lives on the ground all the year round, and gets to know the habits of the deer, and his instructions should be followed to the letter. He will point out which stag should be taken, and it is very important that the right stag should be shot. Once the herd has been spotted, considerable time may be spent in deciding which is the most suitable stag for the larder. The shot should be taken either lying prone, or, for a downhill shot, sitting up with the elbows supported on the knees.

The sport of deer stalking forms part of the necessary annual cull, and is by no means indiscriminate slaughter. The season starts on 1 July and continues to 20 October in Scotland. The rut or mating season will usually be well under way in October. (The hinds on the forest may be culled in the winter.) Only mature red deer are stalked, and of those the stalker will pick out an animal which is beginning to 'go back' (i.e., is past its best) or, because of some weakness or deformity, is not suitable for breeding. Sometimes a stag will be seen alone on the open hillside, but more often they gather in small herds of up to about forty animals, stags and hinds together; in bad weather they will sometimes collect in larger numbers for warmth and shelter. They have an extremely acute sense of smell, more so than of sight or hearing, and the ability to judge the eddies of the wind and their direction is a dominant part of the skill of stalking. This is not to say that deer are deaf and blind; on the contrary, they can certainly see and hear as well as a man, and stealth and camouflage are to be remembered at all times. Often the stalker is crawling either on all fours or flat on his stomach over any sort of terrain, even occasionally bog, and anyone who is expecting a gentle stroll over the hillsides is in for a surprise—it is usual for ten miles or more to be covered in a day. Nevertheless a good day out on the hillside with the weather right and a successful stalk completed is as enjoyable as any other outdoor sport, and with good company and a comfortable lodge to return to in the evening it is hardly surprising that deer stalking remains as popular as ever.

The Glyndebourne Festival

Everything about Glyndebourne is so romantic, so magical, that after the first visit one is tempted to believe that it never happened. And its whole idea and realization could only have happened in England. A Tudor manor set in the rolling Sussex Downs and approached by a narrow lane, with a full-scale opera house attached to it, seems impossible—but it has been a reality since 1934.

The founder of the Glyndebourne Festival Opera was Mr John Christie, one of England's great eccentrics and a very rich man. He had been a chemistry master at Eton, was passionately fond of music (especially Wagner's), and always seemed convinced that everything he was doing was beyond argument. He generally carried a pug dog about with him under one arm and in later years wore white tennis shoes with evening dress; but he had a truly scientific mind and a reasonable baritone voice.

Mr Christie encouraged private performances of opera in the organ room (a Christie organ) at Glyndebourne until one day in 1931, shortly after his marriage to Audrey Mildmay, a soprano from the Carl Rosa Company, he decided he would plough up a vegetable garden and build a small theatre next to the house.

Had it not been for Mrs Christie the theatre might have been no more than a folly, but she suggested that as he intended to build one anyway, why not make a proper opera house. Christie saw the sense in this, revised the instructions to his own builders, and at once began planning public performances of German operas by Wagner and Richard Strauss until the fortunate co-option of three professional theatre men from Germany. They undoubtedly saved the whole venture from foundering on the rocks of amateurism.

Fritz Busch, Chief Conductor of the Dresden State Opera; Professor Carl Ebert, producer from the opera in Berlin; and Rudolf Bing, Viennese impresario and later a disciple of Ebert in Berlin insisted upon a transfer of allegiance from Wagner to Mozart, and upon unlimited rehearsals. They piloted Mr and Mrs Christie safely into the first Glyndebourne season that lasted for two weeks and opened with *Le Nozze di Figaro* on 28 May 1934. This was followed on the next night by *Così fan Tutte* and the two operas were then given alternately.

From this frail start the Glyndebourne Festival Opera was established and was very soon world famous. The solid and successful enterprise of today calls for no burden to be placed upon the taxpayer, nor has any ever been there except for the Festival of Britain year, 1951, when the Treasury generously supported festivals all over the country. Today the deficit at Glyndebourne is willingly covered by commercial sponsorship.

As a matter of tradition at Glyndebourne, the soloists are drawn from all over the world, and offer exciting opportunities possibly to hear next year's queen of song before she has reached that exalted level in popular esteem. But the chorus is British. There are five operas every season, with at least one by Mozart and the rest Italian or by baroque or modern composers.

Very little has changed, or has been changed, outside the opera house itself (with greatly enlarged stage and auditorium increased from three hundred to eight hundred seats since 1934) so what Mr Christie wrote for his original publicity leaflet applies equally today:

> The Opera House is surrounded with beautiful lawns and gardens which will be at the disposal of the public. Within a quarter of a mile's stroll of the house is a chain of woodland pools following the course of a Downland stream, leading to coppices with wild flowers. The grounds are encircled by gracious hills and in whichever direction one looks the eye is met by views of unspoiled natural loveliness.

Mr Christie always regarded any visitor to Glyndebourne as his personal guest, even though nominal control passed from him with the establishment of the Glyndebourne Arts Trust in 1954; and when his son George (born in 1934) officially succeeded him in 1958, the Founder lived another four years and died during a performance of *Così fan Tutte*.

It is always a treat, even an honour, to be a 'guest' at Glyndebourne, with all the excellent amenities that the fastidious Christies enjoy so much themselves. The restaurants are run to a very high standard with exceptional wines, but many people prefer to spend the long interval of seventy-five minutes picnicking in the garden.

Evening dress is recommended and is polite, but it is not compulsory. Special trains are run from London to Lewes (and back again after the performance); and because the operas start round about five in the evening, passengers suitably clad

The beautiful lawns and gardens surrounding the Glyndebourne Opera House where members of the audience can stroll before, during and after performances. On a fine summer's evening many people take a picnic supper to eat on the lawns.

for Glyndebourne make an astonishing spectacle on Victoria Station in the middle of a humdrum summer's afternoon.

There are good hotels in Lewes and in the surrounding towns with Brighton only a dozen miles away. The Festival runs from the third week in May to the first week in August, and tickets are not easy to secure. Information is available from The Glyndebourne Festival Opera, Glyndebourne, Lewes, Sussex.

Puppy Shows

Every year all packs of hounds have a puppy show at which they show the young hounds, known as 'the young entry' to their supporters. These shows are usually held at the kennels and are by invitation (if you can persuade the Master that you are very keen it may well produce an invitation). The best hounds in the pack from the point of make and shape are also shown at the four major hound shows. The premier of these is the Peterborough Royal Hound Show in July. Any interest in hounds and their breeding will demand a visit to this great gathering of hunting people and their hounds.

The Welsh packs show their very distinctive hounds in their own ring at the Welsh and Border Counties Hound Show at Builth Wells. The other main hound shows are the South of England at Ardingly, the Great Yorkshire Show at Harrogate and the West of England Hound Show at Honiton. All these shows are advertised in advance in *Horse and Hound* and the *Shooting Times*.

The Eton and Harrow Cricket Match

The Eton and Harrow cricket match is played at Lord's Cricket Ground on the first Saturday after the end of the summer half (as terms are called at Eton) in mid-July, and is hotly contested by the two schools.

Writing in 1897, R. H. Lyttelton in his book *Cricket* includes a short analysis of the number of Oxford and Cambridge Blues produced by the public schools between 1861 and 1897: 59 from Eton, 46 from Harrow, 24 from Rugby, 23 from Winchester, 18 from Marlborough and so on. These figures show that the match was more than just a social gathering; it was a chance to see some of the finest young cricketers in the country.

It is still, however, as much an occasion for meeting old friends as it always was. In the days before motorized transport spectators would range their carriages along the boundaries and perch on the tops to watch the match. Nowadays it is an informal and friendly day out with spectators dressed casually and usually bringing a picnic hamper to eat on the lawn behind the Warner stand. Tickets can be obtained from The Secretary, Lord's Cricket Ground, St John's Wood, London NW8 (01 289 1615) or in advance by post.

George du Maurier's 'Reminiscence of Lord's cricket ground'
during a late Victorian Eton v. Harrow match, showing the
spectators watching from their carriage roofs.

The Royal Show

Held at Stoneleigh in Warwickshire in July each year the Royal Show is the largest and most prestigious of all British agricultural shows. The show season starts in May and goes on through to September, nearly every county having its own agricultural show, or combining with other counties as do Gloucestershire, Herefordshire and Worcestershire to form the Three Counties Show, held at Malvern. Agricultural shows are very much part of the British country scene, although in many cases these days they encompass aspects of urban as well as rural life

The Royal Show has been held at its permanent showground at Stoneleigh since 1962. Before this date the show travelled around the country, as did many others, but the cost of moving it began to become prohibitive, and it made economic sense to establish a permanent site. Its geographical position in the middle of the country makes it relatively easy for both exhibitors and the general public to attend, and such is its popularity that coaches are run to the Show from all over the country.

It runs from Monday to Thursday of the first week in July and certainly takes the best part of a day to explore. Main ring attractions are always top class here with exhibits and demonstrations of the highest calibre, although the main emphasis of the Show is on livestock and agricultural machinery.

The ambition of every breeder and exhibitor of livestock is to win a class at the Royal Show, where the very best in the country will be competing. Understandably the entries for classes are high, which causes grumbles amongst the competitors. The kudos of winning a class, or even just competing at the Royal Show, far outweighs the cost of entries and transport. From the point of view of the public it is possible to see the very best cattle, horses and ponies in the country, which is a chance that should not be missed.

One would imagine that being so vast, crowds would not be the problem here that they are at shows with smaller sites. This is not the case, however, and it is advisable to arrive at Stoneleigh as early as possible to avoid the worst of the rush. As the Show remains open fairly late it should also be possible to stagger the time of departure.

At the Royal Show, like most other agricultural shows, you will certainly find something to please all the family. As at most major shows the Rare Breeds Survival Trust always has an excellent display which gives the opportunity to view some of our endangered species. Rural skills are always much in evidence and for the uninitiated provide an insight into British country life. Although the trade-stand area is also huge the displays are usually varied and some of the factual ones most interesting.

Dress is generally smart, particularly on the first day, although it is noticeable that the general standard of dress at agricultural shows has declined over recent years. Ladies are usually seen in summer dresses and some wear hats. Gentlemen will mostly be wearing tweeds.

As Stoneleigh is the headquarters of many cattle-breed societies, houses the British Equestrian Centre and the head office of the Young Farmers' Club, it is hardly surprising that the emphasis at the Royal Show has not moved away from farming to the degree that it has at other shows.

A particular feature, mainly due to the permanent showground, is the feeding and grass experiments. Although this is of particular interest to farmers, who are always endeavouring to improve their methods, the experiments make most interesting viewing.

Show-jumping, like all the other equestrian events, is always of the highest standard and proves to be quite a crowd-puller in its own right. It is advisable to secure reserved grandstand seats if main-ring features are to be watched. Another advantage of a reserved seat is the fact that you are sure of somewhere to sit and recover during the day. It is best to reserve your seats well in advance.

Many of the foreign touring main-ring features appear at the Royal Show, such as the *Cadre Noir* from France and the Hungarian Whip Crackers, and the King's Troop, the Royal Horse Artillery and the Household Cavalry also appear periodically.

In short the Royal Show, being our most important agricultural show, is well worth a visit for a town or country dweller. The important points to remember are:

1. arrive early to avoid traffic queues and to facilitate viewing.
2. buy a catalogue to ensure nothing of interest is missed.
3. wear comfortable footwear.

Details of membership, which is the cheapest means of admission if attendance is to be on several days, are available from The Secretary, The Royal Show, Stoneleigh, Warwickshire. Membership also secures admission to the Members' Enclosure where it is usually easier to obtain refreshments and a seat than at the public bars which are positioned throughout the showground.

The parade of Shire horses at the Royal Show.
These dignified animals are a perennial attraction at shows all round the country.

The Open Golf Championship

The world's oldest golf championship, 'The Open', by the very omission of the designation of the country where it is held, unlike the other eighteen or so Open Championships throughout the world, is acknowledged as the major international golf championship. It is the one contest that the game's superstars just dare not miss.

Henry Cotton explained its importance when he wrote, after winning his first Open at Sandwich in 1934:

> I feel very much like a medical student or any other person who has passed an exam. That person is just as clever some months before the exam as he is immediately afterwards. But once he has passed that exam he is qualified; there is now a rod by which his skill may be measured. I do not think I am a better player today than I was a week before the Championship, but I am qualified . . .

That memorable victory in which Cotton returned a shattering 65 in the second round was permanently commemorated in a well-known brand's '65' golf ball.

From all over the world professional golfers and amateurs with a handicap of one or better converge on a chosen rugged British links course for this event. Since 1920 it has been promoted and organized from the home of golf, Scotland's Royal and Ancient Golf Club of St Andrew's. However, despite its long association with The Open, The Royal and Ancient was not its instigator. It began at Prestwick Club in 1860 when eight professionals played three rounds over the

The first green at the Royal and Ancient Golf Club of St Andrew's in 1798. This famous course is considered to be the home of golf, and has a long and distinguished history.

The Ladies' Championship winners at Portrush in 1895.

twelve-hole links. The prize was a challenge belt of red morocco leather—a sort of golfing Lonsdale Belt—to be held for a year. The next year it was decided to admit amateurs. (Meanwhile the belt, having been won three times in succession, had become the property of a young champion called Tom Morris.)

For the next twenty-two years the championship rotated between three Scottish Clubs and the prizes were a silver cup for the winner to hold for a year and a gold medal for him to keep. In 1892 it was extended to seventy-two holes and the winner also received a prize of £100. Two years later it was played in England, at Royal St George's, Sandwich and since then it has been played alternately on Scottish and English courses.

It is always played on a links (seaside) course and, throughout its history, only thirteen of these seaside courses have been considered suitable. Today the rota has been reduced to just eight links which are judged to be of a high enough standard in terms of playing conditions, spectator facilities and accessibility.

The venue is chosen four years in advance to give the club, which for eight days will be the focus of the golfing world, time to ensure that the course is in peak condition and to prepare to accommodate more than 130,000 paying spectators during the week including over 25,000 on each of the last four championship days. Moreover, many spectators will need accommodation within reasonable distance of the course.

As for the competitors the prize money totals £309,000 of which the winner receives £45,000. Some competitors, by virtue of their record, are exempt from taking part in the qualifying rounds. After two rounds the top eighty play a third round and finally the top sixty play the fourth round. In 1982 at the Royal Troon Golf Club, 1120 players from many different countries fought to qualify.

There, for the price of a day ticket, spectators could move freely to all parts of the course. A season ticket with a reduction if bought several months in advance, is a popular way of covering the week's matches. Reserved stand seats on the eighteenth green are difficult to come by and composite tickets, which include access to all the facilities and reserved stand seats around the eighteenth green are available from the November prior to the Open. Demand is heavy and all the tickets are sold within a few months.

At The Open controlled fairways and a mapped route of the course make it easy to follow a complete round from the first to the eighteenth tee and there are plenty of vantage points, including stands, at each hole while strategically placed electronic score-boards display the overall state of play at various points on the course.

Despite its well-organized television coverage The Open seems to attract an increasing number of spectators who enjoy watching superb golf played, usually, in ideal seaside conditions although an umbrella and a light raincoat are essential pieces of equipment. Like the United States Open it has so far managed to resist sponsorship. The only financial concessions are some seventy marquees where companies and organizations can entertain their guests. There are also public bars and refreshment tents, usually with television sets so there is no need to miss an important moment of play. There have been countless magical moments including more than a dozen holes in one, none more memorable than Gene Sarazen's at Troon in 1973 at the age of seventy-one.

'That'll be ten thousand gin and tonics,' shouted a wag from the crowd, reminding the popular American of the traditional forfeit for such a feat.

Applications for details of The Open should be made to The Secretary (Dept GM), Royal and Ancient Golf Club, St Andrews, Fife KY16 9JD, Scotland (0334 72112).

Henley Royal Regatta

Henley Royal Regatta is the crowning glory of the English rowing season and has always been accorded the respect and social cachet due to Ascot. The first Henley Regatta was held in 1839—as its founders hoped, not only 'to be productive of the most beneficial results to the town of Henley' but also 'from its peculiar attractions ... a source of amusement and gratification to the neighbourhood, and the public in general'. Seldom have modest hopes been more abundantly fulfilled, for when you go to Henley today you are attending the only provincial town regatta in two hemispheres at which Olympic and World Champion crews are proud to compete. Unlike the University Boat Race, Henley Royal Regatta (the 'Royal' came in 1851, when HRH Prince Albert became the Regatta's first Royal Patron) has been held every summer without a break since 1839, with the sole exceptions being the interruptions of the two World Wars.

The Regatta is always held in the first week of July, with qualifying races (necessitated by the ever-growing press of entries) taking place in the previous week. Seeding has been introduced in recent years for the leading crews and scullers. The draw for the order of racing is held in Henley Town Hall on the Saturday before the Regatta, with the competitors' names traditionally drawn from the imposing Grand Challenge Cup, the Regatta's first and senior trophy. As with every detail of the Regatta, all of them supervised or performed with faultless efficiency, the draw is held under the aegis of the Regatta's Committee of Stewards.

The Regatta itself spans four days, Thursday to Sunday (racing starts after church on Sunday), with nearly all the finals being raced on the Sunday. Saturday

ABOVE:
On fine days many visitors to the Regatta set out elegant picnic lunches
in the car park enclosures.
BELOW:
A supporter wearing the colours of her team watches the approach of
the race.

and Sunday are inevitably the Regatta's most popular and crowded days, but an opportunity to visit the Regatta on the Thursday should not be missed. Apart from the air of excitement generated by the much higher number of races in the first heats (when there arc always two and frequently three races on the course at the same time), there is a mint-like freshness, before the crowds have left their inevitable mark, to the colourful canvas town which has been created on the Berkshire bank of the Thames.

The first part of the Regatta complex, proceeding from Henley Bridge and Leander Club, consists of the long row of tenting which houses all the competitors' boats and oars. The Boat Tents are also equipped with changing areas, showers and lavatories, the boats being launched from fixed wooden jetties built out from the towpath.

Walking on from the Boat Tents, the core of the Regatta complex is reached next: the Stewards' Enclosure, commanding the finish of the $1\frac{1}{4}$-mile, two-lane straight course. Here are the Regatta Office, Trophy Tent, bandstand, bars, and cloakrooms, and a generous choice of covered and open spectator accommodation, either standing or sitting. A separate entrance leads to the Luncheon and Tea Marquee. The Stewards' Enclosure is not open to the public, but restricted to Members and their guests. Generally speaking, however, it is not difficult to gain the entrée by discreet enquiry two or three months before the Regatta. Devotees of Henley who are Members of the Stewards' Enclosure are usually only too happy to extend their pleasure to interested friends.

Though tickets for both luncheon and tea may be obtained in the Stewards' Enclosure, many Members and guests prefer to picnic in the adjacent car park. It is by no means unusual to see such a party sitting down to a fine table spread in the shadow of the Rolls. Others prefer to picnic further down the course, on the grass at the river's edge or even in a punt. The greatest advantage of the Stewards' Enclosure is, however, the comfort it offers when the elements are unkind.

First-time visitors to the Stewards' Enclosure should make a point of inspecting the superb array in the Trophy Tent, which immediately says more about Henley and its history than anything else could. The trophies for the élite events, which attract top-ranking competition from all over the world, are the Grand Challenge Cup for Eights; the Stewards' Cup for Coxless Fours; the Prince Philip Cup for Coxed Fours; the Silver Goblets and Nickalls' Cup for Coxless Pairs; the Double Sculling Challenge Cup, and the beautiful Diamond Challenge Sculls for single scullers.

For visitors to Henley who do not have the entrée to the Stewards' Enclosure, the facilities in the fee-paying General and Public Enclosures still offer good value for money: bars, cloakrooms, cover from the elements in the event of rain, and always close at hand *a place to sit down*—either in deckchairs at the river's edge or on the raised stands. All enclosures are served by the Public address system, and visitors to all three should bear in mind that bar takings in cash are a vital element in the Regatta's finances. To prevent Regatta visitors from running out of ready cash, a temporary bank branch is opened outside the enclosures for the duration of the Regatta.

On the other bank of the river are several private and club tents and buildings with admission by invitation or membership only, such as Phyllis Court which is opposite the finishing line.

Visitors to Henley who come by rail, changing to the Henley branch line at Twyford from their Paddington 'special', get the most exciting first view of the Regatta complex. This bursts on the eye with its full colour and bustle during the walk from the station over Henley Bridge. Cars arriving at Henley turn off the Oxford–London road (A423) at Leander Club, on the Berkshire bank. Approaches to the car parks are well signposted and cars are efficiently marshalled in the parks to avoid congestion. From the car parks it is only a short walk to the enclosures or the towpath.

If you decide to picnic at Henley, the car parks and towpath are not the only options. You can hire a boat from the Town side of the river, above and below Henley Bridge, moor on the booms beside the course and enjoy a matchless view of the racing—not to mention the ever moving kaleidoscope of activity in the enclosures across the water. Shallow-water punters beware; the river deepens considerably during the crossing to the booms. If you go afloat, it is essential to have someone in charge who can really manage the craft; you *must* keep well out of the way of racing boats coming off the course or leaving the Boat Tents on their way down-river to the Start. At Henley the starters wait for no one, and a competitor delayed by an incompetent spectator unable to control his boat could easily arrive too late at the Start and find himself disqualified. It bears repeating that pleasure boats are far more robust than racing shells, and what for you may be no more than a jolly bump in midstream could cause thousands of pounds' worth of damage.

Owners of pleasure launches should also take extra care during Regatta Week on the Henley Reach; the river is patrolled by the Thames Conservancy, whom it is well worth consulting on progress and moorings. Heavy pleasure craft are not allowed to moor at the booms and piles of the course, because of the leverage they exert. All craft making fast to the booms or piles should remember that the passage of the Umpire's Launch which follows each race is accompanied by a

The Henley Regatta of 1906. Flat-bottomed skiffs, then as now, were a popular means of river transport and for getting a good view of the races.

wash which lifts the sliding booms by some three or four feet—so leave a generous length of painter, and if you make fast to one of the piles do so with a loose knot which can slide up and down with the wash. Failure to take this precaution could, with too short a length of painter, result in a swim for you and your party, not to mention unkind mirth from the enclosures across the course, so take extra care with your mooring.

On the subject of costume, the Stewards are less strict than they used to be; but guests to the Stewards' Enclosure who favour the more outrageous fashions can still be politely asked to leave. Ladies are still not admitted in trousers, and men must wear their jackets unless in exceptional heat it is announced that they may be removed. Denim trousers cannot be worn in any circumstances. Henley Royal Regatta is the last bastion of summertime Victoriana, when the ladies are obliged to compete for attention with the peacock splendour of the rowing men. Ladies should remember that the car parks and enclosures are turf-floored while the towpath is gravel. In dry weather this presents few problems, but a spell of wet weather inevitably results in mud. Low-heeled shoes are therefore to be recommended in all weather conditions, on grounds both of comfort and practicality.

With these observations borne in mind it is hoped that the visitor to this great Regatta, entering the colour and camaraderie of the Henley scene for the first time, will share a sense of having stepped back to the gracious years of England such as few other events of the English Season can impart.

The Royal Tournament

The Royal Tournament was first held in June 1880 at the Agricultural Hall, Islington, as 'The Grand Military Tournament and Assault-at-Arms' under the then Commander-in-Chief of the Army, the Duke of Cambridge, in order to raise money for military charities, in that year the Royal Cambridge Asylum for Soldiers' Widows. (Lord Chalfont, in his book *The Royal Tournament 1880–1980* says the Duke's 'personal and entirely laudable commitment to this charity led him on one occasion to express the well-meaning hope, received with mixed feelings by his audience of married soldiers, "that every Regiment in the Army would soon have a widow in the Institution".') Unfortunately the earliest Tournament, far from benefiting the soldiers' widows, lost considerable sums of money, but by 1882 the organizers had widened the scope of the events and competitions from specialist hand-to-hand fighting with sword, lance and bayonet, to include gymnastics and the eternally popular Musical Ride of the Life Guards. Among early events was one known as 'Cleaving the Turk's Head', in which a mounted soldier galloped past a model of a Turk's head, complete with turban and stuck on a post, and attempted to split it in two with one stroke of his sword. Later, when Turkey became an ally of Great Britain, this rather barbaric event became 'Cutting the Lemon', and the turbaned head was no longer seen. Another spectacle dating from this time was the 'Balaclava Mêlée' in which soldiers wearing protective masks tried to knock off the plume of each other's headdress with single-sticks. (This terrifying event was discontinued after 1911.)

By the end of the century the Royal Navy events had become major attractions

'Cleaving the Turk's Head', a military exercise dating from the
Crimean War. Later a lemon was substituted for the 'head', making a
less gruesome if less spectacular event.

The Windsor Ladder display by the Royal Navy requires immaculate timing and co-ordination, and especially a good head for heights.

at the Tournament, and during Edward VII's reign their Inter-Port Field Gun Competitions became regular displays of skill and speed. In 1906 the Tournament was so firmly established that, as the Royal Naval and Military Tournament, it opened in its new premises at Olympia. It included, as an important part of the proceedings, displays such as the Musical Ride, Musical Drive, Gymnastics and a Pageant.

After the First World War the attractions included the new Royal Air Force, the Machine Gun Corps and Tank Corps, and even a display by women drivers.

As the Second World War drew nearer motorized transport in various forms was increasingly being seen in place of the traditional cavalry displays, and in the 1930s motor-cycle display riding became more and more popular with the spectators.

Although both World Wars temporarily closed the Tournament its popularity survived unimpaired, and in 1950 a new venue was established at Earls Court, where the ever-increasing crowds could be accommodated. It is still one of the major features of the varied Earls Court programme. Today's Tournament is a marvellous and colourful display of skill in every military discipline from the Commonwealth and beyond. The massed bands with their intricate marching formations are a yearly feature, supported by demonstrations of terrifying daring by the Royal Marines and the Royal Navy, tests of physical fitness and horsemanship, and above all the pageantry and breathtaking display of the combined armed forces and police forces with a common tradition of discipline, dedication and teamwork, which make the Royal Tournament such an exciting spectacle.

The Tournament runs for about three weeks in July, and the Sunday before it starts there is a ceremonial march down the Mall for all those taking part. Tickets, including a very limited number for the Royal Enclosure, can be obtained from the Box Office at Earls Court in advance or during the Tournament.

The Lakeland Rose Show

The Lakeland Rose Show is held every year over a weekend in the second half of July in the deer park of Holker Hall, the home of the Cavendish family, near Grange-over-Sands on the southern edge of the Lake District. The name is slightly misleading since there are also showing classes in flower arrangement, sweet peas, fuchsias, geraniums and honey as well as general horticultural and flower displays, but above all, it remains the highlight of the year for the Royal National Rose Society as its Northern Show. Three months after the Harrogate Spring Show, it is an important occasion in the social calendar of the northern counties, with visitors coming from all over the country and overseas.

Unlike the Chelsea Flower Show, the Lakeland Rose Show puts on a varied and much admired programme of entertainment including military brass bands, aerobatic displays, police dogs showing off their remarkable training, motor-bike stunt riding and RAF displays. There is a children's playground, and in the Function Marquee experts give demonstrations of various kinds. On Saturday evening charity events are also held in the Function Marquee, where smartly dressed guests (by invitation only) are entertained while enjoying delicious home-cooked food provided by local ladies.

This show is a very special occasion with a delightful relaxed atmosphere in a particularly attractive part of the country, and it is well worth making the journey to get to it.

Holker Hall is four miles south-west of Grange-over-Sands in Cumbria (junction 36 on the M6 motorway), half a mile north of Cark on the Haverthwaite Road (the B5278).

The Bisley Summer Meeting

Although not strictly speaking an essential part of the English sporting scene, Bisley is the internationally renowned Mecca of target rifle and pistol shooting, and lies only thirty miles west of London. It is an enormous and seemingly bewildering complex made up of Victorian pavilions, large and small club-houses, private shooting-lodges, huts, tents and caravans, to say nothing of the enormous ranges, which together cover an area the size of a small town.

During the second two weeks in July it seethes with activity, with a cacophony of rifle-shots as a continuous background noise. Nowadays, the Bisley fortnight tends to be a family affair—though not so long ago ladies were not permitted to enter the camp until after nine o'clock or they were likely to be offended by the sight of the gentlemen performing their morning ablutions in shallow hip-baths in front of their huts or tents. Modern Bisley is very different, for competitors as often as not bring their wives and children along for a camping holiday, though the families seldom take much interest in the shooting, preferring to tour the area, visiting Windsor and Eton and even the London shops. Although the main Bisley meeting is held during the middle two weeks of July, the ranges themselves are in use throughout the year by military marksmen during the week and bunches of enthusiasts who belong to rifle clubs from all over the country at the weekends.

The land on which the Camp stands is owned by the Ministry of Defence, and it adjoins the ranges belonging to the Brigade of Guards at Pirbright. Run on

Pistol-shooting at Bisley
at the 1910 summer meeting. Members of the armed forces
have a distinguished record in marksmanship,
but civilians have taken their share of the honours.

military lines, it is a truly egalitarian world, for nobody cares a jot about your social background so long as you are either a keen shot or are prepared to show a true interest in the whole affair. But it fosters extremely good international relations, with teams coming from all parts of the globe—several members of the Commonwealth even have their own club-houses where lavish entertainment is dispensed, the contention being that a hang-over promotes good shooting—less pulse to shake the trigger!

If you decide to pay Bisley a visit, then write to The Secretary, The National Rifle Association, Bisley Camp, Brookwood, Woking, Surrey, (048 62 2213), and he will send you a copy of the Bisley Fortnight timetable—known as the 'Bisley Bible'—and this will tell you what competitions are going to take place, and on which ranges, and will provide a lot more useful information, including a map.

Should you enjoy your visit so much that you wish to take an active part yourself, the Secretary will provide you with a list of rifle or pistol clubs in your own area, depending on where you live or work. For a relatively modest annual subscription you can become a member of the NRA when you will recieve its quarterly magazine, be entitled to vote at the annual election of the Council, and attend the Annual General Meeting which is held during the July meeting. When you have joined a club, its members will advise you on the technical aspects,

Prince Charles trying his hand at rifle-shooting.

choice of weapons, etc. The most usual thing is to start shooting with a service rifle at distances ranging from a hundred yards upwards in the prone position, i.e. flat on your stomach. Later on you may wish to graduate to the Match Rifle where competitors as often as not lie on their backs—needless to say thus being the subject of many cartoons!

There are several ranges, each catering for different distances (Running Deer, Pistol, Clay Pigeon) but the main ones are the Century with its hundred targets going up to 600 yards, and Stickledown which is for the long-range enthusiast, going up to 1200 yards. During the July meeting there will be competitions going on up and down the ranges at every distance, but generally speaking, the international ones provide the most interest for a newcomer. The triangular blue and yellow flags—the NRA colours—which fly on tall flagpoles up and down the ranges, are not put there to provide colourful decoration, but perform a vital function. By carefully watching the angle at which they are flying at any given time, an experienced shot can make a reasonably accurate guess as to the strength and the direction of the wind. But it is perfectly possible to see one line of flags blowing to the east, the ones on the opposite side of the range blowing to the west, while those in the middle have flopped altogether, this state of affairs having been brought about by a sudden ebb and change in the wind. Although a bullet is fired with sufficient velocity to reach its target and far beyond, its speed and direction is affected not only by the way the wind is blowing, but also by its force, which means that certain adjustments have to be made in the sighting apparatus on a rifle to allow for these variations: on bad days this can be before each shot.

It is perhaps unnecessary to stress that a red flag means keep out!

Clothes worn at Bisley during the day by the marksmen are casual, inconspicuous, waterproof and comfortable, but you will notice that the recumbent figures lying on the ranges have badges on their backs. These show which clubs they belong to, where they come from and whether they shoot for an international team. The Great Britain team sports hats with navy-blue and silver striped bands round them. Spectators are also wise to be waterproof and comfortable, brightly coloured golfing umbrellas and shooting sticks being part of the general scene. There is a general smartening-up for the evening, even though the black-tie rule in the club-house for dinner went out several years ago, as there are several parties each evening during the fortnight.

Every day at Bisley is a great day for those who shoot, especially if their name figures on the prize list, but the greatest of all for everybody is the last one, when one hundred competitors, who have shot their way through several eliminating stages during the week, lie down on Stickledown at 900 and 1000 yards to shoot for the coveted Queen's Prize. This is the day when all those shambling old tramps and untidy young men you have seen on the ranges throughout the fortnight emerge as smart gentlemen in well-pressed suits or blazers and shining shoes. The ladies wear their best clothes, and there is a feeling of gala about the place, with great crowds gathering on Stickledown. The rotating targets manned by squads of paid schoolboys or a battalion of soldiers seconded to Bisley for camp duties during the fortnight are watched eagerly as after each shot the target disappears and is replaced by a board with black squares along its bottom edge— one in the far right-hand corner denotes a bull's eye, and the further to the right the square appears, the worse the shot. On a scaffolding platform at the top of the firing point is a gigantic scoreboard soaring high above the crowds on which a minute by minute state of affairs is recorded as information comes in via field telephone from the butts and is conveyed to the scorers by fleet-footed messengers. Should there be a tie-shoot at the very end, then follows a few moments of tension hardly to be experienced in any other sport, until at last the outright winner is declared, immediately becoming one of the mighty elect in the shooting world—for the winner of the Queen's Prize at Bisley has achieved world-wide fame for ever. It must surely be one of the greatest tests, not only of skill but also of nerve and concentration in the face of the enormous interest it arouses.

After the winner has had the coveted gold badge pinned on his lapel, he sits in a sort of sedan-chair, which is lifted triumphantly shoulder-high by his exultant fellow club members (only one woman has won the Prize) and off they march to the strains of 'See the Conquering Hero Comes' played by a military band. Then follows a never-to-be-forgotten progress through the camp with a stop at each club-house for a toast. The following day must also be memorable for the winner!

The whole thing ends with a mighty prize-giving when a vast array of hugely impressive silver trophies are handed over to the winners by a visiting dignitary from the international, political or military scene.

So do go to Bisley in July: it is well worth a visit and lies only a few miles away from the Guildford turning off the M3 on a well signposted route.

Croquet

There are some doubts about the true origins of croquet as we know it today, but it bears striking similarities to the game of 'Pall Mall', or 'Pele-mele' which was played at least as early as the seventeenth century. (When St James's Park was laid out for King Charles II as a private royal park, the avenue running through it became known as the Mall because it was specially laid down for regal games of Pall Mall.) This game was played with mallets and hoops similar to those of croquet, but only one or two hoops were used, and the object was to go straight down the course and back again using as few strokes as possible. It seems clear, however, that in spite of similarities of equipment Pall Mall was a more likely precursor of golf than of croquet, and the development of the unique rules of croquet remains obscure.

It is certain at least that croquet in its recognizably modern form was being played, first in Ireland, and later on the mainland of Great Britain, by the middle of the nineteenth century. The game became more popular as the formal Victorian age limited the number of physical and outdoor leisure activities which could be decently undertaken by mixed sexes. Croquet was always eminently

A late seventeenth-century etching showing the Court playing 'pell-mell' down the Mall in St James's Park.

The Hurlingham Club in 1910, now the headquarters of the Croquet Association.

decorous, but at the same time it offered scope for developing a genuine skill within a pleasant social setting. It took several years for the rules to be standardized but by 1865 the first croquet club was founded at Worthing. In 1867 the first Open Championship was organized at Evesham and in 1869 the All England Croquet Club was established, moving to Worple Road in Wimbledon in the following year. In the remaining years of the nineteenth century the fortunes of the game were wrapped up in the struggle for supremacy between the All England Club and the National Croquet Club, and it gradually lost ground to the newly introduced game of lawn tennis. In 1882 tournament croquet at Wimbledon ceased although members still had the right to play the game in private matches. In the following years the game fell into decline as an organized sport except in a few diehard centres like Oxford, Cheltenham and Budleigh Salterton, but in the 1890s it was noted that croquet was becoming more popular again and new club tournaments were organized, culminating in a public tournament at Maidstone in 1895. In 1900 the newly named Croquet Association (whose present patron is Her Majesty The Queen) established its headquarters at Sheen House, later moving to Roehampton where in 1905 the Open Championship was moved from Wimbledon. This remained the headquarters of the Association until 1959 when it moved to its present premises at the Hurlingham Club on the north bank of the River Thames in Fulham.

Croquet tournaments had been held at Hurlingham since 1901 in the grounds of a Georgian mansion which had previously been a pigeon-shooting club and (as it remained until the Second World War) a popular centre for polo.

The highlight of the modern tournament at Hurlingham is the President's Cup which is the highest achievement and, with the Open Championship, the most coveted prize in the sport.

Tickets for the Open Championship at Hurlingham can be obtained from the Secretary, The Croquet Association, The Hurlingham Club, Ranelagh Gardens, London SW6 (01 736 3148) or from the club premises.

The tournament takes place over a week in mid-July and play starts each morning at 10 o'clock. Refreshments are available in the club room, or people often bring a picnic with them. There is an attractive and slightly old-fashioned air to the tournament, slightly at odds with the intensely competitive matches, which makes the occasion a delightful experience.

Royal Garden Parties

'The Lord Chamberlain is commanded by Her Majesty to invite ...'. Those words printed on a white card engraved with The Queen's cypher in gold represent the first intimation to some forty thousand people that they have been selected to attend one of the three Royal Garden Parties held each year at Buckingham Palace. Ten thousand people from every walk of life who have rendered service to charity or the community or perhaps merited some recognition are invited to each mid-week party and their invitations extend to any unmarried daughters over the age of seventeen.

Invitations are sent out one month in advance and there is no need to RSVP unless the recipient is unable to attend. A few distinguished personalities receive invitations year after year but otherwise only members of the Government are automatically invited each year. A similar Garden Party is held annually at the Palace of Holyroodhouse.

The parties were instigated by Queen Victoria towards the end of her reign and, in those days, were called 'breakfasts'. The last she gave was on a brilliantly hot day in July 1900. Watermen in scarlet uniforms rowed on the lake as the Queen was driven among her five thousand guests at walking pace in a small open carriage drawn by two grey horses and preceded by an out-rider on a white steed. The Queen was accompanied by the Princess of Wales and wore a black silk dress and cape, a rose in her feathered bonnet, pearls at her throat and carried a white lace-covered parasol. Behind her carriage walked the Prince of Wales wearing a white hat, the Duke and Duchess of York and the old Duke of Cambridge. The Queen, a frail figure, entered the Royal Pavilion on the arm of her Indian attendant. At about twenty minutes to seven she left for Windsor accompanied by the cheers of the crowd along Constitution Hill. It was one of her last public appearances before her death six months later.

'Morning dress, Uniform or Lounge Suit' is the required dress, according to the invitation, and the party is timed 'from 4–6'. But there is no question of arriving late, or even on time: soon after three o'clock a stream of guests, some wearing colourful national costumes and all the ladies in hats, starts to converge in the inner quadrangle before the Grand Entrance to the Palace and strolls through the Marble Hall and the beautiful Bow Room with displays of porcelain in its corner cabinets, and out on to the terrace. From there the view of the unique forty-acre private garden in the heart of London is startling in its beautiful simplicity.

Sweeping lawns (including camomile which remains green all the year round) and which sometimes serve as a landing pad for Queen's Flight helicopters are surrounded by interesting trees and shrubs and flower beds. Beyond is an artificial four-acre lake with a small island and a miniature waterfall tumbling into it between mossy rocks and ferns. Exotic pink flamingoes mingle with the ducks and wild birds round the lake. They were introduced here in 1962 and their artificial diet is said to include shrimps from the local fishmonger to improve their colour.

There were no fish in the lake until the last war when chub, roach and perch escaped there from the Serpentine after a bomb fell in Hyde Park and damaged the grid covering the entrance to the underground stream which feeds the lake from the Serpentine.

A Royal Garden Party provides an opportunity for a view of the
normally private gardens and lake behind Buckingham Palace.
At a pre-arranged time, guests divide to make 'avenues' down
which members of the Royal Family walk, stopping at intervals
to meet their guests.

Two military bands play as guests wander through the garden, admiring the
roses and the splendid herbaceous borders, including one of grey and silver leaved
plants given to Queen Elizabeth II and the Duke of Edinburgh on their Silver
Wedding by Lord and Lady Astor of Hever. Little tables in front of the long
marquee where tea, iced coffee, dainty sandwiches and delicious cakes are
continuously available at the buffet, are soon occupied.

Other guests congregate at the foot of the steps leading down from the terrace
where, promptly at four o'clock, members of the Royal Family led by The Queen
and Prince Philip appear. A pause for the National Anthem and then the Royal
Party descend to meet their guests. They divide into separate groups to wend their
way through two or three narrow lanes which suddenly appear as the crowd is
skilfully manipulated by the Gentlemen Ushers in morning dress. They are
usually retired members of the Royal Household and the lanes through the crowd
are kept open by stalwart scarlet-uniformed members of the Queen's Bodyguard
of the Yeomen of the Guard.

Guests arriving for a Royal Garden Party at Buckingham Palace in 1935.

For the next hour the Royal parties slowly progress towards the Royal tea tent, stopping to chat informally to strategically placed guests or those who happen to catch their eye. Their small open tea tent in a roped-off enclosure adjoins a similar tent for members of the Diplomatic Corps.

Just before six o'clock the Royal Family, escorted by the Gentlemen Ushers, return to the Palace by a route marked by the Yeomen of the Guard. The National Anthem is played at 6 pm and this is the signal for the guests to disperse. Those with chauffeur-driven cars wait in the Marble Hall while their names are broadcast to the car parks down the Mall and their cars called to the canopied entrance.

Royal Garden Parties take place regardless of the weather and, apart from the long narrow tea tent which could not accommodate all the guests, there is little shelter from the rain. Then raincoats and umbrellas are a necessity, but it seems that not even the most inclement weather can dampen the spirits of the guests.

The Royal International Horse Show

The Royal International Horse Show is held annually in the third week of July at the White City Stadium. In 1967 it moved indoors to the Empire Pool, Wembley, but this venue proved unpopular with the riders, who found it difficult to adjust to indoor conditions in the middle of the outdoor show season, and so the move back to the White City Stadium, in 1983, has been welcomed by spectators and competitors alike.

Many different equestrian events are featured at the show, but the main attraction is usually a display by the *Cadre Noir* from France, the Canadian Mounties, the musical drive of the Household Cavalry or the like. Horses of every shape and size can be found, and top-class show-jumping with leading national and international riders is always a major attraction very popular with the crowd. The two most coveted trophies of the week are the King George V Gold Cup for gentlemen riders, and the Queen Elizabeth II Cup for lady riders. The competitions work up to a climax on the Friday and Saturday, but events of the very highest standard take place throughout the show. The Puissance, ending with the enormous wall, and preceded by the large spread fence, is the highlight of the competitions.

The show classes are hotly contested and many different breeds of horses from sleek hacks and equally impressive hunters to native breeds of ponies can be seen. The actual judging is a complex procedure, but it is interesting to compare one's selections with those of the judge, and to see how surprisingly often they agree.

Essentially a summer show, dress is on the whole smart, and it is customary for those dining at the show to wear formal evening dress. Members of the Royal Family are often present, particularly at evening performances.

At the White City it is possible for spectators to circulate more easily than at Wembley, because of the outdoor arena and the generally more spacious layout. The collecting ring is within view and spectators are therefore able to see competitors warming up. As at other shows, there are a great many trade stands which are always worth a visit.

The White City Stadium is situated in White City Road, London W12, which leads off Wood Lane. The nearest underground station is White City, situated between the stadium and the nearby BBC Television Centre. For details of tickets and membership apply to The Royal International Horse Show Box Office (open prior to the show) The White City Stadium, London W12, or watch for advertisements and booking forms in the sporting press.

Swan Upping

Late in July members of two of the City of London's ancient livery companies (guilds), the Vintners and the Dyers, confirm their rights, shared only with the Sovereign, of keeping swans on the River Thames between Henley-on-Thames in Oxfordshire and London Bridge.

In July the cygnets are two to three months old and their ownership is established by being rounded up and marked by the Barge Master of the Dyers and the Swan Master of the Vintners who are dressed in their traditional livery colours. These officers are rowed out to the swans by swan uppers wearing colourful hats in skiffs decorated with banners. The swans are marked by nicking their beaks, one nick for the Dyers and two for the Vintners. The Sovereign's birds are unmarked.

The Keeper of the Queen's Swans, who has an official position as a member of the Royal Household, accompanies the liverymen in order to ensure that the right cygnets are marked.

The ceremony, which takes place over six days, is an entertaining occasion and also serves a useful purpose. The elegant birds, so much a part of river life, are given a good looking over and a count is made of their numbers.

The mute swan (*Cygnus olor*) was by tradition first brought to England in the thirteenth century as a present to Richard I from Queen Beatrice of Cyprus and has always been considered royal property. Until recently they were a delicacy much in demand at royal banquets, and as a mark of special favour monarchs in the Middle Ages allowed some noblemen to keep swans privately, which were nicked on their beaks to distinguish them from the royal birds. This privilege now only remains with the Vintners and Dyers Companies.

Members of the Vintners and Dyers livery companies marking cygnets on the River Thames.

The Tall Ships Races

Every year in July and August the Cutty Sark Tall Ships Races start off from various ports in Britain and Europe; in Britain the ports are usually Plymouth, Falmouth and Southampton, and in Europe traditionally the ports of Lisbon and Vigo in Portugal.

The first race in 1956 ran from Torbay in Devon to Lisbon, and was the inspiration of Bernard Morgan, a London solicitor, who saw an opportunity for developing in young people the stamina, personal qualities and physical skills he felt were necessary for a successful adult life. The discipline, self-reliance and teamwork essential on board a sailing ship made this an environment which perfectly answered his requirements, with the bonus of being a healthy outdoor life much enjoyed by the crews.

To further this ideal, the Sail Training Association was founded under the patronage of the Duke of Edinburgh. The Association now runs courses on its own schooners, STS *Sir Winston Churchill* and STS *Malcolm Miller*, which with a permanent crew sail over 30,000 miles each year on training cruises. Both ships are normally entered in the Cutty Sark Tall Ships Races, with about eighty other training ships from various countries.

To qualify for entry to the races a ship has to have at least fifty per cent of its crew aged between fifteen and twenty-five, boys or girls, and must have a minimum water-line length of thirty feet. It also, of course, has to be a ship powered by sail, but the 'tallness' of its mast is not subject to any restriction. Most traditional rigs will be seen in the races, from single-masted cutters to majestic full-rigged ships with up to thirty-two sails on four masts.

There is no doubt that the sight of these magnificent vessels making their way

Fully rigged sailing ships at the start of a race in Plymouth Sound.

out to the open sea is truly spectacular and many people make the journey to one of the ports involved, particularly those staging the starts and finishes of the races.

The major award is the 'Cutty Sark Trophy for International Understanding', which is presented to the crew voted the winner by the Masters of the race fleet. The trophy is a solid silver model of the clipper *Cutty Sark* donated by the sponsors, Cutty Sark Scotch Whisky. (The original clipper can be seen at Greenwich, where she is an enormously popular public attraction.)

Details of the races can be obtained from the Secretary of the Race Committee, The Sail Training Association, 2a The Hard, Portsmouth (0705 832055).

Goodwood

The 5th Duke of Richmond who had been wounded in the chest by a musket ball at the battle of Orthez in 1814, was responsible for establishing racing at Goodwood three miles to the north-east of Chichester. When he succeeded to the dukedom he was informed by his doctor and by his wife Caroline, daughter of the famous Marquess of Anglesey who had lost a leg at Waterloo, that his injuries would prevent him from hunting in the future. Consequently the twenty-eight-year-old Duke who appreciated, as did many other English aristocrats, that racing led to the improvement of the thoroughbred, decided to devote his initiative and energy to reviving the racecourse where the first meeting had been held in April 1802 by the Sussex militia and members of the 3rd Duke's hunt.

The Duke's efforts quickly brought success, and the Goodwood turf was so resilient, the gallops so excellent and his hospitality at Goodwood House so lavish that many of his friends, including the diarist Charles Greville and Captain Peel whose brother was to become Prime Minister requested that their racehorses be trained at Goodwood which rapidly earned the epithet 'Glorious'. A French visitor wrote, 'With magnificent scenery, first rate racing and the cream of England's best Society to inspire and gratify him, a stranger would indeed be fastidious who did not consider Goodwood racecourse to be the perfection and the paradise of racegrounds.' By the mid-1840s the July meeting was acknowledged as a highlight of the summer season, and Londoners flocked to the course. There were no trains, and many travellers changed horses and stayed the night at the King's Arms at Godalming. The Duke's guests arrived at Goodwood House on the Monday evening of race-week and at dinner the table was decorated with the gold and silver cups and trophies won by his horses. Traditionally his health was only proposed on the evening of Gold Cup Day and invariably by his highest ranking guest.

Queen Victoria never visited Goodwood, but her son, the Prince of Wales, loved the meeting and was a frequent attender, whilst in later years Queen Alexandra, having stayed at Goodwood House for the races, described her visit as 'the pleasantest week of the year'. At the beginning of the twentieth century King Edward VII was responsible for creating the informal atmosphere of Goodwood by conceding that panama hats and grey flannel suits or white linen suits might replace the tall hats and frock coats which had been the accepted dress for men in the Members' Enclosure. He once wrote to his eldest daughter, HRH

Prize cups at Goodwood Races: the
Chesterfield Cup (far left) and the
Stewards' Cup.

The grandstand and the course at 'Glorious'
Goodwood, one of the most prestigious
meetings in the flat-racing calendar.

the Duchess of Fife, 'I am happiest when I have no public engagements to fulfil . . .
when I can, like plain Mr Jones, go to a race-meeting without it being chronicled
in the papers the next day, "His Royal Highness the Prince of Wales has taken to
gambling very seriously . . ."' King George V stayed at Goodwood on many
occasions, and the royal tradition has continued with the visits of Her Majesty
Queen Elizabeth II. Plaques on the walls of the tapestry drawing room at
Goodwood House record the five Privy Council meetings held there during race-
week by King Edward VII in 1908, by King George V in 1925 and by The Queen in
1953, 1955 and 1957.

The heart of contemporary prestige racing at Goodwood, which consists of a
nearly straight six-furlong course with a triangular right-handed loop circuit, and
is essentially a sharp track, the five-furlong course being one of the fastest in the
country, are the eight Pattern races. Seven, the Sussex Stakes, the Goodwood
Cup, the Nassau Stakes, the Richmond Stakes, the Gordon Stakes, the George
Stakes and the Molecomb Stakes, are held at the four-day meeting at the end of
July and one, the Waterford Crystal Mile, at the August meeting. The new
£3,500,000 Grandstand, opened by The Queen in 1980 and financed largely by a
loan from the Horserace Betting Levy Board, enables racegoers to watch the
racing in great comfort. A contemporary journalist was not exaggerating when
he commented, 'The rolling tree-covered Downs are touched with magic and it
would take the brush of a Munnings to do the scene justice as champion
thoroughbreds race over the turf of Glorious Goodwood.'

August

The Game Fair

The Game Fair, traditionally one of the most important dates in any field sportsman's calendar, is held at the beginning of August each year. Organized by the Country Landowners' Association, the Game Fair does not have a permanent site but moves around England, Scotland and Wales to a different venue every year, usually the grounds of a country house. Northern Ireland now has its own fair, held at Clandeboyne each July.

The Game Fair began in 1958 and was intended by the Country Landowners' Association, its organizing body, to provide its members with an annual centre from which to gain advice on their shooting and fishing. Since its inception other events such as gundogs, archery and clay-pigeon shooting have been added. It was decided to place the emphasis on shooting and fishing as other field sports, such as hunting, are well represented elsewhere. Having said this all other field sports are represented at the Game Fair, although less prominently. The majority of sports will be illustrated for the benefit of the uninitiated as the Game Fair acts as a medium by which town and country can be brought together.

The idea of a 'travelling' game fair works well as it means that every few years the fair will be within reach wherever one lives in the country, although many people make an annual pilgrimage irrespective of the venue. Auchterader in Scotland is the furthest north that the Game Fair travels and Broadlands in Hampshire the furthest south. Generally speaking the Game Fair will be held on a large country estate which provides good vehicular access. A bonus is that the country house is usually open to the public and adds another dimension to the event.

Stout and comfortable walking shoes are essential as there is so much to see over an exceptionally wide area. There are more trade stands alone at the Game Fair than at any other event and it is possible to buy anything from a sporting magazine to a full shooting kit. For convenience similar exhibits are grouped together, Game Farmers' Row, Gunmakers' Row and Fishermen's Row being some of the most famous. At the Game Fair it is all too easy to spend money, be it on a new gun, sporting picture, book or piece of jewellery.

The emphasis is on shooting and fishing, although other field sports are represented. The hawk ring is always a popular feature as it enables the public to see live hawks flown—an all too rare event these days.

Naturally one would expect to find fly-casting competitions and demonstrations, clay-pigeon shooting, gundog trials and the like at the Game Fair. These events are often situated slightly away from the trade stands, making it absolutely essential to buy a catalogue where the times and venues of all the events will be clearly marked. Although some of these events are rather lengthy to watch they are a must for those who wish to see the experts at work.

Apart from the field events and trade stands there are always many interesting static displays mounted by organizations such as the World Pheasant Asssoci-

ABOVE: Prince Charles at the Bowood House Game Fair.
BELOW: Part of the grouse exhibit at a Game Fair,
with some of the many and varied stalls in the background.

ation, the National Trust, the British Association for Shooting and Conservation and the like. Until one has visited the World Pheasant exhibit it is hard to comprehend how many different breeds of pheasant there are.

As all our traditional field sports are under great threat in Britain recruiters of the field sports organizations will be found in force at the Game Fair, and most of the organizations' exhibits show items of great interest to the field sportsman and are certainly worth a visit.

The Fair is held over three days and because of its considerable size it is best to spend more than one day there if possible. Accommodation nearby is always booked much in advance of the event and it is certainly worth while watching the sporting press for accommodation advertisements. It is always advisable to get to the Game Fair as early as possible to avoid the long traffic queue which always builds up. People often arrive as early as seven o'clock in the morning to avoid the queues. In recent years, the Game Fair caravan site has become increasingly popular, enabling people to be within walking distance of the event.

Refreshments are always easy to get as there are plenty of bars where it is possible to obtain both food and drink fairly cheaply and without having to queue for too long. There are always ice-cream vans and the like which do good trade as it seems as if the Game Fair is invariably held during a heatwave. For those staying on site it is worth remembering that it is virtually impossible to obtain fresh food at the Fair, other than from the restaurants.

People from all walks of life attend the Game Fair as there really is something to interest everybody. Every other person you see seems to be leading a dog, springer spaniels being the most popular. It is the focus for an annual pilgrimage of gamekeepers, owners of shoots, farmers or simply interested onlookers, and all kinds of dress can be seen, but waxed cotton jackets and shooting waistcoats are particularly in evidence.

For details of membership apply to the Country Landowners' Association Game Fair (Director R. Rees-Webbe, Esq.), The Game Fair, Berrington House, St Alkmunds Square, Shrewsbury, Shropshire.

Cubhunting

During the autumn (from as early as the first week in August) the foxhunters of England are about their task. In order to educate the young hounds, get the horses fit, and give us all once more the thrill of the chase, hounds meet early in order to catch the better scenting conditions. Although less formal than hunting proper, all the normal hunting rules are in force. As always especial care must be taken to shut gates, for there is still much stock in the fields at this time of year.

Both men and women wear ratcatcher dress, that is, men wear tweed coat, bowler hat, collar and tie, breeches and boots. Women wear the same as the men. Horses' manes are not plaited.

It is important to remember that when cubhunting you are the guest of the Master. He starts when he likes and finishes when he thinks that hounds have had enough. As with all hunting you must ask the Master's permission before going out. Meeting times vary from a 6.30 am start, generally finishing by 10 am at the latest in August to a start at about 9.30 am in October, finishing at 4 pm. At the earliest meets you will not normally be capped, but many packs now expect a contribution at meets in late September and October.

Do not expect to gallop or jump fences until the end of October. Generally speaking cubhunting is an exercise to find out where the foxes are and to cull some and to enter the young hounds, and so leave the country well but not over-foxed. It is the time to see hounds and huntsman working in harmony.

The Eisteddfod

The Royal National Eisteddfod of Wales is held every year as a contest for poets, singers and musicians alternately in North and South Wales for the first full week in August.

It has a long and romantic history, with the earliest recorded mention of such a contest in Cardigan in 1176. The word 'eisteddfod' means any kind of session, but it acquired a specific meaning restricted to a session of bards meeting to discuss the organization of their guild. Celtic 'bards' are poets, singers and musicians, and even before the Roman occupation of Britain they were important figures in the religion of Druidism. By the tenth century the Pencerdd, or chief bard, had established himself in a place of honour at the King's Court, a position which he won in contest with competitors who had to be free men. The symbol of office was a harp, given to him by the king who then expected him to sing the praises of God, and to extol in song the king's valour and wisdom. When the king died, the Pencerdd composed and sang his funeral elegy.

By the Middle Ages, there were bards or mendicant minstrels wandering about the country seeking patronage, and most of them were treated with respect as they played an important part in recording traditions, historical events and genealogy in a largely illiterate age, as well as for their skill with song and harp.

In the sixteenth century efforts were made to regularize the bardic order under royal warrant and a system of apprenticeships was set up, and only students who reached the standards set by the Chief Bards were allowed to recite or sing in the halls of noblemen at the main religious festivals of Easter, Whitsun and Christmas.

The leisured and scholarly poets of the eighteenth century established as compulsory the ancient rigid alliterative formula by which modern Welsh poetry is composed, and the Chair Bard of today is as much bound by these rules as were his ancestors of ten centuries ago.

The ruling body of all bards, the Gorsedd of Bards, was founded in 1792, and, as well as its responsibility for the main ceremonial part of the organization of the National Eisteddfodau, it is an effective force in ensuring that Celtic culture and

The Eisteddfod plays an important part in keeping alive the language, customs and ancient traditions of the Welsh people. Music, drama and dance are strongly represented.

Bards at the Royal National Eisteddfod of Wales in their traditional robes.

its languages flourish. The Gorsedd is also responsible for the traditional announcement to the Archdruid of the programme for the next year's Eisteddfod a year and a day in advance. This is a ceremonious and formal occasion, usually in the open air, and follows a set pattern of ritual and traditional prayer. This ancient custom was revived at the end of the eighteenth century by the society of Welshmen based in London known as the Gwyneddigion. During the nineteenth century several area eisteddfodau were held but by the 1860s the National Eisteddfod of Wales was officially established by the National Eisteddfod Association and the Gorsedd of Bards, who now jointly organize the festival under the title of the Court of the National Eisteddfod of Wales (Llys yr Eisteddfod Genedlaethol).

The Eisteddfod of today attracts thousands of people to the Great Pavilion, the Eisteddfod Field, the Arts and Crafts Pavilion and the various fringe pavilions, to see and hear the best of traditional and modern Welsh music, poetry, literature, art, craft, dance and drama.

Each day in the Great Pavilion, which holds five thousand people, competitions in singing, dancing, music, prose and poetry are judged. The two main awards, the Bardic Chair and the Bardic Crown, are the most ceremonial and the bards dress in their traditional coloured robes. The winning bards are 'chaired' or 'crowned' on a platform in the Pavilion, and all the proceedings are in the Welsh language with instant translation facilities provided for all who do not understand the language.

After the competitions during the day, visitors can attend traditional entertainments, drama, dances and musical performances in local centres. Details of the programme can be obtained from the National Eisteddfod Office, 10 Park Grove, Cardiff.

Cowes Week

Although known as Cowes Week, in reality this annual yachting festival and regatta takes place over nine days, the Saturday and Sunday at either end having been added to the week. Today racing may even take place on the Glorious Twelfth of August, unheard of in bygone days as there would have been a mass exodus to the grouse moors. Cowes, on the Isle of Wight, with its thirty miles of sheltered tidal sea surrounded by natural harbours, forms the ideal location for this spectacular event.

The name Cowes comes from the two fortresses built by Henry VIII to 'cow' anyone with ideas of a southward invasion of England. In later times forts, which can still be seen today, were built by Lord Palmerston, in the nineteenth century, to discourage the French from invasion, and during the last war Winston Churchill devised a system of oil pipes which would set fire to the sea around the town in the event of a German attack.

The fame of Cowes stems mainly from the time of Prince Albert, Consort of Queen Victoria, whose great passion for boats gave it the Royal seal of approval. At this time most of the sailing activity was based on East Cowes, which is the side of the Medina river nearest to Queen Victoria's Osborne House. It was while

King George V aboard the Royal Yacht *Britannia* off Cowes in 1924.
The Royal Family's interest in sailing off the Isle of Wight dates
from the time of Prince Albert, who sailed at Cowes from Osborne House.

at Osborne during Cowes Week that the Queen, when asked of the whereabouts of the Prince of Wales, was heard to reply, 'He's gone yotin with his grocer.' The grocer was Sir Thomas Lipton, whose commercial empire was based on the tea clipper races of the nineteenth century.

Today West Cowes is the centre of Cowes Week, the emphasis having moved away from East Cowes in the 1930s and '40s. Here the yacht clubs are to be found, dominated by the Royal Yacht Squadron in the castle which is its headquarters. Cowes Week is organized by the Cowes Combined Clubs, a representative body established in 1964 of the eight yacht clubs and Cowes Town Regatta Committee involved in the arrangements.

Over the years the whole shape of the regatta has changed from its leisurely and gentlemanly Victorian and Edwardian days. No longer can it be considered to be only a playground of the idle rich, as competitors are now found from all walks of life who take the sailing very seriously indeed. The leading sailors of many countries congregate at Cowes where the standard is as high as anywhere in the world.

The Royal Family have not severed their links with Cowes since the days of Prince Albert, and it is not unusual to see them, particularly Prince Philip, competing in the races which now attract entries of over seven hundred and fifty yachts. A mass of people wearing sea boots and sweaters, smart reefer jackets and those dark Breton red trousers, so popular with the nautical world, fill the narrow streets, and anyone not conforming to the uniform, whether spectator or competitor, will feel quite out of place!

The best way to enjoy the regatta is to own a house in town and to use a yacht as a day boat, before returning homeward to a hot bath before the exhausting evening activities. (Throughout the week there is a continuous round of receptions, dinners and balls, with the Squadron Ball, which is usually held on the Monday night, regarded as the most prestigious.) The most sought-after location for property is along the waterfront, giving a grandstand view of the waterborne activity.

To rent a house during the regatta is always difficult, particularly on the waterfront, and demand considerably outstrips supply. The situation is even worse in years when Admiral's Cup events are held at Cowes, but in any year inflated prices for accommodation are to be expected with rents often double normal summer rates. Hotels are generally booked up over a year in advance. Probably the best prospect of reasonable accommodation for the average enthusiast or competitor is to live on your own boat.

Cruisers and racers are moored either on swinging moorings in the Roads, in

OPPOSITE ABOVE:
Ocean racers making a spectacular display with their colourful spinnakers on a lively reach in the Solent.

OPPOSITE BELOW:
Cruisers and ocean racers crewed by some of the world's leading yachtsmen fill the harbour and marinas at Cowes during Cowes Week.

the Harbour or tied up alongside each other outside Groves and Guttridges marina situated below their boatyard. To ensure a mooring, applications must be made at least the previous year direct to the Harbour Master, the marinas and boatyards in Cowes. Addresses for accommodation can be obtained from the Isle of Wight Tourist Board, The Esplanade, Sandown, Isle of Wight (0983 403886).

For those mooring below Groves & Guttridges it is vital to return as early as possible after each day's racing before the Harbour Master has a chance to hang 'No Mooring Alongside' notices on the outside boat.

Other mooring is available at the new marina up-river on the East Cowes side or on piles on the west side above the floating bridge which links the two towns.

Wherever you are moored, the evenings could prove something of a logistical problem. Restaurant places are always at a premium, but for a minimal fee the Island Sailing Club makes all visiting crews honorary members for the Week, which at least provides the chance of a meal and a drink, as well as often much-needed washing facilities. The majority of sailors on the Isle of Wight belong to the Island Sailing Club which is really the heart of nautical Cowes. Since its foundation in 1889 the Club has grown in size and stature considerably and its present membership is over 3500.

Without doubt every bar and restaurant in Cowes will be crowded by early evening; although the first Saturday is always comparatively quiet as many crews do not arrive until the next day. The Three Crowns, in the High Street, is one of the most renowned pubs with its small back bar known as DOBYC. (Dot's own bloody Yacht Club), named after the landlady. Licence extensions are the norm in Cowes Week, although little drinking will be done by Solent competitors in ocean racers as soon after crossing the line these boats disperse to their home marinas. Nevertheless the party atmosphere prevails with nautical tales and songs being swapped.

Another feature of Cowes is that because of some of its complicated racing procedures it is an advantage if at least one member of any foreign crew can speak English. 483 racing courses are listed in the Programme and Sailing Instructions for the week!

Racing starts daily at 10.30 am, and before every race there is an air of bustle which increases to fever pitch before the major events. The two top races of the week are for the Britannia and New York Yacht Club Challenge Trophies. Full details of all the races can be obtained from the Cowes Combined Clubs, 18 Bath Road, Cowes (0983 293 303).

On the Friday evening a firework display is held, and spectators line every available viewpoint, including the battlements of the Royal Yacht Squadron's Castle. During Cowes Week badges of different colours for men and women are issued by the Squadron and these have to be worn by all guests to the Castle. Entry to the Royal Yacht Squadron is by a member's invitation, and it is a highly exclusive organization of which membership can be obtained only on the personal recommendation of an existing member. All the other Clubs in Cowes issue temporary membership badges for a minimal fee.

Undoubtedly the best way to travel to Cowes is by steamer or hydrofoil as taking a car to the Island during Cowes Week can be something of a problem. If absolutely necessary, a car passage should be booked on one of the car ferries, from Southampton, Lymington or Portsmouth as early as possible.

The Three Choirs Festival

This is Britain's oldest music festival, for in Handel's time amateur choirs performed his larger choral works all over the country, in the manner of elementary festivals, and especially in the three cities of Gloucester, Worcester and Hereford. In about 1715, a society called the Sons of the Clergy and Saint Cecilia (patron saint of music) organized for charitable purposes an annual meeting of the joint choirs from these three cities. By 1752 secular music was also included in the programme, and gradually important works from Europe and the USA were introduced. It became the custom for the performances to be held in each city in rotation, the 'home' city providing half of the 280-strong choir, with a quarter of the strength coming from each of the other two. The title 'Three Choirs Festival' developed during the nineteenth century.

In 1911, Edward Elgar first conducted at the Worcester Festival and continued in this post until 1933, the year before his death. There was a gap during the last war, but Hereford reopened the Three Choirs in 1946.

Recitals and lectures between the music make this a gentle festival for the visitor, who should, all the same, visit the three cities that are set across the Malvern Hills. Hereford is overlooked by the impressive Black Mountains, and this city boasts a fine collection of mediaeval maps and a chained library; the fifteenth-century Booth Hall, the Raven Inn (David Garrick's birthplace); and a number of interesting churches, quite apart from the mainly Norman cathedral with its carved stalls and its *mappa mundi* in the south transept that dates from the fourteenth century.

Gloucester was once a Roman city called Colonia Glevum and sits astride the River Severn. The Norman cathedral contains the tomb of King Edward II, murdered in 1340; and there are some fascinating eighteenth-century and older houses including several which are now museums.

Worcester, higher up the River Severn, is famous for its porcelain. The Royal Porcelain Works has a museum which may be visited with prior notice. The Early English cathedral has an eleventh-century crypt, choir stalls dating from 1379 and a fourteenth-century tower. The visitor can also see the earliest royal effigy in England, that of King John who died in 1216. Worcester is also the site of an important battle in the Civil War when Cromwell beat Charles II, who was supported by a Scottish Army, soon after the latter's coronation as King in Scotland. This was in 1651 and traces of the scene as it was then can be discerned if the visitor has contemporary maps.

The Music Festival lasts for a week between mid to late August, and while musical preparation is in the hands of the three conductor-organists, the Festival Director is Donald Hunt, 25 Castle Street, Hereford, who will provide details of the next Festival on application.

Grouse, Blackgame and Ptarmigan Shooting

Grouse suddenly appearing over the hill closely hugging the contours of the heather, a cock pheasant climbing ever higher on a frost-coated November morning, geese lit by a full moon—these are the perfect moments in the shooting man's life. Others appreciate the countryside but remain spectators, for carrying a gun restores man to his natural role as a hunter.

The first step in a shooting career is a visit to the local police station in order to obtain a shotgun certificate. This permits the holder to own a shotgun and is usually granted automatically to reputable persons.

The second stage should be to join the British Association for Shooting and Conservation (the BASC). This body protects the shooter's sport, undertakes major conservation work and insures its members against third party claims.

The novice has now to choose a gun. A visit to the local gunshop will allow him to handle many guns and obtain good advice. The owner will probably recommend a 12-bore, double-barrelled side-by-side (with the barrels arranged side by side) game gun. This has been proved by generations of sportsmen to be the gun *par excellence* for British shooting conditions. However, the customer may be offered a pump-action or semi-automatic gun, or perhaps an over-and-under (where the barrels are fixed one above the other). The first two are seldom seen on game shoots, as they cannot immediately be seen to be unloaded. The over-and-under needs more careful consideration. Often offering good value for money, they are now very popular and many shooters do experience a marked improvement in their performance when using one. Moreover, they share the side-by-side's features of being demonstrably safe and having a two-shot capacity. However, over-and-unders are used mainly in clay-pigeon shooting and have competitive connotations alien to the British shooting scene and unacceptable to many hosts. They are also uncomfortable to carry for a long period.

If the novice is of average stature, an 'off the peg' gun should fit him adequately. If not, he should consider having the gun altered by a competent gunsmith. Alternatively, he can have a gun built for him by one of the London or provincial gunmakers. These are always costly and a gun from Holland and Holland, Purdey or Boss would be beyond the reach of most sportsmen. However, these firms build 'best' guns only—guns that cannot be improved by expense or labour. Such a gun should serve at least three generations and will always hold its value.

Choice of clothing is much simpler. It should be muted and unobtrusive and, like all other equipment, be of good quality. Waxed cotton coats, thornproof trousers and lightweight gumboots are standard kit on most shoots with the tweeds being brought out for the more formal days. Hats are normally worn and here the shot is allowed a degree of individuality being restricted only by colour which, like his other garb, should blend with the countryside. Although common abroad, camouflaged clothing is rarely seen on an organized shoot.

If he wishes to shoot game, the sportsman must also buy a game licence which is available from post offices. The following are classified as game: pheasant, partridge, grouse, woodcock, snipe, ptarmigan, blackgame, capercaillie, hares and deer.

Shooting arrangements should be finalized during July. If the sportsman has a

Grouse shooting on the Scottish moors. Grouse are very fast fliers and present a difficult target to any marksman trying to be the first on the 'Glorious Twelfth' to supply the nation's dinner tables.

number of private invitations this presents few problems. For the majority of shooting men, however, shooting has to be bought. The classified columns of the *Shooting Times* offer the best selection of shooting by the day or full and half guns for the season. (A full gun will usually give ten days shooting, a half gun five.)

The final preparation is a visit to a shooting school. This gives the experienced gun a warm-up and is vital for the novice. There is little point in taking up the sport and then shooting badly: this disappoints those who provide the sport and causes unnecessary wounding of birds. More importantly, the shooting school provides the perfect place for learning shotgun safety. Unless this is practised until automatic, the novice should never shoot in company.

Far away, the beating line can be seen moving slowly down the glen. The sun's warmth, the smell of heather and the steady indolent hum of insects all create a slight drowsiness. A flash of a flanker's flag dispels the torpor and against the purple haze a series of black dots rapidly materialize into a pack of grouse flying incredibly fast, skimming the hill's contours. Two hurried shots and more by luck than skill a bird bounces on the heather and the Glorious Twelfth has been celebrated.

Lasting from 12 August to 10 December, the grouse season provides some of the best sport in the world and attracts many foreign visitors, for the red grouse is found only in Britain, mainly in Scotland and the North.

Grouse can be walked-up, shot over pointers or setters, or driven to the guns by a line of beaters. Each method has its own attractions. Walking-up allows the gun to wander the moors and work for his birds whilst pointers and setters can give a display of unequalled working elegance. Both these methods give superb sport at reasonable cost, although shots tend to be of the simpler going-away type.

There is nothing simple about driven grouse: they present some of the most testing and varied shots possible. This, together with the incomparable scenery in which they thrive, is why driven grouse shooting is in such demand and therefore expensive.

Those fortunate enough to have a day's driven grouse should ascertain whether sufficient birds are expected to warrant a double gun day. The novice, even if he has a beautifully matched pair of self-opening Purdeys, would be well advised to take only one gun. Using a pair and a loader takes practise and it is difficult enough to connect with two shots, especially if he has not experienced before the excitement of game shooting.

This is something that no shooting school can simulate and any transgressions of the safety rules will endanger other guns and often end in the culprit being sent home. Especially, the tyro must remember not to swing through the line.

Almost as important as safety is sportsmanship. This is a general consideration for the quarry and fellow guns. The sportsman does not fire at birds outside effective range (forty-five to fifty yards) nor at very close birds if there is a risk of smashing them. All sitting birds are of course left. He knows how to despatch wounded game quickly and efficiently and always treats dead quarry with respect: there are few sights more unseemly than a pile of dead game slung on the ground.

Sportsmanship among guns is basically a matter of good manners. Birds which are clearly the neighbouring gun's or which would provide him with a better shot are best left. This can be difficult to judge but shared birds should be avoided.

Whilst a little light-hearted rivalry adds to the enjoyment of the day, competitiveness should be resisted. Shooting is a test of quarry and gun, not fellow sportsmen. The novice should also have a good general knowledge of natural history and the countryside as this will greatly enhance his appreciation of the sport. It will also help him to avoid the embarrassment of shooting non-quarry or out of season species.

Three other gamebirds may also be found on the moors: the black grouse (commonly known as blackgame), the snipe, and the ptarmigan.

Blackgame are slightly larger than grouse and favour the moor/woodland fringe country. The male, the blackcock, is unmistakable having black plumage trimmed with white and a lyre shaped tail. The female, the greyhen, is less distinctive and is occasionally mistaken for the grouse. The blackgame season opens on 20 August and finishes on 10 December. As the opening date is eight days after the Glorious Twelfth, it is essential that the gun can differentiate between the two.

The snipe season also opens on 12 August but finishes on 31 January. Weighing little more than four ounces, it is immediately distinguished by its long bill and amazingly erratic zig-zag flight.

Inhabiting the moors in August, the snipe moves later in the season to marshy and boggy lowland areas throughout the country, but it is Ireland and the West

Country that attract the largest numbers, shooting often being rented for the snipe alone.

Presenting a consistently difficult target due to its small size and jinking flight, the snipe gives excellent sport but there are many who consider it 'not worth the shot' because of its small culinary value. As a result, snipe shooting can often be very reasonable although costs are far higher if the birds are driven.

The ptarmigan is another member of the grouse family but is unlikely to be found in the course of a normal grouse day since it inhabits the highest mountains. These peaks are usually snow-covered in the winter and the ptarmigan would be easily spotted by predators in its dark summer plumage. As a defence, the ptarmigan turns white. This process usually starts in October and is completed by late November. Highly prized in its winter plumage, most ptarmigan shooting does not start until then although their season starts on 12 August. Since it ends on 10 December, ptarmigan shooting expeditions need nice timing.

A difficult quarry to find and shoot, an experienced guide is necessary and only a very few of the sporting agencies can offer good ptarmigan shooting.

Autumn Staghunting and Hindhunting

The 'Autumn Stag' is the common West-Country term for a mature stag with a good head which will be hunted in the autumn. The season runs from the first hunting day in August to the end of October.

The stags are fat and well-fed after the summer of plenty and seldom does one get a long hunt early in the season, but to see hounds rouse a big stag is very exciting and anyone hunting at this time of year will see plenty of deer on Exmoor.

The hunting of the autumn stag is the same as for spring staghunting both in method of hunting, dress and excitement, so it gives one a chance to talk a little about the red deer himself. A mature stag has a head with large horns. Unlike the horns of cattle these are shed in the spring and regrow during the summer. Out hunting the stag is recognized by the make-up of his head. You may hear someone say 'He's got all his rights and three' or 'Brow, bay and two'. The brow point is the lowest one which stretches forwards from the main beam of the horn. The one above it is the bay and the one above that is the trey. These terms are derived from the old Norman French. At the top of both main beams are the crockets or points. Stags can have many crockets, but like all sportsmen, hunters often attribute to the animal more points than he has, until they are close to him. When a stag has brow, bay and trey on both beams he is said to have all his rights.

The best hunts in autumn usually occur during the rut or mating season. The older stags travel a long way to find their hinds and, because they have other things on their minds, hardly eat at all and are much fitter.

Watching deer on Exmoor is best and easiest during the rut, but the stags can be very belligerent and should be treated with respect.

At the end of the autumn staghunting around the end of October hounds and hunt staff have a break, so don't plan to go staghunting without checking on this.

The Devon and Somerset staghounds of 1908
on Exmoor, the main centre for staghunting in England.

Around mid-November the opening meet of hindhunting takes place and from then until the end of February only hinds are hunted. As deer are herd animals they are inclined to run to fresh deer and this complicates the hunting. In many instances the fresh deer will push out the intruder, but many a good hunt has been foiled by the interference of fresh stags or a herd of hinds running across the line of the hunted animal.

The dress for hindhunting is the same as for foxhunting on the moor. That is, only the Joint-Masters and the hunt staff wear red coats. The men who follow should wear black coats, bowler hats, white breeches, white hunting ties and black butcher boots. For ladies the correct dress is a black coat, bowler hat, hair net, white hunting tie and breeches and black butcher boots. You may see some less sartorially correct men riding—these will usually be the local shepherds and farm workers having a day out on their ponies.

A pleasant way to spend some time after hunting is to go to any of the many sporting pubs for a warming drink and talk of the day's sport. Most will welcome the hunter straight from the Chase and a whisky by a log fire is a grand way to finish a hard day's galloping and dry your breeches.

The most knowledgable man on deer-hunting and the ways of the deer of Exmoor is Mr Dick Lloyd, who is also secretary of the Masters of Deer Hounds Association. You will find him most helpful when planning your holiday hunting the wild red deer. His address is Mr Dick Lloyd, Honeymead, Simonsbath, Minehead, Somerset.

The best centres for staghunting are: Devon and Somerset Staghounds, Exford; Tiverton Staghounds, Tiverton and Bampton; Quantock Staghounds, Bridgwater and Williton.

Highland Games

The Highland Gatherings or Games of Scotland have their origins in the ancient musterings of the clans, often for military purposes, when the clan chief would summon his followers, often from far-flung and remote corners of the Highlands, to confirm his leadership and establish the military strength available to him. From very early days the gatherings were important social occasions (as they still are), in a time when communication over the wild reaches of the Highlands was extremely limited. The contests of skill and strength so much a part of the modern games also started for military reasons, and today contests are still held in the traditional sports of running, jumping, putting the weight, throwing the hammer and tossing the caber (the trunk of a pine or fir tree which is about nineteen feet long and weighs about one hundred and fifty pounds).

The gatherings have always given Highlanders an excuse for playing the traditional music of the pipes (the *piobaireachd*), singing and dancing, and today pipers and dancers are still a very popular and colourful part of the programme. There are more than seventy Highland Gatherings held in Scotland, the most famous of which is the Braemar Gathering near Balmoral. The importance of these games in the social calendar came about when Queen Victoria and Prince Albert bought Balmoral Castle in 1852, and fell in love with all things Scottish (or

Queen Elizabeth the Queen Mother with the Princess of Wales at the 1982 Braemar Games, traditionally visited by the Royal Family during their summer holiday at nearby Balmoral.

The Highland Games at Dunkeld in 1842, on the occasion of Queen Victoria's
first visit to the Scottish Highlands.

at least Highland Scottish). The Royal Family today are always at Balmoral for
their summer holiday and will certainly pay a visit to the Braemar games which
coincide with their visit, usually taking place on the first Saturday in September.

Gatherings are held in different places throughout the summer from May to
September, and for details of dates and places it is best to contact the Scottish
Tourist Board, 23 Ravelston Terrace, Edinburgh (031 332 2433) or to watch the
Scottish press.

The Edinburgh International Festival
and the Military Tattoo

Founded in 1947 under the artistic direction of Sir Rudolf Bing, the Edinburgh
International Festival and Fringe occupies three weeks every year over the end of
August and the beginning of September and could be considered the most
important arts festival in Britain, with some two hundred events ranging from
opera, orchestral and chamber music concerts to ballet performances, drama and
art exhibitions. It has been well described as 'a gesture of cultural defiance in a
world made weary by war'.

The Festival is officially opened by a cavalcade consisting of representatives of
the main elements—the Festival, the Fringe and the Military Tattoo—including
marching pipers and bands, which makes its noisy and colourful way along
Princes Street, the main street of the city.

There is also a Festival Service in the twelfth-century St Giles' Cathedral
attended by the Lord Provost and Councillors of the City of Edinburgh.

The floodlit Military Tattoo under the battlements of Edinburgh Castle, where the stirring music of the pipes can be heard on most evenings during the Festival.

Once it is under way, the Festival lives up to its reputation for presenting musical performances, drama and dance of the highest international standards, with artists from all over the world converging on this most romantic of cities for a few weeks of hectic activity and excitement.

The Fringe, which came into being in 1949, has almost taken over from the main Festival as the major attraction of the programme since it became the place for 'non-establishment' groups from the universities, amateur playwrights and actors, jazz musicians and poets to try out their wares on interested and largely sympathetic audiences. Since the success of Peter Cook and Dudley Moore in the satirical revue *Beyond the Fringe* Edinburgh has attracted a truly phenomenal number of unusual and often extremely lively and talented, shows. The Fringe has a separate programme (it needs to—there are several hundred Fringe events from Great Britain and abroad) which can be obtained from The Secretary, The Festival Fringe Society Limited, 170 High Street, Edinburgh (031 226 5257). There is also the Fringe Club which is a popular place to spend the evening. (Details of membership are also available from the Fringe Society Offices.)

It might also be worth joining the Festival Club (write to the Secretary, 54 George Street, Edinburgh), a building which was once a favourite haunt of Sir Walter Scott.

Other events which take place while the Festival is on include the Royal Scottish Academy's Summer Exhibition, an International Film Festival, and of course the famous Military Tattoo.

This spectacular floodlit extravaganza, set on the Castle Esplanade against the backdrop of the ancient fortress is a unique opportunity to hear the stirring music of the Scottish regiments in their native setting. There are performances on most evenings during the Festival, with the massed bands of pipes and drums marching with swinging kilts to traditional reels and strathspeys.

Details can be obtained from the Tattoo Office, 1 Cockburn Street, Edinburgh (031 225 1188).

During the Festival the city is much busier and fuller than usual, but it should not be too difficult to find somewhere to stay and the Scottish Tourist Board at 23 Ravelston Terrace, Edinburgh (031 332 2433) will always help and advise. The Festival programme is published towards the end of April and can be obtained from The Edinburgh Festival Society Ltd, 21 Market Street, Edinburgh 1 (031 226 4001).

The British Jumping Derby at Hickstead

Hickstead is situated on the A23 Brighton road in Sussex and houses one of the few permanent show-jumping arenas in the country. It was started in 1961 and has increased in size and prestige since its inception. The most impressive feature of the huge international arena is the Derby Bank, used only in the British Jumping Derby each August. There are other natural obstacles in the arena, including the Devil's Dyke (a treble over water ditches), the Cornishman, which is a Cornish-style stone wall, and the Irish Bank.

When Hickstead first started it caused much controversy as it was widely regarded as half way between a cross-country course, with its natural obstacles, and a show-jumping course, with its coloured poles. This controversy went on into the 1970s with some riders refusing to bring their top horses to Hickstead as they regarded the course as too punishing.

Throughout the history of the British Jumping Derby few clear rounds have been achieved and on many occasions the event has been won with a round of four faults or more. Some horses have established themselves as real Hickstead specialists over the years, but none more so than Marian Mould's superb 14.2hh pony Stroller who set Hickstead alight in the 1960s and early '70s.

There is always a strong foreign contingent present as the Jumping Derby is one of the most prestigious and richly rewarded competitions in the world, although the home team are always in strong opposition.

The Hickstead Derby meeting lasts for three days, from the Saturday till the Monday of the last weekend in August. Although the Jumping Derby forms the climax of the meeting, exciting show-jumping can be expected on the other days as well. At Hickstead there are several rings in operation at any one time and it is possible to watch showing classes and other events besides show-jumping.

The whole setting of Hickstead is typically English, with Hickstead House, the home of its founder Douglas Bunn, in the background. The public are well catered for with ample seating and car parking and relatively easy access by road. It certainly is worth a visit and no knowledge of horses is strictly necessary. The rules of show-jumping are simple to follow and the whole procedure is easy to understand.

People from all walks of life attend Hickstead and you are quite likely to run into a famous film star or two, socialites and big businessmen. The whole atmosphere of Hickstead is free and unregimented and the public are able to

The terrifying Derby Bank at the annual British Jumping
Derby at Hickstead in Sussex, an obstacle to try the
strength and ability of some of the greatest show-jumpers
ever seen.

wander at leisure collecting autographs and inspecting famous horses at closer
quarters.

As with all similar shows there are many trade stands which certainly merit
inspection as there are always some real bargains to be found.

Other show-jumping meetings take place at Hickstead from Easter to
September, which are less crowded than the Derby Meeting and also provide
excellent entertainment, although the spectacle of the Derby Bank can only be
enjoyed at the Derby Meeting on August Bank Holiday weekend.

For details of membership apply to: The Secretary, All-England Show
Jumping Club, Hickstead, Nr Bolney, Sussex.

September

Partridge and Wildfowl Shooting

September 1 used to be eagerly awaited as the start of the partridge season. The 'little brown birds' were considered the archetypal English gamebird and were a major part of British shooting with good partridge shoots or 'manors' being carefully cultivated and whole books being devoted to the art of partridge driving. Sadly, few shoots now offer a reasonable showing of partridge.

Their decline is partly because the chicks are highly susceptible to bad weather; heavy rain during Royal Ascot may be bad for Ladies' Day hats but it is a disaster for the partridge. But inclement weather is not a new phenomenon; the main reason for their modern decline is agricultural change. Farmers now have to utilize their land fully; hedges are removed or rigorously trimmed, the corn stubble is cut short or burnt, insecticides and artificial fertilizers are extensively used. The partridge has suffered as a result but there are still shoots which hold a few partridge days.

These are normally small affairs although at least one partridge manor had a two hundred and fifty brace day last season. To take part in such a day remains the ambition of many shots for driven partridge shooting is not only extremely exciting but has a unique aura of English tradition.

Two main species are shot: the English or grey partridge (also known in America as the Hungarian partridge) and the red-legged, often referred to as the Frenchman. Both give superlative sport but the grey is usually considered to show itself better.

Many shoots are now raising a few partridge as a side-line to the main pheasant rearing programme and it is to be hoped the partridge will be restored to its former numbers.

September 1 is also the start of the wildfowling season. For many, this is simply the most exciting sport available. The quarry is truly wild and is hunted in the wildest places.

Nine species of duck may be shot: the mallard, wigeon, teal, pintail, common pochard, tufted, gadwell, shoveller and goldeneye, together with four species of geese: the pinkfoot, greylag, whitefront (in England and Wales only) and Canada. The golden plover is also a quarry species. As with game, wildfowl are not subject to bag limits.

Wildfowl may be shot on much of Britain's foreshore: the land lying between ordinary low water and high water marks. At one time much of this shooting was free but the recent popularity of the sport and the irresponsibility of certain elements has led to much of the foreshore shooting being controlled, often by wildfowling clubs. The keen newcomer would do well to join such a club and accompany someone who really knows the ways of fowl—how they will be affected by the tide, the moon, the wind, food supply and the general weather conditions. In every club there is usually one person who has this knowledge and

Wildfowling on an estuary after the morning flight.

the beginner would be well advised to persuade him to share it. Unfortunately, many clubs have restricted membership and long waiting lists although some do operate a day-permit system. Those with some experience can take advantage of this but the novice really is wasting his time wandering onto a strange marsh. He would do better to hire a local guide or perhaps take one of the fowling holidays advertised in the *Shooting Times*.

Though the wildfowling season may have started, the real sport will not begin until the wintering population arrives in late October. For the most part, September fowling is restricted to the home-grown mallard.

Mallard feed during the night and rest during the day. If the shot knows where the mallard are heading then he can intercept them. Unfortunately, they have a wide range of food and without good local knowledge will be difficult to locate. An inland flight pond removes much of the guesswork, providing both feeding and a place to rest. Shooting flight ponds can give very fast sport but in the excitement the novice should remember to let the duck come well in and not to shoot low. He should avoid taking part in some of the 'duck shoots' that are occasionally offered, often as a supplementary to a pheasant day. The guns are placed round the pond and the duck are then forced off the water by the beaters. As tame as those in St James's Park, the duck then make a few circuits before dropping down again. Some guns seem to relish this sort of shooting but most find it embarrassing.

The woodcock season also starts on 1 September but only in Scotland. Therefore the species will be discussed when it comes into season for the rest of Britain on 1 October.

The Royal Opera House, Covent Garden

Gala nights at the Royal Opera House, Covent Garden, with the audience in full evening dress, are infrequent occasions but perhaps three or four times during the forty-six week season they recapture, better than anything else, the glorious days of the London theatre before the Second World War. After the war, as far as audiences were concerned, informality in dress took over. Nevertheless, gala performances apart, an evening of opera or ballet at one of the greatest and best beloved opera houses in the world is invariably a memorable experience.

For more than two hundred and fifty years this theatrical Mecca has dominated London's famous Covent Garden but, in that time, both have changed: the fruit and vegetable market immortalized in Shaw's *Pygmalion* (and later in Lerner and Loewe's *My Fair Lady*) has been moved and replaced by a piazza of little shops and restaurants, and the Opera House is the third Royal Theatre on the site, its predecessors having both been burnt to the ground. However, the new setting for the impressive building which backs on to the market, its main entrance dominated by six great columns, is a great improvement. The conglomeration of attractive little shops stays open until late at night and the cosmopolitan restaurants offer a choice of places to eat after the theatre, when this part of London comes alive and quite a holiday atmosphere prevails.

Refreshments are also available in the Opera House itself; cold buffets can be obtained for an hour before the performance and in the interval while cold suppers may be ordered in advance on the day of the performance.

The first theatre on the site opened in 1732 and earned the title 'Royal' merely by virtue of being licensed by the Lord Chamberlain for all types of theatrical performances. Before the end of the century it was enlarged and remodelled four times whereupon the actress Mrs Siddons described it as 'this vast wilderness'. It was burnt to the ground in 1803 after a performance of *Pizarro* but its successor re-opened just ten months later.

Here Queen Victoria gave a more literal endorsement to the title 'Royal Opera House' when she visited it for the first time at the age of fourteen and wrote in her Journal; 'Pasta sang *beautifully*, Paganini played *wonderfully*, Malibran, like Pasta, sang beautifully. . . .'

The Queen and her beloved Albert, the Prince Consort, regularly occupied the Royal Box. At that time the theatre was reconstructed and called The Royal Italian Opera with an all-Italian repertoire or one in which non-Italian works were sung in Italian. The Royal interest established it as an integral part of the London social scene and Court visitors were entertained there at splendid gala performances including ones for the French Emperor Napoleon III and the German Emperor Wilhelm II.

However, in 1857 the building was again burnt to the ground and Queen Victoria was escorted round the ruins. But within a year the manager had raised £120,000 for a new theatre—the one that stands today—designed by E. M. Barry, son of the architect of the Houses of Parliament.

Its acoustics were unrivalled and many of its star performers including Dame Nellie Melba, thought of Covent Garden as home. In 1892 it no longer performed all works in Italian and became The Royal Opera. At least forty new works were

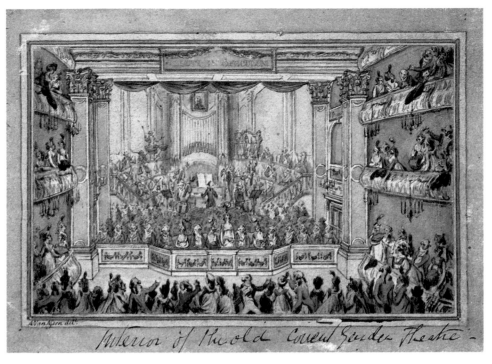

ABOVE:
A view of the interior of the old Covent Garden Theatre which was destroyed by fire in 1808.

LEFT:
Inside the Royal Opera House at Covent Garden. The present building replaced an earlier one burnt out in 1857, and was designed by E. M. Barry, son of the architect of the Houses of Parliament.

In the days when London's fruit and vegetable market was situated at Covent Garden opera-goers could be seen picking their way in their finery past the stalls and covered carts.

presented there and great singers including Caruso, Antonio Scotti and Beniamino Gigli made their debuts. Ballet was introduced there in 1911 when Diaghilev's Russian Company danced for a season and, apart from a period during the First World War when the Royal Opera House became a furniture store, it flourished as a distinguished home for both art forms.

During the Second World War the building served as a dance hall for the troops. Afterwards it re-opened with the ballet *Sleeping Beauty* when the Sadler's Wells Company, directed by Ninette de Valois and led by Margot Fonteyn and Robert Helpmann, transferred there from their home at Sadler's Wells. For a time after the war British operas were performed there and during the 1960s work by outstanding British composers included Britten, Vaughan Williams, Bliss and Tippett. This, allied to the willingness of British opera singers to perform foreign works in their original language, led to the Royal Opera House re-emerging as one of the world's leading permanent homes of both international opera and ballet.

Its small Royal Box at the side of the stage, often occupied by Queen Victoria, is inadequate for present-day gala occasions such as the one which marked the Silver Jubilee of Queen Elizabeth II. Then twenty-six members of the Royal Family were accommodated in a flower-banked Royal Box improvised at the back of the Grand Tier.

Although the theatre has a seating capacity of more than two thousand, tickets for all gala performances held for charity, for special celebrations like Joan Sutherland's Thirtieth Anniversary Concert or premieres of new productions like Puccini's *Manon Lescaut* with Kiri te Kanawa in the title role, are most expensive to obtain.

The programme is announced in May or June for the season which runs from

September through to July but as the major artists are booked two or three years ahead, there are inevitably changes—as when, for instance, three sopranos became pregnant in the same season. Mailing List Subscribers receive about three months' notice of programme changes, with details of booking arrangements and prices which vary for different performances.

Postal bookings are accepted a month to six weeks prior to a performance and car parking spaces may be reserved at this time. Personal bookings can be made a fortnight later. Priority, however, is always given to The Friends of Covent Garden, a society launched some twenty years ago as one way of supplementing the financial support given to the Royal Opera House by the Arts Council of Great Britain. Privileges attendant on an annual subscription of £18 (£6.50 for those under twenty-six) include the virtual guarantee of a seat at most performances if booked in the priority period, invitations to 'open' rehearsals, lunch-time recitals, discussions and interviews with musical celebrities. Details of all schemes are obtainable from The Royal Opera House, Covent Garden, London WC2E 7QA.

However, even with an insatiable demand for tickets for most performances, it is possible to gain admission on the day, except for galas, proms and Sunday concerts. Sixty-five Rear Amphitheatre seats are sold for most opera and ballet performances, one per person, from 10 am on the day of the performance and a limited number of standing tickets are sold if the House is sold out.

The Ryder Cup

'The great thing is not winning but taking part' is how a participant described this five-day contest between teams of twelve professional golfers from Europe and America which takes place every two years, alternately in England and America. The sentiments may well have been expressed by an Englishman because Great Britain—and recently Great Britain and Europe—have won only three of the twenty-three fixtures and tied one.

The American-based fixture is usually held in October, and in September in Great Britain. It is held at some of the most beautiful golf courses in the country, and attracts crowds of some size.

Professionalism takes second place to patriotism for there is no prize money, just the honour of winning the magnificent gold cup first competed for in 1927. It was donated by Samuel Ryder, a wealthy seed-merchant who played a little golf but presumably made a good deal of his money by selling seed for golf courses. Until his death in 1936 he also contributed generously towards the expenses of the British team.

This sporting fixture which, in Britain, rotates between leading inland courses, also demonstrates how the status of the professional golfer has altered over the past century. Then an artisan, the 'pro' touched his cap to the gentry, maintained the course, played with a member for a shilling or two, gave lessons and sometimes made and repaired clubs—all for a weekly retainer of between five and ten shillings. Today even Samuel Ryder might envy the more successful.

Details of British fixtures can be obtained from the promoters: The Professional Golfers' Association, Apollo House, The Belfry, Sutton Coldfield, West Midlands, BT6 9PT (0675 70333) or from leading ticket agencies.

Doncaster

Racing had taken place on Town Moor, half a mile to the south of the centre of Doncaster, in the final decades of the sixteenth century and records show that the local Corporation contributed four guineas towards a race in 1703. The Doncaster Gold Cup was instituted in 1766, but like the majority of races, was run in heats, with the competing horses being owned by aristocrats who lived in the locality. One of them was the eccentric Lord Rockingham, twice Prime Minister of England and a founder member of the Jockey Club. In 1776 Rockingham, bored by the innumerable heats and matches contested by his horses, decided upon novel conditions for a new race at Doncaster. The race was a sweepstake of twenty-five guineas each, for three-year-olds, colts to carry 8st and fillies 7st 12lb over two miles. The fact that the heroine was Alabaculia, owned by Lord Rockingham, was of less importance than the realization by Doncaster Corporation that the event was obviously popular. With wisdom and foresight they appreciated that a new era in northern racing was heralded. In consequence forty-eight hours after the race they adopted a resolution that a new racecourse and grandstand should be built. Two years later Lord Rockingham proposed that the popular sweepstake should bear the name of his friend General Anthony St Leger who lived at nearby Park Hill. His proposal was accepted, and the first St Leger Stakes was run on Tuesday, 2 September, 1778, although at the time no one was aware that the race was to acquire a significant place in Turf history as the first of the five English Classic races.

In the early years of the St Leger, Doncaster Corporation organized balls at the Mansion House during race-week, and each morning crowds of racegoers followed the local hunts, including the Badsworth of which Lord Rockingham was Master. Every afternoon the nobility would attend the races, accompanied by an entourage of liveried servants. The Duke of Devonshire would come from Chatsworth; the Duke of Portland from Welbeck; whilst Earl Fitzwilliam would arrive in splendour, his coach drawn by six bays decorated with favours and rosettes, and accompanied by twenty outriders. The crowds cheered the nobility, but gave hero worship to the racehorses, for Yorkshiremen are renowned horselovers. It has even been claimed that if a bridle was waved above a Yorkshireman's grave he would rise up and search out a horse!

In 1853 West Australian became the first thoroughbred to win the Two Thousand Guineas, the Derby and the St Leger—the races collectively known as the 'Triple Crown'. Since then eleven colts including Ormonds, Flying Fox, Diamond Jubilee, Bahram and Nijinsky have taken the Triple Crown. When Diamond Jubilee triumphed in 1900 his owner, the Prince of Wales, was prevented from attending the races owing to Court Mourning for his brother, the Duke of Edinburgh. In the 1980s there is far less chance of a colt being hailed as a Triple Crown hero. Firstly because the immense monetary value, which could reach ten million pounds, placed upon a Derby winner brings the temptation to retire him to stud without risking subsequent defeat. Secondly the prize money, prestige and date of the Prix de l'Arc de Triomphe at Longchamp run early in October overshadows the St Leger. Europe's richest race comes so soon after the St Leger, which in the 1980s is held on the final day of the four-day meeting in mid-September, that it is inevitable that many owners and trainers set their sights on the French race and consequently bypass the Doncaster Classic, the highlight of the September meeting which also includes four other important races, the Laurent Perrier Champagne Stakes; the Park Hill Stakes; the Doncaster Cup and the Flying Childers Race.

Doncaster is a left-handed course with a straight mile and a round circuit of approximately two miles on which all races beyond a mile are run. Horses trained in the north of England clash at Doncaster with those from Newmarket and the south so that competition is always strong.

'The Race for the Great St Leger Stakes, 1836.' The
first St Leger Stakes was run at Doncaster in 1778,
and is now the first of the five English Classic races.

The Scarborough Cricket Festival

Since 1876 Scarborough Cricket Club's annual Festival has been a place of pilgrimage for cricketers and cricket lovers. It is the oldest and only surviving cricket festival and is steeped in cricket history and legend. Just about all the great names of cricket have played here, and all the touring sides. Many cricket lovers return each year, booking their holidays to coincide with the Festival.

The Festival is held right at the end of the season (usually the first fortnight in September). The format has changed over the years, reflecting, to a large extent, the changes that have taken place in cricket generally. From 1950 to 1963 the Festival comprised three three-day games: MCC v. Yorkshire, Gentlemen (amateurs) v. Players (Professionals) and T. N. Pearce's XI (an invitation side) v. the Touring Side.

In 1971 the Fenner Trophy Knock-out Competition was introduced, played between invited county sides, and continued until 1981.

The Festival fixtures for 1982 began with Brian Close's XI playing the touring team (Pakistan), followed by a knock-out, limited overs tournament (sponsored by ASDA Stores) between Yorkshire, Lancashire, Derbyshire and Nottinghamshire. The Festival concluded with the Courage Old England XI playing the John Smith XI (a team made up of some of the best players from the various Yorkshire leagues).

Traditionalists may disapprove of this new format, but it is totally in keeping with the historical aims of the Festival.

Cricket lovers will find the atmosphere much more relaxed than, say, at a Test

The Scarborough Cricket team of 1874.

The Scarborough Cricket Festival
has attracted the greatest players of the day:
Jack Hobbs and Herbert Sutcliffe opening the innings
for the Players against the Gentlemen in the 1931 Festival.

Match or a Schweppes County Championship game. The Festival has been described as 'first class cricket on holiday' and this does to some extent sum up the whole event. The cricket is always first class, in both senses—this is after all, Yorkshire, but there is an end-of-season, sea-side informality about the Scarborough Festival that is quite unique.

The 100th Festival will take place in 1986 (ten years were lost during the two World Wars).

For further information regarding fixtures and tickets write to: The Secretary, Scarborough Cricket Club, North Marine Road, Scarborough (0723 65625).

Beagling

This is a sport much to be recommended if you have not been hunting before. It is the hunting of the hare with small hounds (fifteen to nineteen inches at the shoulder) by hunt staff on foot. Beagles are the most friendly and happy little animals—hence the nickname the merry beagles.

Much keen interest by the followers means that the expenses of keeping a pack of beagles can be kept down and so colleges, schools and the services have packs kept by students and serving officers.

Many famous Masters of Hounds have started off by hunting their school packs. Eton, Britain's most prestigious public school, has a pack of beagles whose history goes back to 1857. Captain Ronnie Wallace hunted the Eton beagles before going on to hunt famous packs of foxhounds, topping his career by hunting the Heythrop hounds for twenty-five seasons. He is now Joint-Master and Huntsman of the Exmoor Foxhounds. Alastair Jackson, a famous huntsman in the making, hunted the Marlborough College beagles before going to Cirencester Agricultural College and hunting their famous pack. He is now Joint-Master of the Grafton hounds.

What is so pleasant about beagling is that an enormous cross-section of people have the chance to become a Master. Many are of the landed gentry, but there is a publican in Dorset and a milkman in the Midlands, both of whom command much respect from the local community for what they do for hunting.

You will be told that a hare always runs in circles. Generally speaking this is true, but don't rely too much on this as many hares, especially in the spring, will run straight.

In beagling hunting etiquette is still observed, but to a lesser extent than in foxhunting. The Master is still called Master or Sir, and is in complete command. It should always be remembered that one is hunting at the invitation of the farmers so care must be taken to shut gates and not to damage fences. Dress is more informal; gym shoes and lightweight trousers are the best attire, but you

ABOVE
A meet of the Stowe beagles.

OPPOSITE
The Old Berkeley beagle pack.

The beagles of Eton College were established in 1857. Eton is one
of the great public schools, as is Marlborough College in
Wiltshire, with a strong tradition of beagling.

may have to stand around for a while, so a good, warm coat is always useful. At
the meet you will usually see three types of followers. There are the young, hard-
running enthusiasts. They will be hard on the heels of the hounds all day and at
the end will try to give the impression that they have done nothing. They are
nearly always non-smokers. The second type is a progression of the first. They
both smoke and drink and stay up late. Much speed and keenness is shown for the
first two fields, after which they tend to lean on a gate, light a pipe and take out
their hip-flasks. They are great fun to spend the day with and will put you right
for the best pubs in the area. The third type of beagler is the older, more mature
follower who seldom moves out of a walk. They have been beagling for years,
love their hunting and know exactly where to stand. They see nearly as much of
the sport as the huntsman and are generally happy to share their considerable
knowledge.

All hunting should be fun, but beagling—without the glamour of foxhunting or the challenge of riding across country—can give a wonderful insight into hound work and also a chance to meet the people.

Hunt staff generally wear green coats, white breeches and green stockings with good running shoes, but there are exceptions, such as Eton who wear brown velvet coats.

While talking of hunting the hare one should mention harriers. They are larger hounds and are hunted on horseback with a mounted field. Many packs of harriers now hunt foxes.

One of the most famous packs of harriers, which was started in 1745, is the Cambridgeshire. Mrs Hugh Ginyell has been Master and huntsman since 1942 and there is no greater lady to breed a harrier or a horse.

The other hounds used to hunt hares are bassets. Few have remained of the original type as deep plough makes it difficult for a long-bodied, heavily-boned dog on 4½-inch legs to cross country. Bassets have a marvellous, rich tone to their cry and are much slower than beagles, ideal for the less energetic who want to follow hounds.

It may be useful to know one or two of the terms used in hunting the hare. First, the hare, whether male or female, is always known as 'she' or 'puss'. When a hunted hare thinks she is well in front of hounds she will squat or lie down. It will pay to take binoculars out hunting as hares are very well camouflaged when squatting. Another rule when hare-hunting, and one which applies equally to all forms of hunting, is to stand very still if the hare is on foot near you. She won't take any notice of you if you don't move. It is a grand sight to have both hare and hounds not ten yards away from you at the height of a hunt. However, a hare will notice even the slightest movement from a long way off and give you a wide berth. Then you will probably be blamed for turning, or heading, her.

Beagling meets are advertised in the sporting and local press and you will be very welcome for they are all very friendly people. Indeed, you may be invited to a beagling tea afterwards by a friendly farmer and this is an experience not to be missed, so don't make any early evening dates that would make you miss it.

Further information may be obtained from the Honorary Secretary of the Masters of Beagles Association, Mr John Kirkpatrick, Fritham Lodge, Lyndhurst, Hampshire. The Honorary Secretary of the Master of Basset Hounds Association is Mr Rex Hudson, Yew Tree Cottage, Haselton, Cheltenham, Gloucestershire.

The Last Night of the Proms

The Henry Wood Promenade Concerts were inaugurated in 1895 and are now performed yearly in the Royal Albert Hall in Kensington between the middle of July and the middle of September. The 'Proms' have a particular appeal for the young because of the unique atmosphere of the concerts and because tickets are relatively inexpensive. An important part of Henry Wood's contribution was his introduction to the general public of the works of many relatively unknown composers as well as the great masters, and during the season the musical programme ranges from modern and classical opera to orchestral works and solo performances. It involves about thirty conductors leading fifteen orchestras and some two hundred singers in the circular hall which was opened in 1871 in memory of the Prince Consort.

The concerts first took place at the Queen's Hall in Langham Place with Henry Wood (later Sir Henry) as conductor. This remarkable man started conducting operas in 1889 at the age of twenty, and from the age of twenty-six in 1895 almost until his death in 1944 aged seventy-five he conducted his Promenade Concerts. When the Queen's Hall was destroyed in the blitz of 1941 they moved to the Royal Albert Hall and have continued uninterruptedly every year since.

The auditorium seats 5,600 people and, on the last night of the Proms at least, a great many more are packed into every available standing space as well. There is a strong tradition of audience participation, and the occasion of the last night is treated like a vast party with everyone throwing streamers, singing, and waving flags, banners, hats, umbrellas and anything they can lay their hands on. The climax of the evening comes when the orchestra plays the familiar strains of patriotic and traditional songs, notably 'Land of Hope and Glory', which are sung over and over again by the highly excitable audience.

Apart from the orchestra, who are in immaculate evening wear, dress is like the occasion itself, informal and relaxed.

Bookings should be made well in advance from The Box Office, The Henry Wood Promenade Concerts, The Royal Albert Hall, Kensington, London SW7 (01 589 8212), or it is possible to join the mailing list for tickets on application to the same address. A programme of the concerts is published each May and is widely obtainable from newsagents and tourist agencies, or direct from the Albert Hall.

ABOVE:
The Last Night of the Proms has a unique atmosphere of
informality and enjoyment in which the audience plays as much
a part as the performers.

OPPOSITE:
Sir Henry Wood, first conductor of the Promenade Concerts,
conducting in 1942, two years before his death. In 1941 the
original venue of the concerts, Queen's Hall in Langham Place,
had been destroyed by German bombs and they were immediately
moved to the Royal Albert Hall.

October

Capercaillie and Woodcock Shooting

The slight chill in the air and the turning of the leaves announce that the shooting season proper is about to start. On 1 October, the capercaillie and pheasant seasons open and woodcock may now be shot in England and Wales.

Of the three, the pheasant is by far the most important to the British shooting scene as it is the mainstay of most shoots. Although it can be shot in October, most shoots wait until the 'leaf is off the tree'—which usually means early November and therefore pheasant shooting will be discussed in that month's section.

Compared to the ubiquitous pheasant, the capercaillie is something of a rarity and was indeed extinct in Britain before its re-introduction in 1837. It has since flourished in certain coniferous areas in Scotland but there are still comparatively few sportsmen who have shot a capercaillie.

The largest member of the grouse family, the caper averages twelve pounds in weight although it can reach fifteen pounds. Usually driven, it is often missed, its size belying its speed, but if the sportsman gives it plenty of lead he should be rewarded by a most satisfying thud.

As they are found in specific areas, the best way of obtaining a caper is through a reputable sporting agency.

The woodcock is far more widespread. With its exquisite mottled plumage, large eyes and long bill, the woodcock is a most beautiful bird. It is also superb eating and is highly prized—so much so that perfectly safe guns can be dangerous when a 'cock appears.

Favouring sheltered, secluded places, they often appear on pheasant shoots but during hard weather they move south and westwards. Some shoots then receive a 'fall' of woodcock and they may be found in large numbers. Eventually they end up in Ireland, the West Country and some of the warmer Scottish and Channel Islands.

Their awkward bat-like flight and the excitement they engender make them difficult targets so that if the gun succeeds in taking a right-and-left he is entitled to membership of the exclusive Bols Snippen Club, established solely for those who have managed this feat.

If one is fortunate enough to shoot a woodcock, the pin feathers—the small feathers at the wing joint—can be placed in the gun's hatband, a mark of his achievement.

Nottingham Goose Fair

On the first Thursday, Friday and Saturday of October the Forest Recreation Ground in Nottingham is taken over by the remarkable event known as Goose Fair. People come from miles around to join in the fun on the eighteen-acre fairground, where traditional entertainments, games, stalls and sideshows compete with the helter-skelter, big wheels and merry-go-rounds to attract the crowds.

On the opening day at 12.00 noon sharp, the Lord Mayor of Nottingham, accompanied by the Sheriff and other dignitaries, rings a pair of silver bells after the reading of the Proclamation and the fair is declared open.

No one really knows how the fair came to be called Goose Fair, but it is possible that it was named after the old custom of selling geese for the Michaelmas feast, and very likely there was once a market for the geese of the surrounding countryside. The earliest known mention of Goose Fair dates from 1541 where there is a note about an allowance of 1s 10d for twenty-two stalls taken by the city's two Sheriffs on Goose Fair Day, but it is also known that in the thirteenth century a fair was commonly held on the Feast of St Matthew (September 21), the date on which, until 1752, Goose Fair was traditionally held.

Until the nineteenth century the fair was primarily a trading centre, although there would certainly have been sideshows and entertainments as well, but by the time the railways were established and dramatic social changes were taking place

The Nottingham Goose Fair of 1910, showing the first helter-skelter. At this time the Fair was still sited on the Great Market Place in the centre of Nottingham.

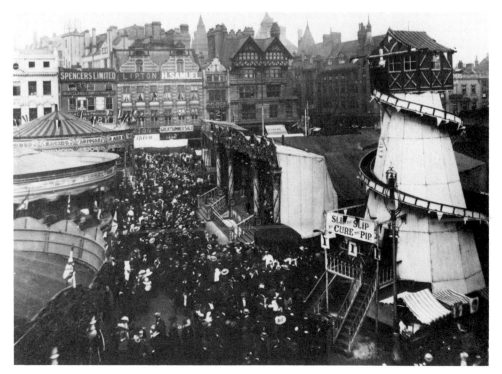

Part of the entertainment at Nottingham Goose Fair
—an actor giving a recitation.

as people became more mobile, and the movement of goods became easier, the fair lost its traditional *raison d'être* as an important part of the preparations for the hard winter ahead, when everyone stocked up with provisions and equipment. By the 1880s complicated mechanical amusements, and especially merry-go-rounds, were firmly established, many of them run by steam, and the fair's popularity as a place of entertainment grew every year, so much so that by the 1920s it had outgrown its original site on the Great Market Place and was moved to its present position about a mile away to the north. Today the advantages of being able to park the car, or use one of the shuttle buses from the city centre, make a day out at Goose Fair a thoroughly enjoyable experience. Further details about the arrangements for Goose Fair can be obtained from the Clerk of the Markets, Victoria Market Offices, Glasshouse Street, Nottingham (0602 417324).

Real Tennis and Rackets

There could be no more contrasting foundations for the British popularity of these two games whose governing body in England is the Tennis and Rackets Association, formed in 1907. Their origins, however, date from centuries earlier when one was the preserve of the nobility, the other of the poor.

More than six hundred years before modern (lawn) tennis was invented about one hundred and fifty years ago, only one game called tennis existed. But the modern version grew so popular that the older one, which originated in France, had, reluctantly, to distinguish itself as Real Tennis in the United Kingdom, Court Tennis in the United States and Royal Tennis in Australia.

In Britain, the game was popularized in the fifteenth and sixteenth centuries by the Tudor kings. Henry VII was a keen exponent and Henry VIII equipped all his palaces with tennis courts including two open and two covered ones at the Palace of Whitehall. None of these survives and the only open court existing in Britain today is the one built by James V at Falkland Palace in Scotland.

Meanwhile within easy reach of London is perhaps the most famous real-tennis court in the world and thought to be the oldest surviving purpose-built ball game court of any sort still in active play. This is the one at Hampton Court, built by Henry VIII in about 1530 and renovated during the reign of William and Mary. All courts are of slightly different dimensions but this royal court is the largest and with the two at The Queen's Club, London, rates as chief among the eighteen courts in Britain. To arrange to play there, which is done by contacting the resident professional Chris Ronaldson, a world champion who lives at Hampton Court Palace, East Molesey, Surrey (01 977 3015), is to step back in time to the days when the game figured prominently in the lives of English kings.

Shakespeare recorded their interest in several of his plays, as, for instance, the incident when the French Dauphin sent Henry V a set of tennis balls, implying that the recipient was more of a playboy than a statesman. The King replied:

When we have match'd our rackets to these balls,
We will in France, by God's grace, play a set
Shall strike his father's crown into the hazard.
Tell him he hath made a match with such a wrangler
That all the courts of France will be disturb'd
With chases.

These 'chases' are an integral feature of the game and give an advantage to skill over physical strength and to age and experience over youthful enthusiasm. They occur because the court floor is marked with 'chase lines' parallel to the end walls but varying at the serving and receiving end of the court. They constitute the main difference between real and lawn tennis. The scoring is similar but in the former a ball can bounce twice before it is returned and if it bounces in the parallel lines, 'makes a chase' when neither player scores. The point goes into cold storage to be played off either when one player has scored forty or when there are two chases in cold storage in the same game. Then the players change ends and play off the chases.

The nearer the chase is to the back wall the better and the player who made the

Prince James, Duke of York,
later King James II, playing real (or 'royal')
tennis in the mid-seventeenth century.

original chase must improve on it to win the point. The marker at the net names the chases as well as keeping the score.

Another difference between the two games is the court itself. A real-tennis court is a stone surface, rectangular in shape, surrounded by four high walls with a sloping roof around three sides at a height of about six feet. The ball is served and played off this sloping roof. On the receiving side the main wall projects into the court by about eighteen inches creating a vertical surface off which the ball may be played for unusual rebounds. The court is divided by a net five feet high at the ends dipping to three feet in the middle. The game is played with an asymmetrical racket and a set of nine dozen tennis balls. They are particularly hard and usually collect in a channel cut out of the floor along the length of the net. From time to time they are collected by the marker and tipped into an open channel at the serving end, called the Dedans.

In its sixteenth-century heyday, when the game was played throughout Europe by kings and courtiers, a less sophisticated form enjoyed by the general public was frequently banned by royal edict in favour of sports of more military value, like archery. But in royal circles it retained its popularity throughout the reign of the Stuarts and in the time of King Charles I the royal coach, John Webb, received a wage of £20 a year.

Today the professional still performs a vital role in a game that has retained its

A nineteenth-century game of rackets. Acknowledged to be the
fastest ball game in the world, the game has similarities to squash
but is played on a much larger court.

amateur status. Each club normally has its own professional or, in larger clubs, more than one. Apart from scoring and calling out the chases, he maintains the court, repairs the rackets and gives lessons in the game. His role is similar to that of a golf professional.

There are thirty-two real-tennis courts in the world and, in Britain, some of today's clubs are based at the courts built by Victorian noblemen when the game, which declined in popularity in Hanoverian times, regained favour. In the nineteenth century club courts were also built at Lord's in London, Manchester, Leamington, Oxford and Cambridge.

This minority sport is growing in popularity in Britain although at each of the two major venues for the main competitions and occasional international matches, The Queen's Club, London, and Hampton Court, there is room for less than two hundred spectators. The principal annual competitions in England include the Amateur, Professional and Open Singles and Doubles Championships and the Ladies' Doubles, Open and Handicap Singles. The World Championship is held on a challenge basis, like boxing, usually every eighteen months.

Details of all aspects of the sport and of rackets may be obtained from the Secretary of the Tennis and Rackets Association, c/o The Queen's Club, Palliser Road, London, W14 9EQ (01 381 4746).

But if real tennis was the sport of kings, rackets was first played in England in the mid-nineteenth century by their most humble subjects. Open courts existed in the backyards of inns and taverns but it was most popular among debtors in the Fleet and King's Bench prisons, as described by Charles Dickens in *The Pickwick Papers*:

> The area formed by the wall in that part of the Fleet which Mr Pickwick stood was just wide enough to make a good racket-court; one side being formed by the wall itself and the other by that portion of the prison which looked (or rather would be looked, but for the wall) towards St Paul's Cathedral.... Lolling from the windows which commanded a view of this promenade were a number of persons ... looking on at the racket-players.

Rackets—an extended form of squash—is played on a court about two-and-a-half times the size of a squash court and using an elongated squash racket. The ball, which is the size and texture of a golf ball, is probably the fastest moving ball used on any court. The two dozen rackets courts in the United Kingdom belong to public schools with the exception of one at The Queen's Club, the Manchester Tennis and Racquet Club, Seacourt Tennis Club at Hayling Island, and ones at Cambridge University, the Dartmouth Naval College and the Sandhurst Military Academy.

There are also flourishing rackets clubs: the Clifton Boasters, the Harrow Thursday Club and the Wykeham Rackets Club which use the school courts at Clifton, Harrow and Winchester respectively. Any adult wishing to take up the game should write to one of the Secretaries c/o the school concerned.

Most major British racket events take place at The Queen's Club but the World Championship, dating from 1820, is fought on an irregular basis when the reigning title holder accepts a challenge. Decades have passed, however, with hardly a tilt at the title and the World Challenge Trophy introduced by the Tennis and Rackets Association. This was to commemorate the remarkable seventeen-year reign of the longest title holder, Geoffrey Atkins, who retired in 1971.

Ironically, only modern technology has saved the historic game of rackets from extinction. In 1950 the original type of hand-made ball with a stitch-on cover of kid leather was out of production and remaining stocks were dwindling. However, experiments with a ball built round a moulded polythene core were successful and a new type of ball was produced comparatively cheaply in large quantities which made the game even faster and truer. It is estimated that the ball travels at speeds of up to 140 miles per hour in the acknowledged fastest ball game in the world.

The Horse of the Year Show

Held annually at Wembley during the first week of October the Horse of the Year Show has very much an end of term feel. In the past this show marked the end of the show season, but now there is an extensive winter circuit at home and on the Continent which many of our leading show-jumpers follow. For riders of animals in show classes the Horse of the Year Show still marks the end of their season.

Although by tradition this is our British Horse of the Year Show there are always famous foreign show-jumpers visiting. Throughout the season there are qualifying rounds for finals to be held at the Horse of the Year Show. Most of these qualifiers are held at county shows throughout the summer months and it is for this reason that several virtual 'unknowns' appear at the Horse of the Year Show.

An impressive display of working
horses in the Horse of the Year Show
at the Empire Pool, Wembley.

The Show runs from the Monday through to Saturday and during the week the marvellous versatility of the horse becomes clear, both as marvellous entertainment and as a unique partnership with its rider when it can achieve remarkable feats of strength, co-ordination and skill. The first night traditionally is gala night in aid of charities such as the Army Benevolent Fund, Riding for the Disabled and the Injured Jockeys' Fund. On the first night the Jockeys' and Jumpers' Relay between leading show-jumpers and jockeys provides a good curtain raiser.

This is a very well balanced show, staging events which cover most equestrian disciplines. Events start very early in the morning, sometimes as early as 7.0 am, and can finish as late as 11.0 pm. During the early part of the day preliminary rounds take place for trials to be staged in the matinee or evening performances.

Although the majority of events are held at Wembley the dressage events are held at Park Farm, Northwood, Middlesex. In some classes at Wembley an outdoor arena is used for parts of the competition. The turnout and dressage of the Police Horse of the Year and the Shire Horse of the Year are all judged outside.

As the week progresses the tension increases and the prize money in the jumping classes increases to the conclusion of the show, the Radio Rentals Grand Prix, held on the Saturday evening.

The show-jumping week is busy for both experienced and novice horses. The Foxhunter Championship, named after that great horse of Colonel Sir Harry Llewellyn's, takes place on the Tuesday night. This competition is for novice horses which have qualified at shows of varying sizes up and down the country. For the internationals there are many competitions to be fought, although the leading show-jumper of the year is restricted to national riders only. One of the crowd's favourite competitions is the Puissance held on the Thursday evening where the fearsome wall can rise to over seven feet. In the last rounds of this competition only a spread fence and the mighty wall are left in the ring. A special kind of horse with a big, bold jump is needed in this competition which really captures the imagination of the audience.

The juniors have their own 'Junior Show Jumper of the Year' competition which is always interesting to watch. It seems incredible to see ponies jumping such large fences. These juniors are the stars of tomorrow in the making and most will switch to horses when they are sixteen years old.

The show classes reach their conclusion at the Horse of the Year Show. On Wednesday it is 'Pony Day' with the Pony of the Year being selected. On Thursday the hunters have their chance as do the shire horses. Friday is hack day and also the final of the Lloyds Bank In-Hand Competition for led horses.

The Police Horses of the Year always attract attention as after doing a dressage test the horse has to enter the main arena and negotiate some hazards, which can be surprising, but represent typical disturbances such as football hooligans, flapping sheets, carol singers and the like. These highly trained horses rarely mind any of them.

The Pony Club Mounted Games take place all week with the championship on the Saturday. These children have been successful in area finals all around the country to qualify for Wembley and represent Pony Clubs throughout Great Britain. Most children are mounted on small Welsh ponies and the whole event is highly entertaining, especially when a pony takes a violent dislike to one of the games. The standard of the games is exceptionally high and these children ride very well.

Another feature of the Horse of the Year Show is the shire horses. These 'gentle giants' come into the ring between classes to rake the arena ready for the next class.

The Scurry Drivers also seem to capture the imagination of the audience. Scurry Driving is a competition where teams of two ponies, usually very small, negotiate a timed obstacle course. There are some real thrills and spills and the excitement in this event, both for the competitors and the spectators, can reach fever pitch.

A popular feature for matinee audiences at Wembley is the Riding Club Quadrille. Clubs qualify for Wembley throughout the summer and this event is for teams of four horses. A quadrille, which is a display enhanced by various costumes, provides a colourful spectacle.

Another popular feature of the show is the Personalities Parade which may contain Olympic Medal Winners, world champions, Grand National winners and other famous horses. This event is held nightly before the interval. Each personality in the parade has his own signature tune played when he enters the ring, and over the years some very clever tunes have been thought up. 'Strolling' was an obvious choice for Stroller, Marian Mould's phenomenal jumping pony of the '60s and '70s, whereas former top show-jumper Merely a Monach earned 'If I ruled the World'.

On the last night the final event at the close of the show is the Cavalcade, where every discipline and facet of the equine world is represented in a united tribute to the horse.

The trumpeters of the Household Cavalry enter the arena in darkness and are suddenly illuminated by the spotlights in the centre of the arena. They take up their places at the entrance, making a gateway, and blow a fanfare. Each group is announced and then enters to its own music.

When everyone is assembled in the ring the star of the Cavalcade takes his place in the centre of the ring. This may be the winner of an important championship, a famous racehorse or a victorious team.

When the Cavalcade is complete as many as 120 horses may be in the ring and at this moment we pay our special tribute to the horse in the words of Ronald Duneran:

Where in this wide world can man find
nobility without pride, friendship without envy,
or beauty without vanity? Here, where grace is
laced with muscle and strength by gentleness confined.
He serves without servility, he has fought
without enmity. There is nothing so quick,
nothing more patient.
England's past has been borne on his back.
Our history is his industry. We are his heirs,
he our inheritance.
THE HORSE!

The Horse of the Year Show, which started in 1948, provides a view of equestrianism at its best in this country. During the evening performances it is possible to dine in the restaurant whilst watching the events in the main ring. Over the years facilities have improved somewhat, although the grooms have to work long hours, often by torchlight in the dark stable area. A 'rover' ticket has recently been introduced which admits the bearer to all areas of the show, thus eliminating the rather closed-in feeling that an indoor show can give. Purchased in advance only, these tickets have certainly proved very popular.

Trade stands can be found at the Horse of the Year Show in abundance and it is most enjoyable browsing through them while stretching your legs after a dose of the hard Wembley seating.

Members of the Royal Family are often to be seen at the Horse of the Year Show where Princess Anne and Captain Mark Phillips have competed. The best tickets, particularly around the Royal Box, sell out quickly, so an early application is advised. Tickets are obtainable from The Horse of the Year Show Box Office, Empire Pool, Wembley, Middlesex (01 902 1234).

The State Opening of Parliament

Since the sixteenth century the ritual of the State Opening of Parliament by the Monarch and the reading of the Gracious Speech from the Throne has taken place almost unchanged, and has become an essential part of the ritual of government. Since Guy Fawkes's unsuccessful Gunpowder Plot of 1605 the vaults under the Houses of Parliament have been searched the night before by Yeomen of the Guard, the Beefeaters of the Tower of London.

The Houses of Parliament were built on the site of the mediaeval Palace of Westminster which, with the exception of the still standing Westminster Hall, was burnt down in 1834. Rebuilt by Sir Charles Barry and Augustus Pugin it contains the two 'houses' or chambers—the House of Lords and the House of Commons—as well as that symbol of the nation, Big Ben.

For the State Opening of the new Parliament each year at the end of October or the beginning of November The Queen rides in the Irish State Coach from Buckingham Palace down the Mall and Whitehall. She enters the Houses of Parliament at the Royal Entrance under the Victoria Tower and goes in to her Robing Room, where she puts on her Royal Robes and the Imperial State Crown before proceeding through the Royal Gallery to the House of Lords. When she has ascended the Throne members of the House of Commons are summoned by Black Rod to the Bar of the House to listen to the Speech, which outlines the Government's plans for the coming Parliament. (Black Rod's part in the ritual is an interesting one, dating at least from the reign of Charles I. When he reaches the door to the House of Commons it is slammed in his face and he has to knock loudly on it three times before it is opened again. This ceremony signifies the Commons' independence from the Sovereign.)

The only way for a member of the public to attend the State Opening is as the guest of a peer in the Strangers' Gallery overlooking the Chamber of the House of Lords, but failing that it is still worth braving the crowds to watch the procession making its stately way to the seat of government.

The Queen reading the Gracious Speech at the State
Opening of Parliament. The Duke of Edinburgh sits in
the second throne and the Prince and Princess of Wales
on her right. On Prince Philip's left is Princess Anne,
with Captain Mark Phillips standing beside her.

Troopers of the Household Cavalry
arriving at Westminster in the procession
to the State Opening of Parliament.

November

Pheasant Shooting

Many shoots will now be holding their first pheasant days. First recorded in Britain in 1059, the pheasant has since thrived and the wild stock has been greatly supplemented by reared birds so that it is found on nearly every shoot. These vary greatly, from the small rough shoot where maybe five birds are shot in a day, to the big organized days where as many as four hundred may be put in the game-larder. Those new to the sport should be able to find something that exactly suits their tastes and pocket.

Most shoots are now syndicated, the guns sharing the rent and rearing costs. A good syndicate provides good sport and company but the newcomer should carefully inspect the ground and the game records before committing himself; a shoot that seems to have a high turnover of guns should be approached cautiously. Similar precautions should be taken if a single day is bought.

Having secured his shooting the gun should ensure that he arrives in good time. If the birds are to be driven, pegs will be drawn. These determine where the guns stand during the drives and the new gun should make sure he knows where he is supposed to be. On a strange shoot it is as well to also check whether the drives' beginning and end will be signalled and whether the host will wish vermin and ground game to be shot.

Edwardian beaters bringing up the refreshments
on a great shooting estate.

If the gun owns a dog he should ensure that it will be welcome and that it is good enough. On some rough shoots the cover is so thick that almost any dog is an asset, but on driven days there are usually pickers-up with very good dogs and guns' dogs are not necessary. There are few people more unpopular on a shoot than a gun whose dog is wild and spoils others' sport.

Not all shoots can show consistently high birds and the low ones must be left. Killing birds a few yards up is not clever, although some shooters appear to enjoy shooting large numbers of very easy birds. Low shots should specially never be taken in front; the beating line may be close but hidden by the cover.

Although shoots are sometimes very formal, the gun should try to relax— tension is detrimental to good shooting. If pegs are well spaced and birds are plentiful, it is best to take the first bird well out in front, leaving plenty of time for the second barrel. This is far easier than taking birds behind. On smaller shoots, particularly if pegs are close, the gun would do better to wait until birds are overhead and definitely his. In these circumstances, taking birds well in front can be very close to poaching neighbouring guns' birds and perhaps their only shot of the drive.

The gun is only a part of the whole shooting operation and he should always consider those working for his sport. Birds should be accurately marked for the pickers-up, pricked birds especially. Undue lingering over lunch may allow one more glass of port but the beaters have probably walked through wet crops and would like to press on. Keepers should be thanked and tipped if the sport has been good.

ABOVE:
Autumn pheasant shooting is still highly organized. Pheasant populations are kept at a high level
by reared birds, although the wild bird thrives in spite of the spread of urbanization and modern
farming methods.

OPPOSITE: A pheasant shoot of 1911 at Stonor Park, Henley-on-Thames.

Foxhunting

Although hunting takes place in most rural areas of the British Isles there are certain districts particularly renowned for foxhunting. The Shires of England are famous the world over in hunting circles, for they house most of the fashionable packs.

The Shires, well-known for their old turf, jumping and consistently good sport, are regarded by many as being the centre of foxhunting. Many of the fashionable hunts based here have interesting histories with people in the public eye both past and present figuring in their stories.

Many regard the Monday and Friday countries of the Quorn as the smartest place to hunt in Britain. The Quorn country is in Leicestershire, with some country in Derbyshire and Nottinghamshire. Although hunting takes place on four days a week, the Monday and Friday country is the most popular with an average mounted field of 170.

Hugo Meynell is reputed to have started the pack in its present form in 1753, although a Mr Boothby had been Master since 1698. The famous 'Squire' Osbaldeston was Master from 1813 to 1821 and the list of Quorn Masters is full of the names of rich and famous men and women from England's heartland. In modern times the Quorn has had a professional huntsman and, today, Michael Farrin is well aware of the great men who have preceded him, men like Tom Firr, Walter Wilson and George Barker. Even as late as Barker's term of office (1929–59) the huntsman had his own gardener and, as the bell-board in his house gives evidence, his own household staff.

On Tuesdays and Saturdays the mounted field will be about eighty. Also in Leicestershire, but with some good country in Lincolnshire, the Belvoir (pronounced 'Beever') offer good sport. Kennelled at Belvoir Castle, this was the private pack of the Dukes of Rutland from 1750 until 1896. These hounds, darker in colour than other foxhounds, are the foundations of foxhounds the world over.

Although the Quorn and the Belvoir are, in many people's view, the most fashionable packs, the Berkeley in Gloucestershire have had a great influence on hound breeding although they have never shown at Peterborough. At one time their country stretched from Bristol to Charing Cross. Today their country is in Gloucestershire.

Next door to the Berkeley is the Duke of Beaufort's. Since its formation the pack has been under the Mastership of the successive Dukes, and today the 10th Duke is still Master of these hounds. Now in his eighties, he hunted his own hounds for forty-seven seasons and has contributed much to hound breeding. 'Master' is the longest serving Master of Hounds in the country, having taken office when his father died in 1924. The hounds are still kennelled at Badminton, the home of the Dukes of Beaufort.

The Beaufort country, situated in Gloucestershire, Avon and Wiltshire has some distinguished residents. The Prince and Princess of Wales, Princess Anne and Captain Mark Phillips and Prince and Princess Michael of Kent all live in the country and can sometimes be seen following hounds. The Prince of Wales is a keen foxhunter and hunts with different packs all over Great Britain. He keeps some horses at Melton Mowbray.

The Flint and Denbigh Hunt in the Welsh hills.

The Beaufort hunt servants wear the traditional green livery. The blue coat with blue collar and buff facings is a much sought-after honour and may be worn only at the invitation of the Duke and Duchess of Beaufort.

The Williams-Wynn family have maintained one of the most sporting packs on the Welsh Borders since 1749 when the first Sir Watkin Williams-Wynn was killed out hunting. It is, today, one of the very few packs not troubled by corn or plough and is a must for any sporting tour.

Although it is difficult to define a fashionable pack, each area will have some packs that by tradition are regarded as more popular than their neighbours. It is worth remembering that visits can only be made to any pack by arrangement with the Secretary, as the number of strangers is always strictly limited.

Not only is hunting a most enjoyable pastime for all concerned—except perhaps the fox!—but it opens up a whole new sphere of social events for hunting people and their associates.

The most notable function to swell hunt funds is the hunt ball. In most cases this will be held at a large country house with connections with the hunt or at a hotel. The hunt ball is normally held during the hunting season, but this is not always the case.

Traditionally both supper and breakfast are served at a hunt ball, but nowadays this is not always done. Again, tradition indicates that the ball starts around 10 pm and finishes about 3 am. Parties arrive after private dinners beforehand, and many will not turn up before midnight.

The dress at hunt balls is always smart. Ladies appear immaculately dressed and their escorts may be wearing white ties, although dinner jackets are generally accepted nowadays. The whole scene will be made more colourful by members wearing the evening dress of their hunt, usually a scarlet tail coat.

There are many stories of the mischief that the young bucks get up to, but no doubt some are exaggerated. There was a dance in Dorset some years ago which got a little out of hand and, during the early hours of the morning, some younger members totally redesigned the garden. The rose garden was removed to the lawn, the cabbages, sprouts and other movable vegetables were replanted in the rose garden. Like most pranks it was not received as a total success, but it caused a lot of confusion when 'taking the air in the rose walk'.

Hotels, naturally enough, lack a sense of humour when hunt balls get out of hand and a rather smart hotelier in Kent was not amused when some young hunting men let loose nine piglets in his ballroom. If you have ever tried to catch eight-week-old piglets under tables laden with food and drink and with ladies' long dresses getting in the way you can imagine the chaos. Those are the exceptions as most hunt balls are elegant, rather grand and extremely enjoyable.

The people attending the ball will mostly be people connected with the hunt, although a proportion will come from neighbouring hunts and there will be some who have no connection with hunting or the country life.

Like most organizations hunts are short of money today and organize all kinds of events to raise funds. Efforts are twofold—to raise money and to act as a medium whereby supporters can meet socially. Throughout the season film shows, skittles matches, quizzes and a host of other events will be organized and are well worth attending. Most, if not all these events are organized by the Hunt Supporters' Club, an organization mainly composed of people who follow

The opening meet of the Old Berkeley Pack at Shardeloes,
near Amersham in Buckinghamshire, in 1929.

hounds on foot or in a car. The Supporters' Clubs also organize dances during the season. In many hunts a dance will be held the night before the opening meet, which gives members and supporters the chance to get together before the serious business of the following day.

To a lesser extent the terrier show, the horse trials and the point-to-point can be classed as social events. None of these sets out to be a social function as such, but to anyone new in a hunting country they provide an opportunity to meet the hunting people in the area. Help is always needed, particularly at the Hunter Trials, where jump judges are always wanted.

It is worth remembering that the foot packs (beagles, bassets, mink hounds) also have social events throughout the year and in most cases will hold a ball or dinner.

For details of all events in the area the Hunt Secretary is the person to contact and he or she will be able to put you in touch with the secretary of the Supporters' Club. Most Supporters' Clubs have a regular newsletter which is circulated to their members and which provides information about local events.

Normally the opening meet takes place on the Saturday nearest to 1 November. Hounds will generally meet at 11 am. This is the first day of proper

The Cheshire Hunt sets out on a winter's morning.

The Duke of Beaufort, Britain's premier Master of Foxhounds,
who has been in office since 1924.

hunting. From today a full subscription or cap will be expected. Horses' manes are plaited up and riders should be in correct hunting dress.

Ladies should wear a bowler hat, black hunting coat and breeches (white or buff), hairnet and white hunting tie. A hunting whip should be carried but never used except for opening gates and keeping hounds away from the horse's legs. Ladies may wear a hunting cap with the permission of their Master of Hounds as this is really the privilege of farmers and their wives and ex-Masters of Hounds. Men should not wear scarlet as this is a much coveted privilege and is worn only by those who have been given the Hunt button. Ladies who ride sidesaddle should wear a well-cut blue or black habit with a silk hat and a veil. Men should wear a black hunting coat with a top hat or a bowler.

As a visitor you should introduce yourself to the Master at the meet and pay

The Pytchley Hunt Ball of 1844.

your cap and field money. Always remember that the Master is in complete command. Don't overtake the Field Master and *don't* allow your horse to kick hounds. Always turn his head towards them. At the end of the day thank the hunt staff (a financial reward for a good day is much appreciated). If a fox is killed and you are given a pad or brush by the Master it is customary to tip the huntsman.

Remember that most packs pick their best country for the opening meet and you will probably have to ride hard. It pays to fall in behind a regular follower as he will know which way to go, but don't ride in his pocket. If you get left behind don't worry. Country people are always about on a hunting day and can be most helpful.

Although surrounded with tradition, hunting in Great Britain is great fun and you will meet a large cross-section of both town and country society.

Much fun can be had by following hounds on foot. By a combination of judicious walking and driving your car you can see the country, meet the people, and stay reasonably warm without the expense of hiring a horse and so on.

Foot following is a skill all on its own and, badly done, can not only cause much frustration to yourself, but a great deal of damage to the Hunt. Always remember that the order of hunting is quarry first, then hounds, huntsman, Master, mounted field, foot followers. Please be careful not to head the fox by over enthusiastic driving and always turn off the engine of your car when hounds are near.

You will be asked to contribute what you feel you can give at the meet and it is a good idea to ask whom to follow. A good guide is invaluable. You will see more and be less liable to incur the wrath of the Master by making a mistake.

Do remember that the cardinal rule for the field also applies to car followers— gates must be shut and never blocked by a car.

The Lord Mayor's Show

The Lord Mayor's Show is held by Act of Parliament on the second Saturday in November and progresses from the Guildhall in the City to the Royal Courts of Justice in the Strand where the Lord Mayor is sworn in before the Lord Chief Justice and the Judges of the Queen's Bench Division. It has developed from the traditional journey of the mayor, who was elected by the people, from the City to the Court at Westminster to be presented to the king and swear fealty to him. Since 1546 the election of the mayor has taken place on Michaelmas Day (29 September).

The first mayor of London was Henry Fitz Ailwyn in the thirteenth century under King John. London's citizens had supported John in his power struggle against his brother Richard I and when he became King, John rewarded the city by granting it the right to set up a 'commune' along the lines of similar sworn associations of townspeople on the Continent. Later in his reign Magna Carta confirmed the right of the citizens of London to choose their own mayor at an annual election, provided that the mayor was approved by the king and swore fealty to him. In the Middle Ages all the processions were on horseback along the Strand, which in those days was a country road with the great mansions of the nobles on either side, or by boat on the River Thames from London Bridge to Westminster and back via Blackfriar's Bridge. (The most famous Lord Mayor of the Middle Ages was Dick Whittington who held office three times in the early fifteenth century.) By the sixteenth century the procession had taken on certain aspects of pageantry with allegorical plays and speeches organized by the Livery Companies (originally the City Guilds). The Elizabethan pageants were very lively and attracted much interest but by the early eighteenth century they had lost much of their excitement and imagination, and it was not until Victoria was on the throne that the processions once more became colourful spectacles drawing crowds of onlookers.

Since 1756, attended by his bodyguard of pikemen and musketeers, the Lord Mayor has ridden in the marvellous coach so well known today, with elaborate painted panels on the sides (all the paintings are attributed to Cipriani). It weighs well over four tons and until 1951 had no brakes at all. It still has no springs, but is suspended from the wheels on leather braces which cause it to creak and sway ominously as it makes its ponderous way through the streets. During the nineteenth century the main companies and organizations connected with the City arranged mobile tableaux and floats illustrating their particular crafts or businesses, and this developed into the present-day pageant which always has a theme linking the various tableaux. The streets from the Guildhall to the Courts

OPPOSITE ABOVE:
The Lord Mayor's Procession of 1787
up the River Thames to Westminster.

OPPOSITE BELOW:
The Lord Mayor's state coach, which weighs over four tons and
is ornately gilded and decorated with painted side panels. It dates
from 1756.

A 'beefeater' on ceremonial guard at the Guildhall
for the Lord Mayor's Show.

of Justice are lined with spectators, and all the windows in buildings along the route are filled with people cheering and waving. It is as well to arrive in good time on the Saturday morning.

The Lord Mayor's Show is the culmination of the traditional ceremonial of the City, but throughout the year the Livery Companies still keep their rituals and have formal dinners for members and guests. On the Monday after his Show the Lord Mayor holds a banquet in the Guildhall for VIPs and the civic dignitaries of the City of London, some of whom can invite private guests. It is usually attended by the Prime Minister and the Archbishop of Canterbury. Unlike the Livery dinners (with the exception of a few special occasions) women can attend the Lord Mayor's Banquet, and at all these dinners dress is formal.

A Victorian Guildhall Banquet.

The Eton Wall Game

The extraordinary Wall Game which is unique to Eton College is played once a year on the Saturday nearest to St Andrew's Day at the end of November. It is played on a field with a wall at the side and one end, in which is a door acting as one of the goals. A tree at the opposite end represents the other goal. The two sides are taken from the College (boys with scholarships) and the Oppidans (fee-paying pupils), and the game consists almost entirely of a rugger-like scrum (called a bully) which, usually unsuccessfully, tries to propel itself and the ball along the wall to the goals. The end result is seldom a goal, but always two teams of boys so mud-covered as to be almost totally unrecognizable.

It is a remarkable spectacle, and to the uninitiated possibly incomprehensible, but this odd event is not untypical of the strange traditions still alive in the great public schools of Britain.

OPPOSITE:
It is impossible for the players in the Eton Wall Game to avoid being covered in mud to the point at which they are unrecognizable. There is rarely a clear-cut winner, or even any goals at all.

BELOW:
The wall against which the Eton Wall Game is played on St Andrew's Day. It provides a useful vantage point for spectators.

The RAC London to Brighton Veteran Car Run

The Veteran Car Run from Hyde Park Corner in London to Madeira Drive on the seafront at Brighton has been organized by the Royal Automobile Club yearly since 1930. It has its roots in the Act of Parliament of 1865 which required a man walking on foot and holding a red flag to precede all motor vehicles. This obviously restricted the speed of that new toy of the rich, the automobile, to a frustrating four miles an hour, and it was not until more than thirty years later that matters improved. On 14 November, 1896—to be known ever after as 'Emancipation Day'—the Act was repealed and a new speed limit of twelve miles per hour was set.

On that day, a procession of thirty-two horseless carriages made the first historic run in celebration of their newly found freedom.

The next milestone came in 1927 when the *Daily Sketch* organized an 'Old Crocks' Run' to commemorate the 1896 event. The interest this generated prompted the RAC to take over the organization on a permanent basis and shortly afterwards the Veteran Car Club was formed—the first of its kind in the world. To be accepted for membership a car had to be built before 31 December 1904, and this remains the qualifying date to this day.

In recent years the number of entries has had to be restricted to three hundred because so many cars have been rescued from oblivion and rebuilt, and they are all lovingly maintained in a remarkable state of repair that could be envied by owners of cars an eighth of their age. Nor is the restoration of these stylish machines purely cosmetic; over ninety per cent make the sixty-mile run successfully.

It should be stressed that the event is not a race, and it is one of the few 'competitive' occasions when it really is enough to have taken part. Each year the start (at eight o'clock in the morning) is brightened by the elegant dress sported by the drivers and their companions, with the ladies bringing to life Victorian and Edwardian fashion plates in veils, hats and scarves, last seen before the Great War.

The journey can have its hazards, not least being the heavy (modern) traffic and spectators lining the route. Many of the cars have little in the way of brakes and some of the engines are only just powerful enough to negotiate the hills.

As the cars arrive in Brighton throughout the afternoon they are welcomed with much noisy applause and their drivers make their way to wherever they will be spending the night (most people will stay overnight in Brighton) to prepare for the Ball in the evening when awards are presented to successful drivers.

The start at Hyde Park Corner or the finish on Madeira Drive are the best times to watch the run but it is of course much more crowded than on the road between, when a clear view can be guaranteed. Cars reach Brighton from about noon onwards, and so long as they arrive by four o'clock in the afternoon those completing the run qualify for a small commemorative award. The route goes through the suburbs of South London and the commuter lands of Surrey, past Gatwick Airport and into the Downs of Sussex and the Regency town of Brighton.

The Veteran Car Run is a delightful spectacle worth risking the unreliable November weather to see.

Competitors in the Royal Automobile Club London to Brighton Veteran Car Run reach Westminster Bridge soon after the start from Hyde Park Corner.

December

Tattersalls December Sales at Newmarket

The elegant showing ring at Tattersalls in Newmarket, where the cream of racing bloodstock is bought and sold in the December sales.

Tattersalls December sales are generally regarded as the best European outlet for English, Irish and French bloodstock. Held from Monday to Thursday in the first week of December at Newmarket, the home of the British racing industry, otherwise known as the 'Headquarters', Tattersalls sales attract buyers from all over the world to this delightful part of Suffolk.

Horse breeding is an important industry in Great Britain. Every breeder will undoubtedly try to breed a Derby winner, which is a most expensive business, but the average breeder will almost certainly aim to breed a dual-purpose horse that could run on the flat or go hurdling and steeplechasing later on. Many horses which reach the sale ring in the autumn and winter as three- or four-year-olds will often be the horses which cannot continue to survive solely as flat race horses and will reappear as hurdlers and National Hunt horses.

Horses bred with the intention of becoming flat horses will be well 'fed up' in the early stages of their lives, whereas prospective steeplechasers will usually be given more time to mature as they are generally bigger, heavier thoroughbreds than their flat counterparts. Of course there is the exception to every rule as the great Aintree conqueror, Red Rum, ran on the flat as a two- and three-year-old before switching to the winter game.

The December sales always provide a mixed collection of horses. It is quite usual to find horses of all kinds here and of all prices. At the 1982 sales a horse called Tenea became Europe's first to pass the million guineas barrier. At the other end of the scale there were horses changing hands for just a few hundred pounds.

Most of the buying is done by bloodstock agencies buying on behalf of clients. It is quite usual for horses from these sales to be sold to buyers from Australia, Brazil, Belgium, France, Germany, India, Ireland, Italy, Japan, South Africa, Spain, Sweden, Trinidad, Turkey and the United States.

Whether as a prospective buyer, seller or just an onlooker Tattersalls sales are an interesting part of British life. The duels that emerge when two bidders are trying to purchase the same horse, although tense, are most entertaining.

A very assorted collection of people can be found at these sales. Shipping magnates, oil tycoons and businessmen are in abundance and to add up the total assets of some of the bidders would be quite enlightening. The majority of prospective purchasers will be accompanied by trainers, who as well as concentrating on the task in hand will always be trying to pick up a bargain horse.

These four-day sales offer on average about 250 lots a day. At this time of year it is the younger horses and prospective brood mares that usually sell best.

As well as various studs which have a steady stream of horses to sell, horses appear from small private breeders and have often been beautifully produced. Many of the horses intended for flat racing will be bought for syndicates as the price of good prospective flat horses today is so high. It is now becoming more common to find syndicated horses in National Hunt racing thereby allowing people to enjoy owning a horse in partnership with others.

Another reason for the high price which potential flat horses fetch at sales is that after their racing days their stud value will be almost immeasurable. At the other end of the scale most National Hunt horses are geldings, and therefore have no stud value. When Red Rum won his third Grand National he would have been worth no more at the end of the day in real terms.

A view of Tattersalls sales by Gustav Doré.

Horse sales can be a most confusing business to the uninitiated. If you want to buy a racehorse the best recipe for success is to follow these simple rules:

1. Select a trainer.
2. Jointly with your trainer decide what sort of horse you want.
3. Rely on your trainer's knowledge to select a suitable horse.
4. Decide how much you can afford.
5. Do not get carried away during the bidding. In all probability a bloodstock agent will be acting for you which is certainly the best plan.

In selecting a horse the pedigree is all-important and a trainer's knowledge of this is invaluable.

The Tattersall's December sales are a very important and somewhat quaint part of racing heritage and certainly worth a visit by anyone interested in the racing and bloodstock industries.

The Royal Smithfield Show

Every year in the first week of December the Country comes to Town. The impact of the Royal Smithfield Show is felt well beyond the Earls Court Exhibition Centre where it is held. Rosy-faced stockmen and farmers in their country tweeds can be seen in groups, cheerfully losing their way in the Underground or piling into taxis en route to the many conferences and social events that surround this six-day annual event which is the biggest indoor international shop window for British agriculture for livestock and machinery.

It is both an educational and a social occasion. Hotels are booked up from year to year and remember to lay on an extra number of large breakfasts. In the theatres, comedians introduce appropriate jokes and innuendoes into their act, applicable to the farmers and their wives in the audience. For the wives are there; not necessarily at the Show itself but for thousands of them this week constitutes the pre-Christmas shopping spree they would hate to miss.

The National Show, as it was originally called, was first held in December 1799 at Wooton's Livery Stables in London's twelfth-century famous 'Smooth-field' Market and it therefore links contemporary agriculture with an England engaged in war with Napoleonic France and in the industrial and agricultural revolution. It was the time when Robert Bakewell of Leicestershire had changed the mediaeval sheep that looked like goats crossed with dogs to animals more like the woolly creatures of today, and the time when new grasses and root crops meant that cattle could survive the winter to replace the dreariness of salted winter beef. Only two years before the first National Show a wife, according to a lithograph, was sold there 'with ten pounds worth of bad half pence', for half a guinea.

In other respects Smooth-field, or Smithfield, Market was, in pre-National Show days, not associated purely with livestock or agriculture. It was a place of public executions and burning at the stake, conducted alongside archery tournaments and other forms of public entertainment. In the mid-fifteenth century two hundred people were burnt there for their religious beliefs in the space of four years.

In the early nineteenth century the National Show moved to various sites in Smithfield Market and had become a popular annual event, growing in size each

Judging for the champion bull at the Royal Smithfield Show.

year, especially with the introduction of farm machinery in 1806, and later with carcass classes.

By 1840 it was established in the Horse Bazaar in 'the green suburbs of Portman Square' and was visited by Albert, the Prince Consort. From that moment it became an obligatory event in the calendar for leaders of society and agriculture and in 1844 Queen Victoria, escorted by Prince Albert, arrived at two day's notice with 'a long train of German princeling cousins'. There was just time to order a crimson carpet and arrange for a duke and some earls to greet the royal party. The Queen was so impressed by one of her husband's exhibits, 'a black polled ox of the Scottish breed', that she bought it to prevent it from being butchered.

The opportunity of seeing prize cattle, sheep and pigs judged 'on the hoof' after being groomed like beauty queens for months before by their devoted stockmen and trained to walk round the ring to catch the judges' eye, then seeing them again judged 'on the hook' after their journey to nearby abattoirs, is a feature of the Royal Smithfield Show. Housewives are particularly interested in the continuous displays and commentaries on the best cuts of meat to be used for various occasions.

There are also constant displays of various aspects of farming and well-organized and ingenious competitions and demonstrations for children.

Like some of the best British institutions it all developed gradually. In 1862 the show had expanded so much that a permanent home was built for it, the Royal Agricultural Hall in Islington, London, where it was run entirely by the Royal Smithfield Club and was eventually called the Royal Smithfield Show. Manufacturers of agricultural implements and seed suppliers took an increasing number of stands.

The steady growth of farm mechanization and agriculture in general meant that by 1949 a far bigger site was needed and in conjunction with the Agricultural Engineer's Association and the Society of Motor Manufacturers and Traders it moved to Earls Court and signed a lease ensuring that there it will remain until its two hundredth birthday in 1999.

Attendance has reached more than eighty thousand visitors a year including more than six thousand trade visitors from overseas who are admitted free of charge. They come from all over the world and in particular there are large contingents from Norway, Denmark, Germany, Ireland and Switzerland.

For anyone whose business is involved with agriculture Sunday, the preview day, from 11.0 am–6.0 pm is the best day to visit when everything is pleasantly uncrowded. Trade tickets and party tickets at reduced prices are available in advance from the Smithfield Show Joint Committee, Forbes House, Halkin Street, London, SW1X 7DS (01 235 0315). Party tickets are not available for the preview. Tickets can be obtained at the door by the general public and opening times are from 9.0 am–6.0 pm.

The Exhibition Centre is directly opposite Earls Court Underground station on the Piccadilly, Circle and District lines and buses 30, 31 and 74 stop at the door. Special British Rail travel facilities are also available from selected stations and details may be obtained from local stations. Enquiries regarding special travel and accommodation package trips can be made to the Farmers Weekly Travel Service, 136–138 London Road, Leicester LE2 1EN (0533 552521).

The 'Varsity Match

The match between Oxford and Cambridge Universities on the first Tuesday in December is the only major fixture at Twickenham Rugby Football Ground for which tickets are easily available, even at the ground on the day. But although the ground may be less than one-third full, as a curtain-raiser to the International Rugby Season, it is a day to remember. With little hassle or congestion spectators, sporting light or dark blue favours as symbols of their real or instinctive allegiance, revel in the promise and excitement of the series of International matches to be fought at the ground during the coming months.

The background to the annual Battle of the Blues started at Oxford in 1872, just one year after the first Rugby International. Oxford won that pioneer match on their home ground and the Light Blues avenged the defeat at Cambridge a year later. After that it was decided to play the fixture on a neutral pitch.

For the next seven years it was held at the Oval, followed by seven years at Blackheath and thirty-four at The Queen's Club, interrupted only by the First World War. In December 1921 Twickenham became its permanent home for the first or second Tuesday in December. The only exception was in 1947 when, during an economic crisis, the Government appealed to sports' bodies not to interrupt the working week if possible and the 'Varsity Match was changed to Saturday. The dramatic and unexpected fall in attendance figures resulted in the Tuesday fixture being immediately re-instated.

One fringe benefit from holding it on a weekday is the chance to 'catch 'em

The Cambridge side (in the light stripes) determined to gain possession of the ball from a line out in a 'Varsity Match at Twickenham.

young', as indicated by the many parties of schoolboys shepherded by games' masters who, for various reasons, are not apparent at Saturday fixtures. These, added to the great get-togethers of 'Oxbridge' men, from undergraduates to veterans, at picnics in car parks or around the bars, before the game, emphasize the essential and life-long pull of this great amateur sport which engenders a unique spirit of camaraderie as was indicated by Prince Andrew in his first public speech made in 1981 at the dinner to mark the Centenary 'Varsity Match.

Once upon a time the 'Varsity Match was such an important nursery for Internationals that it was regarded as an extra Trial and many potential 'caps' were excused from showing their paces to the selectors at the regular Trials, providing they appeared in the 'varsity clash. In those days the public saw the beginning of many successful International Rugby careers including those of Rhodes' scholars who introduced several good playing features from their own countries. A typical example of the importance of this match was emphasized at the official opening of the Scottish ground at Murrayfield in 1925 when England played six Oxbridge men and Scotland seven.

Since the 1960s, however, the predominance of 'Oxbridge' players in International Rugby has dwindled, partly because both Universities tend to allocate places to academics rather than to sportsmen. Simultaneously, more players from outside public schools and universities tend to dominate the game.

Nevertheless, for true Rugby Union enthusiasts it remains a vital day in the calendar and, for players, an unforgettable one. S. J. S. Clarke, Cambridge scrum-half in 1962 and '63 and who was capped for England thirteen times between '63 and '66, recalls why he found such a special thrill in playing in the 'Varsity Match:

A whole term is spent training and playing Club sides with one over-riding aim; the defeat of that other place. Great team spirit is generated and, when it comes to the big day at Twickenham, you give your all for the cause.

The build-up includes some psychological warfare. The Cambridge President used to host a dinner in his College a few days before the match which culminated in a solemn toast 'God Damn Bloody Oxford' over a glass of port.

Before my first match the Oxford Captain conducted a subtle campaign through the Press accusing us of drinking nothing but milk; therefore we were 'milk-sops', puny types, whereas his team trained on beer like proper red-blooded Corinthians. It didn't do them any good as we had a handsome victory that year, and his allegation was far from true anyway.

There is a great feeling of elation when you are selected to play in the 'Varsity Match. This was best expressed to me by one of our side who spent the week beforehand wearing, day and night, all his rugger regalia: shirt, stockings, sweater, tie. He was, literally, clothed in his glee.

The feeling of being picked for England is different. Being awarded your Blue puts you on a high which lasts 'till the post-match celebrations are over. Being selected to represent England has a sharp thrill at first which is followed by the realisation of an awesome possibility that you might let everybody down.

My Blue led directly to an England cap and I will therefore always remember the 'Varsity Match and support it with the greatest affection.

The Olympia Christmas Show

The Christmas Show at the Olympia Stadium, Hammersmith Road, London W14 was first held in 1972 and since its inception has gained steadily in popularity with competitors and public alike. This show has a real Christmas flavour and its boast is that it provides all-round entertainment.

One of the more light-hearted features of the show is the Camel Corps, usually under the command of ex-international show-jumper Ted Edgar. The antics of the camels never fail to amuse as the spectators are treated to the sight of well known equestrian and show-business personalities often unsuccessfully trying to ride the animals.

The show-jumping is naturally of the highest standard. All competitors compete by invitation and in addition to our top national riders a nucleus of riders from overseas also take part. The show really is a festival of talent of the highest order.

Although all the major show-jumping events are hard fought, a more light-hearted event is the fancy-dress competition, held on the last night of the show. The riders, and often the horses too, are subject to some sort of cleverly thought-out disguise, and are often totally unrecognizable. The fancy-dress show-jumping competition is a most amusing spectacle, but later on the final night the whole arena becomes tense with excitement at the Grand Prix, the climax of this five-day show.

Although show-jumping is the focal point at Olympia there are many more events providing all-round entertainment. Even Father Christmas turns up in his sleigh, accompanied by carol singers, which gives the audience a chance to air their lungs! Over the years some most impressive equestrian displays have been mounted at Olympia where the public have been treated to such spectacles as the Musical Ride of the Westphalian stallions from Germany, and other such attractions. Another popular aspect of Olympia is the chance to dine by the ringside whilst watching the events take place.

To add to the all-round entertainment it is usual to see such events as the Shetland Pony Grand National or Pony Club Mounted Games, which always 'warm up' the audience before the big show-jumping classes.

Events such as the Dog Obedience classes have also gained in popularity, and are most entertaining to watch. The dogs have to negotiate show jumps, and other hazards aided by their handlers. On charity night it is entertaining to see various personalities from all walks of life having a go at the Dog Obedience class, with their canines.

Members of the Royal Family are often in attendance at Olympia. On the first night, traditionally charity night, personalities from all walks of life can be found at the show.

As at most other shows of this type there is a wide range of trade stands, where it is possible to buy anything from a piece of equipment for a horse for a few pence to a painting costing thousands of pounds.

The Olympia Christmas Show usually takes place the weekend before Christmas and runs from the Thursday through to the Monday night. Information is available from the Secretary, 35 Belgrave Square, London SW1. The nearest underground station to the stadium is Kensington Olympia. This station is open only when an event is being held at Olympia. As there is hardly ever a spare seat in the house, especially towards the end of the week, advance booking is advised.

The Olympia Christmas Show attracts top
international show-jumping stars and presents a
programme of unrivalled variety and spectacle.

The Boxing Day Shoot
and the Close of the Shooting Season

Although most shoots are now concentrating on pheasants, the grouse, ptarmigan and blackgame seasons do not close until 10 December. The moor game will now be more wary and difficult to approach but those that do not mind a smaller bag should be able to find some very reasonable days on offer. All other gamebirds are in season in December and many shoots will carefully be planning the Boxing Day shoot.

For many, this is the most enjoyable day of the year. Christmas cheer is still uppermost and the shooting man has a justifiable reason to escape relatives and small children unless they are also shooting or have been press-ganged into the beating team, for Boxing Day shoots are traditionally family affairs. Some young sportsmen will be enjoying their first full day's shoot, perhaps clutching a newly acquired 20-bore, and they should be given every encouragement. Not that they usually need it. Many a pheasant has run the gauntlet of adult guns only to be neatly felled by a young shot.

The day is equally enjoyable for the syndicate gun. Daylight is now scarce, drives usually over by 3.30 pm and then it is time to return to base and mull over the season's sport and future plans before returning to the anarchy of small children and broken toys.

The wildfowler may have made a foray inland for the occasion but he is more likely to be found on the foreshore for 'proper' wildfowling will now be at its height, the wintering populations being at full strength.

As winter weather is so changeable, plans will have to include the possibility of snow, fog and high winds and perhaps an extraordinarily big tide. Rain and wind can sometimes raise the high water level by several metres and the fowler must take this into account if he is going to have success with the fowl and avoid drowning.

The risk can be minimized by taking a compass, a whistle and a torch and by checking that the route off the marsh will not be stopped by the tide flowing behind the shooting position. Tide tables should always be consulted and someone told of the day's plans.

A more insidious threat is arthritis and rheumatism created by sitting in mud gutters for lengthy periods. The old-time fowlers suffered terribly but with today's clothing it is not necessary to be uncomfortable. A waxed cotton coat, warm underclothes, a thick sweater and waterproof overtrousers are standard, together with waders and something to sit on. Thus kitted out, the fowler can enjoy that coldest of sports, moonlight flighting.

This can only be done when a full moon coincides with favourable tides and cloud cover. The quarry is the wigeon and the geese which use the light to travel to and from their feeding grounds. Often flying low, they provide fast sport and a quick-handling gun can be an advantage.

Choice of a wildfowling gun is always a matter of debate. Duck and geese often fly high and many fowlers use a three-inch magnum 12-bore, some take a 10-bore and a few enthusiasts tote 8- and even 4-bores. An ordinary game gun (of plain quality) is adequate if the fowler can use his skills to get within reasonable range.

Aiming high overhead on an end-of-season day's shooting.

The beaters are not forgotten, and in this December shoot of 1910 they are given
a filling lunch, to keep up their energies for the afternoon's work.

However, he may only be able to shoot where the fowl are flighting high. In this case, a magnum twelve is the answer unless the fowler is of sufficient strength to handle a bigger gun and can afford 10-bore cartridges. Cartridges for 8- and 4-bore guns are not commercially available and have to be reloaded.

Whichever bore is chosen, the newcomer should remember that range is difficult to judge on the foreshore. Out-of-range shooting is commonplace and can lead to wounding birds, particularly geese. Therefore, range judging must be practised.

In January the season draws to a close. All game-bird shooting ends on 31 January apart from the pheasant and partridge, which may be shot on 1 February.

Keepers are now thinking about catching up breeding stock for the next season but will first wish to reduce the number of cock pheasants in order to maintain a good cocks to hens ratio. To achieve this, 'cocks only' days are held.

As they are not full shooting days, these are often offered to friends of the shoot—the farmers, beaters and pickers-up. Sometimes, the roles will be reversed with the guns beating for the beaters. This not only promotes good relations between the two parties but also gives the guns an opportunity to return the caustic remarks on shooting prowess thrown at them during the season.

Often informal and great fun, 'cocks only' days offer many the chance to shoot driven pheasants of a quality that they might not usually be able to afford. They have only one drawback—the single high bird that breaks cover towards dusk, heads straight towards the gun in full view of the line, and, after a superb shot, bounces to the ground having somehow donned hen's plumage.

To escape the rather gloomy end-of-season atmosphere, the more adventurous and hardy head towards the goose grounds in East Anglia, the northern coasts and Scotland.

Every activity has its specialists and shooting is no exception: the snipe shot, the woodcock man, the expert on high pheasants—each has his favourite quarry and shot. But the successful goose shooter is single-minded to an extraordinary degree. He needs to be, for the goose is perhaps the wariest bird of all, matched only by the curlew before it was placed on the protected list. They have excellent sight and prefer to feed well away from any cover. Indeed the professional fowlers maintained that they appoint a sentry, another bird giving it a tap on the shoulder when it is time 'to change the guard'.

Their cunning is only a part of the fascination. They are large birds, and to witness a mass of geese filling the sky with their beautiful cries is an unequalled experience. And sometimes they can be very close. Confident in their senses, they may fly within yards of a well-hidden man, especially if he has set out goose decoys and is adept at calling. In these circumstances, geese can be very easy and although everyone is entitled to a few really good flights, successive shooting is no longer sport but execution. One should stop shooting long before then.

As geese are powerful birds and often fly high, the keen goose shooter is often armed with a 10- or 8-bore, but if it is possible to get within normal range, the object of all wildfowling skills, then a game gun will suffice, although large shot (No. 3) must be used.

Geese, like duck, cannot be shot inland after 31 January. Nor can the golden plover. But both geese and duck can be shot on the *foreshore* until 20 February. This is a real bonus, since all game shooting has then ended.

Before embarking on any major wildfowling expedition, however, the guns must ensure that a wildfowling ban is not imminent. This is enforced after thirteen days of continuous frost, and two days warning of an imminent ban is given. The BASC should be contacted if hard weather persists.

Sitting on the marsh, far from civilization, with the wild sounds all around, the sportsman can then bless his sport, for no other offers such satisfaction and camaraderie. Then, with the last flight over, he can return home, clean the gun, and plan the next season's sport.

Acknowledgements

The publishers would like to thank the following for their assistance in compiling this book:

Colin Adamson, Assistant Secretary of the Scarborough Cricket Club; The All-England Lawn Tennis & Croquet Club; Anna Beadel; The Clerk of the Markets, Markets & Fairs Division, The City of Nottingham; Lord Cottesloe; Malcolm Couch; Cowes Combined Clubs, Organizers of Cowes Week; Mrs Peggy Crooks, The Lakeland Rose Show; the Edinburgh Festival Office; The Hon. Edward Fremantle; The Royal Horticultural Society; W. A. Jackson, Editor of the *Shooting Times* & *Country Magazine*; Emyr Jenkins, Director of The Royal National Eisteddfod of Wales; Sheila Ladner; The Secretary of the Marylebone Cricket Club, Lord's Ground; Mrs Barbara McIlroy; Mrs Margaret McNulty, The Bath Festival Office; Patrick Montague-Smith; Susan Roughton; The Royal Shakespeare Theatre, Stratford-upon-Avon; The Vice Chairman of The Royal Tournament Committee; Dan Russell; Mrs Iris Webb; The Wimbledon Lawn Tennis Museum.

Index